# Levies of Devotion

ଷ

## Matthew Taylor

XOAR PRESS
New York

ISBN: 978-1-7349064-1-7

Any references to historical events, real people or
real places are used fictitiously.
Names, places and characters are products of the author's imagination.

Front cover image and book design by Xoar Press

Printed by Xoar Press in the United States of America
First edition 2020

Xoar Press
2799 Southwestern Blvd.
Orchard Park, NY 14127
www.xoarcom.com

*For Elizabeth Ann*

C３

He lost his virginity to an older woman on a bed across the hall from where his true love slept. His true love lost her virginity some years earlier to a man who worked for her father and drove an Indian motorcycle.

*And her true love*, his was lost before then, in the company of another virgin. They were childhood pals living near on the farm, and both were pubescent savants. In the hayloft together with neither coaxing nor coaching. And having shed their husky innocence in the sour of unripened fruit, that day and beyond their emotions had no scent of bloodguilt. This boy told the story of the hayloft only once in his entire life.

Lost virginity is like the Kennedy assassination or September eleventh. For as long as you live, its memory remains crisp and unsoggied; immune to the wilt of other things that once seemed important. He thought this consummate experience could only be bested by a first time with a true love. It was so with him. There is no memory so pristine as the first time with her. At will, drowning in details, like an effortless soul passing through cinder blocks of time. If one accepts this conjecture, then logically, the paramount sexual experience is virginity lost in the comfort of one's true love. His sister had come into this fortune and in the end, it proved but a reflection.

# 1
# ⊂ℨ A Simple Grave

Two days left in country, according to plan. Tomorrow on his own, making one last trip to the dig. He would tie up loose ends, pay off the locals and sign off on remediation. After that, the repatriation ceremony at Da Nang airport before the flight back to Hickham with the remains. Meanwhile the others would be off to the next recovery, across the Srepok River and deeper into the central highlands. There, left to sift through a swath of jungle, searching for the tiny bits of a soldier's life strewn amidst the wreckage of a Navy Skyhawk.

He took dinner alone at the hotel ordering the summer roll, later finding Bill Johnson in the bar to say farewell. Together downing shots of *ruou thouc* in celebration. The server placed the jug in front of them, on the bar, so they could see. The body of a cobra coiled tightly in the bottle, it's head bobbing in the rice alcohol, almost alive and about to strike. The bartender winked and said it would make them tigers in bed.

It was his third time working with Bill, once before in Vietnam and another time in Korea. After drinks they got around to shop talk and Bill said, "Our boy's a bit of a mystery, right?"

"Nobody's talking, that's for sure."

Bill was a civilian contractor with a background in criminal forensics. He had a keen eye for detail and could pick his way through a bag of bones with the best of them. He said, "Somebody takes the time to hide the grave, clear the brush and keep a marker. He's got three coins in his mouth, but nobody knows anything. Deaf and dumb. I suppose it's divine intervention, plain and simple."

"Oh, I bet there's plenty of folks who know exactly what happened to this kid, including our trusty old friend, Mr. Phan." Mr. Phan was the villager employed to keep watch in their absence.

Bill said matter-of-factly, "They know enough to keep their heads down and mouths shut. Glad to get the monkey off their back."

"Whatever they know, from the looks of that skull, it wasn't pretty. And there's that woman, I think she's got a story."

The first morning they surprised a woman coming down the path from the gravesite. She ducked away suspiciously, cutting off the trail before they could speak with her. When they tried to arrange an interview, nobody could pin her down. She could have been anyone, the locals said.

"Nah, too young, I got a good look at her. Couldn't have been alive then. All she's got is hearsay. She knows what everyone knows," Bill dismissed his suspicions.

"Yeah, well, I think she's got a story to tell. She looked a little *bui doi* to me." He hadn't got a good look at her, but from a distance she seemed taller and lighter than your average village girl.

"So what, you think she's a relation?"

"I'm just saying, I think she's got a story and I'd like to hear it."

"Good luck with that. Ha!" Bill scoffed.

"And good luck with that Skyhawk," he jabbed back. Glad to be out before the muck and the bugs and the sweat of hacking away at an acre of jungle for the next month.

The trip from Hoi An to the dig was less than an hour's ride. It followed the Thu Bon river valley and passed through shadows of hilltops poking up behind rice patties and tree rows. His driver was unusually quiet, sensing there was nothing more to be said between them. Dak's father fought as a sapper with Ho Chi Minh's 812th Regiment and died storming the perimeter of a fire support base in the A Shau valley. In a manner more New York than Da Nang, Dak bragged how his father died heroically.

They passed a village along the way known for making shirts from Vietnamese silk. They had a small reputation with tourists who came specifically for clothes, so there would be larger sizes for westerners. He said they would stop on the way back. He wished he knew sizes for his wife and daughter. All these years and he had no idea what size his wife was.

Today he rode in back, working on his notes and going through the Pelican case one last time. Four bags were marked for collection. They finished exposing and brushing the last of the frags the previous day, setting up a tent and allowing for a day of desiccation. Most of their boy already inventoried and back in the hotel vault, including the shattered skull. From the looks of it, he was shot at close range, execution-style.

For over forty years in the ground, they had a pretty good idea of whose bones they were. The location was reported through an anonymous tip and even came with a name. They said his name was Clark. It was unusual, the grave hidden on a hillside in a bamboo grove and meticulously tended. And it was queer how he was buried with three coins in his mouth, the Vietnamese tradition of mourning a loved one. The elephant grass was tamped down and someone kept a marker. A small, simple cross made from two pieces of rough-hewn ebony and a single nail run through.

A high priority dig, it involved the son of a prominent Western New York family. In the weathered binder PFC Robert Clark's official memory was typed in courier and amended with scribbles across a handful of pages... copies of copies of copies. His parents dead now, the mother a suicide and the father from cancer, he was survived by two sisters. Linda, the official contact, was divorced and living in Florida. They called and said her brother may have been found in the central highlands of Vietnam.

These trips were strictly business and he was seldom bit with curiosity. Discovery, removal and identification, that was the job. Their goal was to provide closure and nothing more. Bagging up what was left and shipping it back for families to mourn. Mourning publicly, what was already known. For closure it seemed enough to know these boys once lived, and how now, they were certainly dead. Casualties of conflicts the world had moved on from; those grievances once demanding capital and blood, no longer important in the big scheme of things. Yet he found himself opening PFC Clark's binder again and thumbing through the pages already read and reread. Aimlessly looking for clues. How did this kid come to find himself here, buried ceremoniously on a hillside in Vietnam?

While most American boys were scheming for ways to evade the draft, Robert Clark enlisted entirely against the wishes of his parents. A transcribed interview with his father mentions how he did his level best to keep his son out of the army; how his wife had forbidden it. Because of the family's social standing, there were any number of dodges to keep him from serving. He could have elected for a deferment and gone to college. Certainly his family connections could have bought him a spot in the Guard, near to home and safe from conflict. Sometimes there's a warrior tradition, sons enlisting in the shadows of fathers, but not here. Both his father and grandfather were too busy building the Clark empire to serve in either world war.

His grandfather, William Clark, patented several improvements in the design and manufacture of iron truss bridges and formed the Clark Iron Bridge Company prior to the first world war. The company flourished, flush with business from the defense department and capital works projects in the depression. They even purchased a steel foundry to augment the bridge business. By the time Robert Clark was born in 1950, his father had taken the helm of an enterprise which employed several thousand workers.

So, openly defying his parents, Robert Clark enlisted before his high school graduation and was shipped off to Fort Campbell, Kentucky for basic training. Just another grunt, the lowest of the low. No different from the thousands of other nobodies plucked off the streets of small town, USA and conscripted to serve in America's least popular war. Arriving in country in January of 1969, he was assigned to the 164th Light Infantry Brigade with the Army's Americal Division. Barely a month into his combat assignment, he was reported missing in action. A parent's worst nightmare.

Dak turned up a small cart path that wound closely through the farming village, before parking in a narrow cut a quarter mile below the dig. For nearly a week they traversed the steep hillside transporting the remains to base camp. Mr. Phan was squatted beside the tent, expecting them. The old man had friends on the local people's committee and was given this plum assignment. They expensed a million dong for his services; a small fortune in the provinces. He kept the money unfolded in the top compartment of his satchel. New, crisp bills, the way the locals preferred

them. They shook hands and he told Dak to express their gratitude. The man placed the money in his breast pocket without
counting and bowed instinctively.

Then he told Dak, "Ask him about the *bui doi.*"

Dak had seen her, too, and there was an uncomfortable resent-
ment that he should press this issue. Of course the villagers knew
something and so what, it doesn't matter now. He knew what Dak
was thinking. *Stupid American, be grateful for these bones. Just
shut up and take them. You're welcome.*

But Dak did press for information about the girl who was seen
on the path. Of course, Mr. Phan had no recollection of any such
girl hereabouts. He should know, born and raised in this place.
Perhaps it was some girl traveling from a neighboring village,
people often pass through. She could have gone up the path to re-
lieve herself and was embarrassed, that's why she avoided them.
Maybe she was lost, the old man speculated. No, there was no girl
like that in this village. All the while the old man kept his eyes to
the ground, watching his rubber boots paw the dirt.

How coincidental, at that very moment, this same girl should
approach, proving the old man's lies. She was coming up deliber-
ately, desperate to not waste chances. In her hands, a faded
infantry field pack, an only remembrance, sacrificed to complete a
story.

As he took the package, she turned away and Dak translated
the soft, but desperate words, "She says this is of the soldier. Of
Clark. The grave."

"Does she know this man?"

"She says this is Clark's bag," Dak translated.

"Ask her how? How does she come by this?"

She was hesitant to answer and when the words came, they
came delicately, her face hidden under the brim of a conical hat.

"She says her mother gave it to her."

Dog tags were strung through a loop on the buttpack and inside
were letters, some in envelopes waiting to be mailed and others
tightly folded. Brittle and faded and shaped in the soldier's pack,
their message a time capsule hidden through fate.

"Was this man her father? Ask her if Clark is her father."

She looked up, olive cheeks wet with tears.

# 2
# ෆ Willardshire

Gee spent most of her life in this house, from the day she was bundled home in diapers until she was on her own. Then again later, after she and Boy bought the house when her parents retired to south Florida, just after Hurricane Andrew. She had traveled and there was something about Willardshire Road on a perfect summer day. It was primal, a feeling beyond holidays abroad in some fashionable destination. It was a smell of wet bounty and the gently pulsing breeze pushing through mature hardwoods, rustling the leaves in passing crescendos.

She and Boy were working in the yard. Their usual mix of pop standards and sixties hits played on deck speakers mounted up under the eaves. It was a perfect summer day, when memories puffed up like dew bugs fluttering out front of footsteps across a morning lawn. It was on perfect summer days she would find herself crying; not for what is, but for what was. Love is like that.

Boy loved her and always had. A love that was faithful, enduring and true as any emotion. It was understanding and patient, beyond reproach. Its purity could not be sullied by the shadows of lesser loves.

He was in the herb patch, behind the sun room, and caught her gaze. "Love you, Gee."

She smiled back and said, "Love you, Boy."

She called him *Boy* since that time he was one. Two years younger, he would always be a boy to her. In their youth together, she would often accuse him of being *just a boy*.

"How do you manage to look so damn good?"

"Go to hell. I look like shit," she said.

"Yeah, I saw that kid looking at you."

"And what kid is that?" Though she knew who he meant.

"That kid at the market. That bag boy. He was looking down your top."

"Go to hell."

"He was. That bag boy, for Christ's sake. You were signing the receipt. Your shirt falls out and the little prick was looking down the front."

"You're full of it." She knew he loved her in that puppy dog way. Sometimes it fed her ego and then there were the times it pushed her away, like a turned back in a December wind.

"I like it. I like having the hot wife."

"You're delusional, Boy," she said dismissively.

"The hell if he wasn't looking, the little prick."

She gave him a half gesture and stretched out the cut of her top, so he could see. She blushed and looked down at herself. Why did she blush? It was true about her looks and she was accustomed to a second glance from even much-younger men.

She was happy today. Happy because of the day and happy with Boy and especially happy because Maddy was coming; at that moment, somewhere in Hartsfield-Jackson making a connection. In less than four hours she'd be on the ground in Buffalo. She wondered if her only child had the same feelings about summer and Willardshire Road. And while Madeline wasn't even home yet, she already felt the loss, knowing how in two weeks the catching up would be done. Then there would be another long time before late morning coffee on the deck in the sun. And a long time before dinners with Madeline and Boy, the three of them together. And it would be a long time before after dinner kisses, as their daughter left with the car for long nights of catching up with her oldest and dearest friends. Boy would fall asleep on the couch, lightly dosing until her safe return, as was his custom. His daughter often back in the twilight before dawn.

"Go to bed, Dad," she would tell him.

"To bed? And miss this beautiful morning?"

And she would always say, "Don't let me sleep too late. I wanna be up by ten or eleven." It was a running joke from the many times she would come in late and Boy would be on the couch. She would always tell him to rouse her at ten or eleven; but Boy would tease and promise to come exactly at eleven minutes after ten. And so it was, the coffee would be brewed and the knock would echo at precisely ten, eleven. This had become a cementing ritual in their lives together.

She and Boy would have their coffee and toast outside, or in the sun room if it was raining, hours before Madeline. Then there would be the special second serving. The ten, eleven serving. Tomorrow and many days over the next two weeks she would prepare Maddy's favorite creamy eggs. Cream and two large eggs in a butter ramekin baked in a water bath. Sometimes she would add chives from the garden and sautéed mushrooms. There would be two slices of toast with elderberry jam, from the bushes in the field beyond the horse fence.

Maddy had grown up a free spirit like her mother. Over forty now, she had been through a string of *Boys* who loved her, but could never tame her. And then there were the men who took her passions without commitment. She married one of those, but it was dead on arrival and so long ago. no one even spoke of it anymore. There were a couple of other fellas with whom she lived, but even that was a long time ago. Now, it seemed, she was quite free of men and content to cut this vein of the bloodline. It was natural she had none of the sticking stuff that Boy had. It could not be grated off and sprinkled upon the salad of life. It had to be passed on chemically through seed and soul. Gee desperately wanted a grandchild, but it wasn't in the cards.

Madeline found a happy life in Pensacola as a project manager with Northrop Grumman. She struggled to get on with it out of high school, but after finally committing to Syracuse and getting a degree in Industrial Engineering, she saw a steady progression in her professional life. Maddy was working with the military and the AWACS program. Lately she spent a lot of time in the Middle East.

Reading her mind, Boy said, "Excited?"

"Can't wait. I wish it was already then. You?"

"I keep watching the clock," he said. He turned away from her, choking up at the thought of seeing his daughter, his face hidden while deadheading the basil tops.

There were times when Gee liked to poke fun at his mawkish side, but today she covered for him and changed the subject, "Do you think if we tried moving this azalea, we'd kill it? I love it, but it's out of control."

He was still choked up and answered in timid little gusts of breath, "Maybe... Might be all right... Hate to chance it though."

Gee came over and threw her arms around him tenderly, "Awghh, Boy. It's okay. We've got two whole weeks. It's gonna be great."

"Look at me, she's not even here and I already miss her. You know, our daughter can be a pain in the ass sometimes, but I'm always at my best when she's around. I'm never the same after she goes. You think I'd get used to it, but I never do."

"Me too, Boy. Me too. It's so sad to put her on that plane."

The phone rang and Boy said, "Let the machine get it."

Gee had already sprung for the door, "Maybe it's Maddy."

It wasn't Maddy. It was sluggish dew bugs trapped under foot. It was a breeze of reversal and a return to perfect summer days past. It was all that once was, and all that is again, recalled from buried memories. It was Maddy's aunt from Florida and she had news about her father.

Linda Clark thought it was appropriate for Gee to hear it straight from the source. It wasn't so much a phone call as a news story. Clean hard facts in descending graphs ranked by diminishing importance. Yes, all these years later and Robbie's finally been found, buried on a hillside in Vietnam. Shot in the leg, he was captured and held. But it was a gunshot to the head that killed him, for reasons unknown. But at last he was found, his remains in Hawaii, and soon coming home to join his parents in Forest Lawn. She thought Gee should know the facts. Just the facts, ma'am.

Without thinking, Gee said to Linda, "What about Debbie? Should we tell her?"

Linda said, "I called you Regina, because I know what my brother meant to you... what you meant to him. I thought you should know."

"He loved her, too."

"Oh, please, one night. She knew what she was doing."

"It was more than that. I believe there was more to it," Gee said, remembering the pain of Robbie's confession the last time they spoke, and how she later denied it.

"Oh, for heaven's sake, she was so young... they both were. He barely knew her."

Then Gee touched a nerve, "And what about her daughter?"

Linda voice's went flat, filtering through without emotion, "I can't go through that again. Wasn't it you, Regina, who said it couldn't be Robbie's? Honestly, I can't go through that again."

When Gee didn't respond, Linda broke the silence, "Anyways, thought you should know. It's final now... no more wondering. We haven't made any plans for a service, maybe something small. I still have some connections at the Basilica and we can get the church if we decide to do something more formal."

And when she thought they were done, Linda added, "There were some personal effects, letters they said. I suspect some are yours and I'll see you get them."

"If there's any for Debbie..."

"If there's anything for you, I'll see you get it," Linda said coldly.

Things can be awkward because of time and things can be awkward because of past grievances and things can be awkward by circumstance. He caught enough of the conversation to understand its nuance. She hung up and Boy took her in his arms.

"I think we should call your sister. Debbie should know."

"Don't," Boy said.

# 3
## ఆ Caz Park

Over the years Debbie moved at least ten times; switching rentals, from one shithole to another while raising her daughter. But alone now, with a steady paycheck, she settled in this Southside flat overlooking the park. The second story apartment had a porch near the tennis courts and you could see the golfers hitting across the creek as they approached the ninth hole. It was awfully nice in the summer to sit out and people watch. Even the toughs as they cussed and smoked, dancing those dances which masked suggestions of a clumsy social existence; even their mischief pleased her. They reminded her of being young once.

While not childless, her friends started referring to her as the *Spinster Donohue* some time in her thirties and she wore it proudly. She laughed about it in her forties, and at fifty she cried, when they no longer mentioned it. Now sixty, she had reached the final phase of spinsterhood; acceptance. And acceptance set her free.

She was not averse to men, and in fact, Debbie was quite capable of finding a man when she needed one. Though it was something done on her terms. She still harbored an active and healthy desire for physical intimacy, though never found a man worth loving. Many of her friends had settled and it made her mad. She wasn't about to settle. Having experienced the depths of true love, dammit, there was no amount of impulse that could account for settling.

Sometimes, still, she missed the feel of a man. That feeling of want and desire and body around flesh. In the early spring she went for drinks with a friend, back when winter's snow still clumped in piles where the plows had stopped. She had the wanting and there was Sam Shea, a warm body.

Sam was in his fifties, a functional alcoholic who found himself along Seneca Street every afternoon until closing time; or a better offer. Sam's wife left him back in his forties, her spirit beaten down by whispers of extra-marital affairs. Now, his looks had not completely left him, but his face had gone ruddy from drink and sun. He was in sales and spent a lot of time involved in golf and ball games, and fishing with clients on the lake.

Debbie and Sue were drinking vodka and cranberry. Sam was drinking highballs. After the first drink, he slithered down to their end of the bar. It was not the first time he hit on her, but she never had the hunger then.

"What's goin' on, ladies?"

"Just looking for a nice guy who'd like to buy a round or two," Debbie's friend, Sue, suggested.

"Oh, I'm not nice, but I'm buying."

"You're a swell fella," Deb smiled.

"You're a hell of a guy," Sue said.

"Set us up," he directed the bartender. "What brings a couple of angels 'round this place?"

"Angels? Hardly," Sue purred, encouraging his generosity.

"Couple of devils then? Even better," Sam bantered.

They had another round more and Sue had gone to pee when Sam asked, "I'm heading down to the Blackthorn, can you come?"

"I'll ask Sue."

"Absolutely, Sue can come if she wants. Sure, bring Sue along. But I was kind of thinkin' about a little us time? Don't you ever just want a little us time, darlin'?"

"I can't just leave her."

"If you could, would you?"

Debbie laughed at the question.

"Well, bring her then. Bring Sue and I'll buy another round. We'll all have drinks and a few laughs. I'll see you down there. We'll drink to something."

When Sue came back Deb told her, "He's gone."

"Fuck, my glass is empty. I suppose he's down the street?"

"The jerk left us dry."

"Every night, the Blackthorn. We should go down and let him buy us another. You think he would, don't you?"

"Should we go then?"

"Did he ask?" Sue wondered.

Debbie skipped a beat and took a breath, playing it cool, "Actually he was trying to get me to come. But I said I wouldn't without you."

"I think he expected something after the drinks and all. Poor guy. I think you should go. You could use it," Sue said.

"And like you couldn't?"

"I've got a boyfriend, you know? It's all I can do to keep him off me for fifteen minutes. A rest is what I need!"

"Stop your bragging. Anyways, I said I couldn't come without you and he said he'd buy us drinks." Debbie rolled the dregs around the bottom of her glass.

"Poor guy. Should we go and keep him company?"

"I'm beat. I think I'll just head home," Debbie said, her appetite rising.

Sue asked the bartender to call a cab and they waited outside. It was cold and wet, the lingering drab of a northern winter.

When the cab came Debbie told her friend, "I think I should walk. I'm spinning. If I don't get some air, I'll get sick when I lay down."

"It's not safe," Sue said.

Deb smiled softly and said, "I'll be okay. Besides, if it feels like trouble, I'll just stop at the Blackthorn."

"Call me when you get home. And make sure you stay on Seneca. Don't walk through the park. It's not safe in the park."

They hugged and Debbie watched the cab pull away. She walked along Seneca towards the park. Empty sidewalks, but for the smokers hunched along barroom stoops. At the Blackthorn three guys she knew were smoking on the railing. Inside the bar was dark and even the television was off. Only the smokers and Sam kept the owner from closing.

"Where's Sue?" Sam asked.

"Went home. Told her I was gonna walk." She huddled up next to him and he went to kiss her, but she turned.

"Still drinking vodka and cranberry?"

"Can't stay. Told Sue I'd call as soon as I got home."

Sam left his drink on the bar and they walked down Seneca, crossing at Cazenovia Street and passing through the pillars of the Masonic temple; cutting through the park. It was quiet there and by the shuttered casino she took his hand and led him up the steps, stopping against the concrete railing. She pulled him to her lips and he pressed himself against her. There were some kids skateboarding in the dark through the empty wading pool and she said, "We've got to go. I told Sue I'd call. She'll worry."

Her door was around the side and the staircase was narrow and steep. After calling Sue, she didn't offer Sam a drink. And in the morning she didn't offer him coffee. She said she had things to do. She told him this when they woke, and again after. She kissed him at the top of the stairs and did not walk out with him. She wasn't sorry for sending him off that way. Also, she wasn't sorry for what they had done at night and in the morning.

Debbie worked alternate Saturdays as a window clerk at the post office and it was her weekend off when the call about Robbie came. That final bit of punctuation following the semi-colon in the longest paragraph of her life.

She was up early making brownies from a mix, as she would be watching her grandchildren all day. Her daughter Bertie, a single mother of three, was taking advantage of Debbie. When Bertie's eldest joined the service, she could no longer help with the younger two, so Debbie gladly shuffled her life around to pick up the slack. It was neither a chore nor a bother, glad for the time with the little ones.

Like Debbie, Bertie was pregnant and still in school. The mistakes of a generation repeated. Barely seventeen, Bertie had already been with two boys and a man. Debbie was stretched thin, struggling to provide necessities at the cost of supervision and direction. Often Bertie was on her own and the boy took advantage, filling her needs. They were naive with the chances they took.

Being a wayward Catholic, Debbie considered an abortion for her daughter. When she met with the boy's parents to decide what should be done, they said off-handedly, like it was a done deal, "Of course we'll pay any expenses you need to have this taken care of."

This assumption set Debbie off, prompting hard memories of her own experience.

When Debbie was pregnant, her mother wanted to have it taken care of. She was told of a backroom doctor who would do this type of thing, but father wouldn't stand for it. It resulted in a ruinous family fight. The final straw in her parents' marriage. Bags were packed and her mother moved out, pulling Debbie from class to have the procedure.

Debbie begged her mother to reconsider. When they stopped for gas, she leapt from the car and ran into a nearby cornfield. She wasn't going to have it taken care of. She could still see the barren spring field and smell the musty dirt. Even at sixty, still haunted by the panic in her mother's voice and the desperate calls of a broken woman. There was a fading terror in the voice as she ran; running through the fallen wintered corn and then into the woods behind the field until she couldn't hear anymore. There was a little stream and she lay down beside the bank, crying a hushed uncontrollable cry. Darkness came and frost covered the ground. She walked the four miles back to town, ducking in ditches at the lonely approach of distant cars.

Finally home, hours past midnight, her father was awake and drinking from a gallon jug of hard cider. Home at last and safe now. But her father spent the night shaking his rage in that pressurized bottle and he called her a little f'in whore and a f'in home wrecker. He was drunk and broken, so he hit her openhanded on the face and when she covered up he punched her on the back. Then when she fell in a ball on the floor, he stewed a moment more and kicked her. But the kick was empty and didn't hurt like the slap and the punch. And he said quietly, to himself, "I oughta f'in kill that bitch." Then he left, she didn't know where. She stayed on the floor in a ball for what seemed like hours, twisted in emotions of pain and joy. Joy that her baby, their baby, would not be taken care of. The pain of her father she could handle.

She was only sixteen and had never been with a boy before. She was a cautionary tale. It only takes once, just look at little Debbie Donahue. Not that anybody truly believed it was just once. But it was her first time and while she was only sixteen, she was as much in love with that boy as she had ever been, before or since. She tried to understand why she could never love again; why all of her left with him. But there were no answers, only conclusions.

Any other love would mean settling and she wasn't prepared to settle.

Bertie worked second shift on the line at American Axle, but she was pulling a double today. She dropped the children just before seven. Each of Bertie's kids had a different father. Not one of these men committed financially or emotionally to the well-being of the children. No one could argue Bertie's poor choices in lovers, but like her mother, she refused to settle.

Debbie was a much better grandparent than parent. She took time to read and explain and love and understand them. She cherished them and protected them in a way she was never able to with her own daughter. She was too busy growing up to be a good mother then.

When the news came to Debbie, they had just cut the brownies and she was stoic in front of the kids. The news was delivered softly, with a yearning to sooth the anger of a grudge never healed. The bonds that separated her from Gee and Boy could not be mended with any phone call, no matter what the intentions and no matter how softly spoken. A grudge like theirs was permanent. It had been built through years of silence and blame, and this breaking of the silence did not crack its wall; it only put light on the wall and each could plainly see the wall they had built.

# 4
# ᨠ Surprisingly Hard

Exams were finished and so was Tommy's junior year at East Aurora High. As his mother put the supper on the table, he was scratching with the giddiness of summer. His little sister had another day of exams before finishing her freshman year and she took her nose out a social studies book as he passed the mashed potatoes.

"Gonna watch *Our World* on Sunday, Dad?" his sister asked.

"I'm gonna watch Bonanza and maybe some Andy Williams."

"Not Sunday, Dad. *Our World's* on. It's a show and it's being shown live around the world. It's the Beatles and Picasso," she added.

"Big deal. A bunch of hippies and a guy who can't draw."

"They say the Vienna Boys Choir is also going to perform the opening song in 22 languages," their mother added.

Jimmy Donohue was a working man with a straight line view of the world. He told his daughter, "And I wanna watch this why, Peanut? What kind of idiots buy this Picasso, you don't know what it is? You kids were drawing better pictures in kindergarten. You could go out and spill paint on a bedspread, it's better than that crap."

"It's satellite, Dad. The whole world's gonna watch. It's broadcasting from a satellite up in space. People in Europe and everywhere are gonna watch at the same time as us; right as it's happening," Tommy said enthusiastically.

"I wanna see the Beatles," his sister repeated.

"Bunch'a goddam freaks, if you ask me. Andy Williams, now there's a singer. You put Williams, a Sinatra, a Eddy Arnold or a George Jones, now there's something the world's gonna watch. Couple of long-haired girlie-boys yanking their gui-tar strings, that ain't music."

"I'd rather see the Monkees." Peanut said.

"I'd rather see the Doors," Tommy said.

"The world's gone crazy. The whole world's gonna stop to watch a bunch'a goddam freaks. They oughta send 'em up into space and have 'em play up there. I'd watch that. So long as they ain't comin' back."

"The new music isn't all bad. I like some of the Beatles," their mother added.

"The whole world's gone crazy. You can't even drive into the city anymore. Goddam niggers'll pull ya outta your car and beat you silly."

"Dear," their mother protested.

"Tell Joe Stevens, one of the drivers at the plant. He's headed down through the east side a couple weeks ago and a bunch of these guys jumped his cab, smashed his windows and tried to rip him right out of the truck. Ol' Joe was ready for 'em, though. He had a gun right between the seat and gearbox. Joe, he pulls that piece and puts it right between their eyes. They disappeared back into the jungle quicker than slick on grease."

"Please, dear. The supper table."

"Tommy, I don't want you driving anywhere near those dark neighborhoods."

"Why would Tommy be anywhere near those places?" their mother said, knowing she couldn't win.

"Tommy's gettin' to be a man now and he needs to know to keep away from the dark side of town."

Ann Donohue took her food with downcast eyes and hoped for a distraction.

That's when Tommy dropped in casually, "I'm going over to Will's house tonight. I'll probably sleep over."

His father gave him a look and he tried not to give anything away. The old man said, "I don't like that Will McIver."

"He's a troublemaker at school," Peanut said and stuck her tongue out at Tommy, when their father wasn't looking.

"I never liked that kid. I think you should stick around here tonight."

"It's the first day of summer, Dad," Tommy pleaded.

His father looked him over again, "All right, but you're not gonna spend the summer hangin' around that Will McIver. You gotta get yourself some work."

"I got a job at Albach's."

"Albach's Chevy?"

"I'm workin' the lot. Washin' cars and stuff. Mrs. Peters got me the job. I told you."

"Well, that's good... I hope you get *a lot* of hours. When you start that job?" his father asked.

"Next week."

"Good. I don't want you hangin' out with that Will McIver all summer."

His father was right to be suspicious of Will. He wasn't a bad kid, but there was no real adult supervision in his life. Will's father was a hard-drinking slacker unable to hold down steady work, often relegated to odd jobs around town. He treated Will more like a contemporary than a son. His mother was a jovial, raspy woman who spent much of her time weaving cups of coffee through packs of cigarettes. She mistakenly fancied herself a confident of her kids.

Tommy grabbed his sleeping bag and flew into his loafers before the old man could change his mind. His biked was propped in the the lilac branches. The blooms were late this year, their scent lingered softly about the front porch. It was only day one and there was the promise of a long summer. Summer was better at seventeen than it was at seven. The loss of boyish innocence gave way to a new magic; a better magic.

Will's house was literally on the other side of the tracks, his driveway cut by a spur line to the feed mill. Old and poorly-kept, its spooky exterior suggested abandonment. Inside, hardwood floors were worn through and the walls were a patchwork of neglect. While some windows didn't open at all, others had to be propped up with scraps of wood.

Tommy laid his bike on the lawn near the back door and entered without knocking. Will's mom was at the kitchen table, a cigarette dangling off the ashtray and two hands around a mug of coffee,

"Hi honey. Will's just down to the corner picking me up some smokes. He won't be long."

He sat on the stoop between the back hall and kitchen.

She asked him, "So you got plans for your summer vacation?"

"I'm working at Albach's as a lot boy."

"Good for you. You got anything fun planned?"

"Just hangin' out. My dad thinks there's a strike coming, so he's banking as many hours as he can. He says we gotta lay low this year."

"If I know you boys, you'll find enough trouble right around here. I know I did at your age," she laughed her raspy laugh. "I know what teenage boys got on their mind."

"There's nothing on our minds," he protested.

"What about girls? You got a girlfriend, honey? You must have a girl, a cute boy like you."

"I ain't got a girlfriend."

"You're just like my Will. If you had a girl I expect you wouldn't tell me anyways."

Will came in, letting the door bounce closed behind him. He threw the carton of cigarettes shouting *catch*. She covered her face and the box skipped off her shoulder, onto the floor.

"Jesus, Will!"

"Gotta be ready," he smiled.

"Where's my change?"

"No change... delivery charge, you know?"

"Hey, where's my change!"

"Allowance. I didn't get no allowance this week."

"Allowance? I was paying my parents rent by the time I was your age." Tommy picked up the carton for Will's mom and she said, "Thank you, honey. I was asking Tommy if he had a girl. I said if I were seventeen he wouldn't have to look too hard. A handsome boy like him."

"You'd have to put out," Will said.

"I was a good girl!"

"Tommy only dates girls that put out."

"Oh, be quiet. Tommy's a good boy."

Upstairs Will had a mickey of Southern Comfort buried in his sock drawer. He took a swig and tossed the bottle to Tommy. "Drink up, good boy."

"Hell yeah," Tommy said, taking a shallow taste and passing the bottle back.

"You wanna see something'?" Will unscrewed the cover over the floor vent and stuck his arm deep into the duct work. Pulling out a photo of his sister, he flicked it across to Tommy. "It's Peggy, no top. I busted in on her and snapped this Polaroid. She turned away, but you can still see 'em in the mirror. It's art."

"Jesus! She looks mad."

"That's 'cause I know how small her tits really are. She's been sniffin' around for this all week. I told her it was just the flash, but she didn't believe me."

"You're a perv."

"Yuppers," he said matter-of-factly. Then, "I know somethin' fun to do tonight."

"Yeah?"

"I know Jenny Pierce has a tent set up in her backyard and I know she and Carol Smith are sleeping out."

"No way! Tonight?"

"You know I sit right behind that beautiful Carol Smith ass in geography and she says to Jenny, *Should I bring anything for tonight?* And Jenny, she says her dad already put up the tent and they already got sleeping bags out there. So after school I took my bike and drove by, you know, to check it out. Sure enough there's a tent way out in the backyard. A long ways back from the house, too."

"That Carol sure is nice," Tommy said.

"That's the only thing I'll miss this summer. I don't get to sit behind that beautiful ass anymore. I never cut fifth period."

"How'd you do in that class, anyways?" Tommy asked snarkily.

"Yeah, whatever. If the final exam was about the geography of Carol's jeans... straight A's, man."

Will fired up a smoke and flicked a Camel across the room to Tommy. Will's parents were resigned to him smoking. Having been poor examples, they couldn't figure their way past the hypocrisy of *do as I say, not as I do.*

"So what, we go out there and what?... Scare 'em?" Tommy said.

"Scare 'em? I wanna screw 'em."

"Better idea," Tommy agreed. "I get Carol, though."

"That don't sound right to me," Will said with a smile.

The boys rolled out their sleeping bags behind the shed under the willow that grew in the swale of the lot line. Will brought the rest of the mickey and they each rolled four Pabst into their sleeping bags; from his dad's stash in the basement.

After dark, Will took the booze and tucked it carefully into an old backpack, except the walking beers they drank on the way. The night was starry with a sliver of moon and the air was heavy with the blossom of summer. Fireflies ignited in tiny blinks over fresh cut grass as brown bats cut jerky paths in the dark above.

It was a lonely road, leading away from the village lights. The road to Jenny's passed the gated drive of the town's wealthiest resident. Moats of pastures and mature woods protected the separateness of success and privilege. Beyond a stone wall and up a hill was the big house of the Clark estate. The distant window lights peeking through the trees, a glimpse at the contentment of wealth.

The boys stopped by some woods near Jenny's laneway. With two fresh beers from the backpack they rested beyond the ditch, in the dim. The night was listening and they spoke seriously in shadowed voices.

"Do you think we'll get drafted?" Will asked.

"It doesn't matter. I'm enlisting as soon as I turn eighteen."

"What the hell?"

"My dad."

"What? 'Cause your old man was in the Army, you gotta be in the Army?"

"The Marines. My dad was a Marine." Tommy said it with pride and he imagined his father's pride, knowing his son would don the dress blues.

"That's messed up. Your dad didn't have to go to Vietnam. Your dad was in World War II, right?"

"He fought the Japs in the Pacific."

"Vietnam, man, that's messed up. Fighting Japs is like, I mean, they attacked us, right? Them Vietnamese, they ain't done nothin' to us."

"They're commies. Are we just gonna sit by and let the commies take one country after another?" Tommy could hear his father's words echoing from his lips.

"I dunno, man. I ain't goin' unless they make me. I wish I could go to college or some shit like that and wait for this war to end."

"The only way to end this is to kill ever one of them goddam commies." Tommy added, "Anyways, my dad always had it in for me bein' a Marine."

Will reckoned, "It don't seem right, your old man sending you off to be killed in a country that we probably wouldn't of even heard of, if it weren't for the commies over there."

"It's an honor to die serving your country."

"Some honor. If I had the grades, man, I'd go to college and get a deferment until that whole thing settles down over there."

"You could join the Coast Guard," Tommy suggested.

"You gotta have the grades and connections to get in the Guard. My old man says guys like us get screwed every which way. Rich guys get the college deferments and the officers' training and the doctor's excuses, but not us. It's like slam bam, you're in the army man."

"Maybe you could go to the seminary, become a priest."

Will smiled and gestured to Tommy in a jerk-off manner. Two more Blue Ribbons in the ditch.

Will threw the pack on his shoulders and together they ducked along the treeline, down the last of the private lane which backed up on the creek. The little split-level was nestled on a woody acre . Will issued final instructions. The best thing to do was to just go up to the tent and call their names in a nice friendly way. When they say who's there, they just tell 'em who it is and let 'em know they got nothin' to be scared of. It was a good plan.

A light ricocheted off the inside of the green canvas walls. They could hear the feminine lilt coming in breaths through the tent pores. The sweetness of it in the night set aside their plan and the boys strained to drink in the stolen marrow of Adam's rib. The discussion was about an unnamed boy and how they were both keen on him. Carol had slow-danced with him at the CYO's teen night and she kissed him under the fire escape steps at the back of the church. She said she could feel his thing against her and Jenny asked if it was a big ten-incher. Their giggles were muted. And this caused Will to gag back a snicker of his own.

There was a "Shhh!" from inside and they cut the light.

"Kevin Lee is that you?" Jenny spoke up. "Kevin Lee, I'll go right in and wake up dad!... Kevin Lee?"

Tommy looked to Will for direction and he put their plan into action. "It ain't Kevin. No, we ain't here to cause no trouble, Jenny. Everybody just stay calm, it ain't Kevin Lee," he announced.

"Whose out there?" Jenny demanded. "I'll scream and my parents' window is right in the back of our house. My dad has a twelve gauge."

"There's no excuse for screaming or anything like that. It's only me, Tommy Donahue," Will said.

They can hear whispers inside the tent. Tommy is glad for the night, to hide his cheeks, flush with anger at having his name spoken.

"And it's me, Will McIver," Tommy countered, talking in his deepest voice.

"Will McIver from geography class?" Jenny asked.

"Yuppers," Will took over.

"I don't know what you're doing here, but you better get out of here, Will McIver. My parents' bedroom is right in that back window and I wouldn't be surprised if they haven't heard you guys already."

"Nah, I doubt it. Your house is pretty far away and it looks pretty dark to me. Tommy and I walked all the way from town to come and see you guys, so maybe you might just let us come in, okay?"

"Will McIver, I'm not letting you in my tent. You are a seriously creepy guy," Jenny said.

"Awghh, now that hurts my feelings, Jenny. I always thought you were a real sweet girl and such. When I heard you were camping out, and seeing how Tommy has this thing for you, I think this is good chance to, you know?" Tommy scowled at Will, who smiled and shrugged with a wink, wanting his buddy to go with it. Will continued, "So, if you won't let us in, maybe you wanna come out? We brought some beer and such and maybe we could go for a walk and hang out for a little while?"

They could hear whispering and a sleeping bag unzipping. Will winked again, like *I told ya so.*

Jenny was first out. She was thick, but not fat. She had thick arms and thick calves and thick thighs. She played sports at school and frequently had a sweaty glow about her, but her face was not un-pretty. In the dimness, as she clutched herself against the sudden chill of the night air, Tommy could glimpse the pretty of her. Carol was second out. Taller than Jenny and lean from head to toe, punctuated with a bottom that kept all the boys attention. She had long arrow-straight dirty blonde hair, parted in the middle. She would spent much the day pushing it back from her face.

When Will took out the beer, Jenny said, "Not here. Let's walk... and keep your voices down."

Back at the road, Will opened beers for everyone, pounding off the bottle caps using the top of a fence post. There was an awkward, adolescent tension that found them trying to remain as outwardly cool as possible, waiting for someone to say something; anything.

Finally Jenny said, "You guys do a lot of stalking in your spare time?"

"Naw, like I said, Tommy's got a thing for you."

"It's more like he likes Carol," Tommy said.

"So you don't like me?" Jenny asked.

"Sure he likes you, he's lying," Will persisted. "He's just a little shy, is all."

Jenny answered, "Nah, I don't think so. I know when a guy's interested and he's not interested." Tommy couldn't look at her now, as she measured him directly. "He doesn't like me at all. You're lying."

"He's shy," Will said again.

The funny thing was, he never thought at all about Jenny, but her directness, right then, was an unexpected turn on. At that moment, she was kind of desirable.

"So, whatta we do now?" Jenny wondered.

Will had a plan and said, "Tommy and me thought we could go climb the water tower. Me and Tommy climbed it three times last summer."

"You're crazy, I'm not climbing that thing," Carol said.

"It's really wild. You can see the whole city from up there."

"Sounds kinda cool," Jenny said.

"You guys go ahead, but I'm not going up there."

"It's not hard," Will told Carol. "I'll climb up behind and catch ya if you fall." He smiled at Tommy.

"I'm not going up the stupid water tower!" Carol said emphatically.

Will had another idea, "You guys ever been up to the Clark estate? I have. You know, there's this big bell up on this pole and there's a rope. It's like a dinner bell or something. It's right up front of the house. We should go ring it."

"Why?" Carol asked.

"Why not?" Will truly wondered and started walking, Jenny following beside Tommy. Carol laid back long enough to underline the stupidity of it.

Jenny asked accusingly, "How did you get up to the Clark estate?"

"It's not hard. There ain't no guard or anything like that. You just jump the wall and walk. There ain't no dogs. Anybody with half a mind can go up and see the place, 'specially at night."

"Special emphasis on half a mind," Carol added.

"It's adventure. Don't you like adventure?" Will confronted her.

"This isn't adventure, it's just stupid. Sailing across the ocean. Climbing a mountain. Flying a plane. That's adventure."

"Well, I ain't got no plane, I don't see no mountains and I can't swim, so this might just have to do for now."

Carol laughed, truly amused, "I knew you were a retard, but I just never realized what a big retard you are."

Jenny was walking close to Tommy now, their hands touching once as their arms swung lightly.

Tommy never had a real girl of his own, if you don't count that night in his cousin Celia's basement. The previous summer Celia's best friend let him finger her, as they sat under the blanket on the barcalounger watching *The Birds*. When he tried to make a further advance in the weeks that followed, she told him she had a steady boyfriend and liked him only as a friend. He wanted to say something about his finger and the depth of their friendship, but just couched his disappointment in a strong face. It was the only basis for a real girlfriend fantasy ever since, but now he was forming a new one with someone he knew, but never considered as *girlfriendish.*

Will stopped to let Jenny and Tommy pass and he waited for the dawdling Carol. He stood right in front of her and as she tried to step around, Will moved to block her. Their eyes met in a confrontational stare, neither about to back down. When Carol made a second attempt, he blocked her again and she pushed him aside saying, "You're such a retard!"

"Yeah, and you've got the greatest ass I've ever seen."

Carol burst into a laugh, but then they were walking as couples. Later, Will took her hand as they jumped the ditch and slid over the stone wall, crossing onto the Clark property. Tommy slouched and checked the road before straddling the wall. He went over with Jenny and they managed an accidental embrace. A little ways up the hill there was a horse pasture and an electric fence.

Will tapped the line in a quick check, then grabbed it fully in hand. "It's okay, there ain't no juice in it," he said. He dropped the pack at the fence post and put the Southern Comfort in his breast pocket.

They crouched slightly crossing the meadow and came to the edge of a pond. There was a small dock with a paddle boat tied up. There was a canoe turned upside down on the grass.

"Look, it's the goddamed ocean at the top of this mountain. Imagine that," Will told Carol who was in his arms and he kissed her.

Tommy was amazed at how quickly she yielded and the audaciousness of the move took him by surprise. He certainly understood his friend was the alpha male, but he marveled at its easy translation to the opposite sex. He felt ashamed for not having the courage to act with similar confidence. It seemed Jenny was into it, yet he couldn't bring himself to attempt a kiss. It was true when he was accused of being shy.

They each drank from the mickey before moving into the trees that surrounded the house. The house was nice, but not as extravagant as imagined. It looked like a really big family home. The few estate-like things were a six car garage set apart from the house and a large basin-shaped inground pool with cabana. The driveway entered a circle between the pool and the house. In the center of the circle was a large pole with a substantial bell perched at the top.

"There it is. Go give it a yank," Will told Tommy.

"It's your idea," Tommy squirmed.

Jenny was watching him and he thought about where his finger once was and he thought about playing sidekick to imaginary boyfriends. Dammit, maybe he couldn't manage a kiss, but by God this was a chance to be perceived as a man of action. He ran hunched towards the bell pole.

The others retreated to the shadows beyond the cabana. The rope was wound and knotted around a metal cleat. It was stiff from disuse and was recently painted over in silver along with the rest of the pole. He used his teeth to loosen the knot. Through a window he could see a lighted hallway and looking back, he was alone now. Why hadn't they come up with a group escape plan?

The loosening of the rope caused the bell to move free and the clapper lightly contacted the mouth of the bell, sending a ting on the wind. Then, taking a higher purchase on the rope, he put his shoulder into it, turning the bell full on the yoke. It was a good and well-balanced bell. It rang out in a bulky bellow with each drum and the volume did not diminish as quickly as one might have expected.

Tommy took off in full stride, seeking the shadows of the cabana house on the way to the wood. There are times in life when you should expect the worst of outcomes. Times when pitfalls are announced by neon signs flashing, *over here, dummy*. Times when things seem as they are and common sense steps aside for a life lesson. As the bell continued to illuminate the presence of a simpleton, he was caught in such a time.

What he didn't expect was to be intercepted and tackled by an obviously, and completely, naked boy. And he did not anticipate the power and strength contained in the frame of a boy of similar years, but shorter. And as he was crushed to the ground and mounted like a horse, he certainly never expected to be confronted by an erection which now pointed at his face from a distance of no more than twice its elongation.

"What're you doin', you piece of shit? Whatta ya think you're doin'?" the boy asked.

"Get off me, freak," Tommy choked out.

"I oughtta kick your ass, boy," the naked kid said. A dog was barking from the house and a spotlight over the garage flipped on. The boy dragged Tommy along the ground into the cabana house.

A woman's voice called from the main house, "Robbie, are you out here?"

The boy released his grip on Tommy's throat and hastily grabbed a towel to cover his late erection as he stepped out from the cabana, "It's all right mother. It was just some kids. They ran off into the woods."

"I'm going to call the police." The voice was getting closer.

"Mother, it was just kids. I saw them," he yelled.

"What are you doing out here, Robbie? Are you alone?" The boy's mother was on the pool deck now, next to him, clutching a coat wrapped around her shoulders.

"Yes, Mother, I'm alone. I was just taking a swim."

"You're sure it was just kids?"

"I saw them."

"I don't like it, Robbie. I think I should call the police."

"Mother, the East Aurora police department does not need to spend the night chasing down some idiot teenagers. It's all right Mom, I saw them. They were just some dumb townies."

She parsed the landscape with genuine concern and then deferred, "Well... it's late, Robbie. You shouldn't be out swimming without telling someone. God forbid, what if you should hit your head?"

As Tommy's eyes adjusted to the darkness inside, he noticed he wasn't alone in the cabana. Sitting on a deck chair was a girl. In the mottled light she suddenly became obvious to him. She was hastily wrapped in a beach towel and watching him. For someone in her predicament she seemed quite calm, almost detached. She had an Ann Margaret, *Viva Las Vegas* thing going on. Poofy auburn hair parted on the side and falling across her forehead; it spilled over her shoulders and down her back in bounding rich curls. She seemed older than him, but he couldn't be sure if it was age or sophistication that begot age. She had a robust upper body that supported the towel and its ample virtues were revealed in its rift. He locked in with a transfixing gaze. She was a girl accustomed to the drooley stare of smitten men and received it with resigned expectation. As his eyes found hers she smiled and touched a finger to her lips, as if to stop him from bellowing in rapture at this lusty discovery.

"Go to bed, Mom. I'm all done here. I just have to change."

"It's getting chilly, put some clothes on, for heaven's sake. Stay out of the pool, now."

"I will, Mother."

And as she started away, with her back to him, she said, "Lock up the cabana. You never know with those kids around."

"Good night, Mom."

The boy came into the cabana, watching through the door until his mother was gone.

"You see that girl over there, boy? She's hot, huh?" He said to Tommy.

The girl was taking it in with a little smile. A cool demeanor belying the tension. The kid pressed on, interrogating Tommy, "Can you imagine what it's like to get with something like that? Something that gorgeous? No? I don't think you've ever got with something as hot as that? Not that hot, right boy?"

"He must have a name. Why are you calling him boy?" the girl said. Her voice had a husky, resonate tone that accentuated her sex appeal.

"What's your name, boy?" the kid asked, like Tommy was some migrant looking for field work.

Tommy didn't answer. He was right. The girl was smokin'. To be made small at that moment was worse than any beating, worse than having his father come down to the East Aurora police station, and worse than being too shy to make a pass at Jenny Pierce. It was about as damned bad as anything could be. Stupid bell.

"I guess I can put my pants on in about thirty seconds. How far can you run in thirty seconds, boy? How long before I catch you if I give you thirty seconds?... Huh?" And when Tommy didn't answer, "You don't say much, do you? Thirty seconds... Ready... Go." And the boy dropped his towel, naked again.

Tommy took one last look at the girl as he steamed out of the cabana, bound for the woods. Never looking back, busting through the coppice, pocketing scratches on his arms and getting poked near his eye by the tip of a pine limb. He half-slid, half-rolled down a dirt embankment.

In the ditch along the road he looked back for the first time, surveying the lonely landscape for any sign of the others.

# 5
# ○8 Albach's Garage

Tommy showed up early for his first day on the job. A freshness of morning he hadn't tasted since the start of summer. Under obligation's thumb, he rode his bike to the dealership with a drudging acceptance.

A friend of his mother worked in the office at Albach's and that was his in. He went to see her at the end of May and she took him into Mr. Albach's office without knocking. He was on the phone, his chair pulled away from the credenza. He looked at Tommy and made circular hand gestures suggesting the caller was a long-winded blowhard wasting his time.

The interview consisted of Albach asking if he had a driver's license and reminding him, "You always gotta be careful when you're working around the cars. It's hard to sell dents and scratches." Then he told him how he liked to take care of his people, "How's a buck, seventy-five to start sound? That's thirty-five cents over the minimum, right? You be good to me and I'll be good to you."

Then he took him to meet Mr. Schultz, the general manager. Mr. Schultz had a glass office in a corner of the showroom. At first glance one could tell that Schultz was a humorless sonofabitch. His veneer was all business and his overriding motivation was to make sure nobody was getting over. Not the salesmen, not the customers and certainly not the new lot boy.

It was clear that Albach forgot his name when he introduced him as, "The young man who was going to work the lot".

Mr. Schultz told him to come in Monday and rolled his eyes when Tommy explained he was still in school and couldn't start until June. The bossman made a derisive little hissing sound and said "I suppose that'll have to do, then. Come see me at 8:30."

Tommy walked through the showroom door at 8:20. Schultz was in his office with one of the salesmen. They locked eyes and the boss set about ignoring him for the better part of an hour. Twice passing by without a blink of recognition, as if Tommy were invisible.

At 9:15 he poked his head in the office door and meekly announced, "Mr. Schultz. I'm Tommy Donahue, the lot boy."

"I know," Schultz said with characteristic annoyance.

At 9:45, and with a great display of inconvenience, Mr. Schultz took Tommy down to the office where the women worked and he filled out the employment forms. It was 10:30 when Buddy, the service manager, showed him where to punch in and he was officially on the clock.

He thought it was a joke when his first official task involved Buddy marching him across Main Street to Russ's Barber Shop.

"Above the shoulder. I wanna see the scruff of his neck," he told Russ.

"I'll make him look like the handsome young man he is," Russ assured him.

Buddy paid the dollar, fifty and told Tommy, "This is an advance. You can pay me back on payday."

Furious, Tommy was trapped. His father would tan his hide if he quit on the first day. Then he would tan him a second time if he quit because he refused to get a haircut. His long hair had been a source of friction between him and the old man for some time. The ruff gradually lengthening between each successive haircut, to where it now touched below his shoulders. This progress came at the price of *little girl* and *pink dress* comments from his father. His mother didn't mind, though, and she loved to run her fingers through it until he kicked up a fuss. Whether through fatigue or resignation, the bar had been lowered with each successive trip to the barber. Years of pounding at his father's resolve would all be for naught in a couple of snips.

After the haircut, he returned to the garage still red with anger and Buddy mussed his hair, telling him, "Now you look like a young man. You should be proud of yourself. You don't know how many kids I've come across who would rather keep their hair than their job."

"It's not fair. Hair doesn't have anything to do with the way I work," Tommy mumbled.

"Sure it does. It says you're a serious person and you respect others enough to sacrifice your own vanity. You'll be all right," Buddy said.

Buddy sent him with a guy from the parts department to deliver a new Chevelle to a dealership in Hamburg. Jesse was driving the Chevelle and Tommy followed in a '62 Bel Air from the used car inventory. Jesse drove fast, like he was trying to lose Tommy, but Tommy stayed right with him, topping seventy and right off his bumper as they floated along a stretch of wide-open two lane. After the papers were exchanged, Jesse let Tommy drive back.

"Were ya scared?" he asked.

"I was right with you... all the way."

"Yeah, but were you scared?"

"I wasn't scared none. I've driven plenty faster than that."

Jesse told him to head along the back road and they stopped on a bridge. "The reason I like to go fast is it gives me time to stop for a smoke."

Jesse offered Tommy a Kool from the cellophane pack and said, "Not in the car. They don't like cigarette smoke in the cars."

They followed a path under the bridge and down by the creek. A heron lifted heavily from its perch in the water. They sat on the concrete umbrella under the bridge, leaning back on their elbows, holding the cigarettes with their lips.

"How's your first day... got a haircut, huh?"

"That really stinks. How can they do that?"

"Buddy's a good guy, he just don't like long hair."

"I would've quit if I had someplace else to go," Tommy said, scuffing the concrete with the soles of his sneakers.

"Your hair'll grow back. Buddy's a good guy. Just keep it above the ears and everything else comes easy. You don't wanna look like a girl, do ya?"

"They shouldn't be able to make a guy cut his hair, is all."

"The Army makes you cut your hair. Shorter than that, too," Jesse said, still pinching the cigarette with the corner of his lips.

"That's different."

"Why's that different?"

"I dunno, it just is. It's for your country. I'm going in the Marines," Tommy added.

"The Marines? How crazy is that?.. Me, I'm married and got a kid, so I got out of the draft. Lucky huh?"

Genuinely surprised, Tommy asked, "How old are you?"

"I'll be twenty next month. I got a two-year-old daughter. Me and her mom, we wasn't married, but with the draft and all, she said we should make it legal. So we did. We didn't get married in a church or nothin' like that, 'cause we didn't have the money. We just went down, got the blood test, got the marriage license and did it right there in town hall with the jay pee. I got my brother to be the witness. There weren't nothin' to it and now I'm married and goodbye Vietnam... You got a girl?"

"Not right now..." Not ever.

Jesse offered, "Albach's got a daughter, Reggie. Maybe you could ask her out?"

"Is she cute?"

"Oh, yeah... You'll see her. Can't miss her, you know?" Jesse flicked the cigarette butt into the creek and added, "She's cool, too. Always says hi, even to us guys in the back. She makes us feel like we ain't just a bunch of grease monkeys."

"Not like Mr. Schultz."

"Schultz? Guy's a dick. Everyone thinks he's a dick. His mother probably thinks he's dick," Jesse said.

"I hate that guy."

"Everybody hates that guy. You can't be a person and like that guy. Stay clear of him. You'll catch hell if he sees your shadow. Guy's a dick, all right."

"For sure. He's a dick," Tommy added.

"Buddy says that Albach's too nice a guy, so he needs a dick to do his dirty work. He says he ran a dick wanted ad and Schultz fit the bill."

Tommy crushed the cigarette butt and Jesse threw a block of loose concrete into the creek, before heading back to work.

Tommy managed to avoid Schultz for the rest of the week. He washed a lot of cars and moved around even more. He made some parts runs and got to drive a new Camaro to a dealership north of the city. Like Jesse said, Buddy was a good guy. He whistled as he worked and possessed a genuine concern for all the guys. He was always first in line to lend a hand. On payday, Buddy said to forget about the haircut money.

Tommy settled quickly into the summer routine. While too busy to live the previously-imagined summer, he was not unhappy. It may have been the haircut or perhaps the job, but his father was treating him more like a man. There was a race riot in the city at the end of June and the old man was up in arms about the *niggers* ever since. His mother spent a lot of time trying to change the subject, or just staring at her food.

The first time he ran into Albach's daughter was on payday. She was in the office handing out paychecks. She wore a fringed leather Indian vest and the top of her head was wrapped with a leather string. She noticed him first and was watching with a confident directness that made him blush.

Intimidated by pretty girls, he kept his head down. She said, "I know you. There's something about you that rings a bell."

She looked much different that night in the dark of the cabana house, and it was only then, he made the connection. The feminine grit in her voice was a ribbon around his fantasies and it was instantly recognizable. Flustered, he stammered, "Sorry," and kept walking.

"Enjoy your weekend, *Boy*," she said with a little smirk.

That night of the bell, when he caught up with the others, it was told as a clean getaway. Neatly painted on a canvas of success. They didn't know of the encounter with the naked boy and they never heard about the redhead in the cabana house. A good story left untold.

Back in the tent, Will got as far as second base with Carol. Tommy got to first and briefly touched second before being tagged out by Jenny, effectively ending the game. Will, on the other hand, spent much of the early summer in extra innings, sliding into home on a regular basis, as he told it. This left Tommy to his own device.

His days were spent working, his nights at home in front of the television and the weekends were duller than imagined. He biked past Jenny's a time or two, but hopes for a chance meeting never materialized. After running into Albach's daughter, he was now trying to duck both her and Schultz. When he did see Reggie

Albach, she would be watching him curiously and his face would redden, certain she enjoyed teasing him.

At the end of July, Albach's held their annual company picnic at Chestnut Ridge Park. A formal invitation was put in his first pay envelope. Jesse said it was a blast, even Schultz managed to drop the dick routine. Around the dealership, it was a summer highlight and everyone was going; everyone but Tommy. The last thing Tommy wanted was to spend the whole day ducking Regina Albach, but she was the one who cornered him as he scrubbed the whitewalls on a '63 Rambler American hardtop.

"Hey, Boy... what's this I hear you're not coming to the picnic?"

"My name's Tommy."

"I know what your name is. So, how come you're not coming... *Boy?*"

Angry at the teasing, he could hardly speak, "I'm just not. I'm gonna hang out with my friends."

"Hang out? Seriously?" She stood over him and her shadow cut across half his face. "You know what I think? I think you're afraid of me. Because of that night. I think you've been avoiding me because of that night. That's what I think."

"I'm not avoiding anyone," he lied. "Besides, I don't have a ride."

"I can take you. Where do you live?"

"I may have to watch my sister," he lied again, pathetically, squinting up at her.

"Where do you live?" she asked, in singing tones, marking her final decision. "Nevermind, I'll check it in payroll. I'll pick you up about eleven. You can help me set up the games."

"I dunno if I can."

"Oh, you can. Bring your sister. Besides, I could really use your help. See you at eleven, Boy . . . Ta, ta, Thomas," she sang and walked away.

# 6
# ᦸ Buffalo Stuff

Regina Albach was made from the stuff that occupies a boy's fancy as he reflects upon the day and seeks the stillness of slumber. Laying semi-conscious and primitive in the art of self-discovery as her voice and face, hair and curves, all become life-like in the clutch of a foam-stuffed pillow. Tommy was flush with excitement in the days before the picnic. Why, it was practically a date, and at her request.

He got up that morning without the customary drowse of an ordinary day and spent some time pondering his wardrobe. Clothes customarily plucked from the top of the heap just wouldn't cut it, for today he was Regina Albach's escort. Perhaps she would find his bell-bottoms cool. Those silly-looking jeans his mother bought because all the kids were wearing them. He stood shirtless in front of the mirror, gawking aghast at his tented ankles and came to a previous conclusion; Tommy wasn't cool. Playing it safe, he settled on cords and a short-sleeved, red checkered grandfather shirt, still in its Christmas box up on the top shelf.

His mom was surprised to see him so nifty at his own shove. She ran her fingers through his hair and he pulled away aggravated, using a comb from his back pocket to fix her mess.

"My, don't you look nice? Now, who is it that's taking you?" his mother asked.

"A girl."

"Oh, a girl," she commented, full of inference.

"Regina Albach," he said annoyed. "I'm helping her set up, is all."

"Oh, Regina Albach. Did you hear that, Jimmy? Tommy's going to the picnic with the boss's daughter."

Tommy's father was half-listening over the paper and his morning coffee, "Don't let that one get away, kid."

"It's just a ride, is all."

"Well, be polite. Don't forget the ambrosia in the refrigerator." His mother insisted on making something for the picnic.

He went out on the porch to wait and Peanut was on the steps.

"Where ya goin'?"

"Company picnic," he said, tucking his shirt into his pants.

"Where's the picnic?"

"Chestnut Ridge."

"Who ya goin' with?"

"None of your beeswax."

When his ride arrived, Peanut was doing her best Lolita, bored and sultry on the porch swing. Regina was driving an Impala convertible Tommy had detailed a couple days before. She dumped the hippy look and was dressed in a floral sundress, cinched at the waste and flowing out in knee-length pleats. Her hair was pushed back with a black headband. To Tommy, she seemed right out of a fashion magazine... even if he had never seen a fashion magazine.

"Hello, Tommy," she said formally and smiled. Then she called hello to Tommy's sister, who responded with a half wave, neither much considering the other. A pause for retrospect.

He blushed as his mother rushed out with the forgotten ambrosia, stating, "He'd forget his head if it wasn't attached to his neck."

"Thank you so much. You shouldn't have gone to any trouble. Tommy's only coming 'cause I made him," Reggie said and smiled at him.

"Don't be silly. He can't go empty-handed. It's just a little ambrosia. An old family recipe."

"Thank you so much. I'm Reggie by the way," she said coming around the car and lightly taking his mother's hand in the way women do.

"I'm Ann. Tommy's mom."

"Nice to meet you, Ann." Reggie looked at the mortified Tommy and said, "It's a picnic, you sure you won't be too hot in those long pants?"

"I'm fine."

"Don't you think he looks nice, though," his mother encouraged.

"He looks great. I'm just thinking, it's gonna be an awfully hot day… we'll just have to loosen that collar."

She came over and popped out the top button on his shirt. "There," she said, satisfied.

The back seat was already bulging with picnic supplies. She sighed and told Tommy, "Wow, I can't believe how much shi… stuff I've got. You'll have to hold onto the ambrosia. You don't mind, do you, Boy?"

Tommy climbed into the front bench beside Reggie, resting the tupperware bowl on his lap and resenting his mother's efforts. Peanut was still posing and his mother was waving on the steps as they pulled away.

"Your mom's nice," Reggie said.

"Yeah, she's nice. You're the boss's daughter."

"She seemed swell. Was that your sister on the porch? She's cute. Guess you didn't have to watch her after all." Reggie couldn't resist the dig.

KB 1520's Bud Ballou finished stepping all over the intro of the Grass Roots *Let's Live for Today*. Reggie spun up the volume and said, "God, I love this song. Don't you love this song?"

"It's all right," he said sitting stiffly, cradling the ambrosia salad.

At the light, she watched him and he looked away. She reached over and pinched him. "You're kind of a square, aren't you? You know, if you're gonna chum with me, you gotta loosen up. Let your hair down a little, Boy. What happened to that intrepid little bell ringer I used to know?"

"That wasn't me. That was just my stupid friend making me do it?"

"Oh, I see?" Regina said with a tease in her voice.

"Yeah, we were hanging out with these girls and he put me on the spot."

"Yeah, you guys do all kinds of dumb shit for girls. Was one of these girls, your girlfriend?"

"I thought maybe, but not really," he lamented, surprised how easily such candor was extracted. All the same, this honest portrayal of personal inadequacies felt damn good. He sensed she liked this.

"Awgghh," she sympathized and pinched him again. *What's with the pinching?*

At the circle, Reggie went towards the city instead of swinging left towards the park. The stone wall of the Clark estate mirrored the road out of town, Reggie turning through the open gates of the main entrance. The property was a working farm and they passed caretaker houses and livestock barns. Angus and shorthorn cattle grazed in pastures along the lane and later, horses. An old hound chased them up from the barn, snapping at their wheels. Reggie knew the turns leading up to the big house.

"Look familiar by day?" she asked light-heartedly. He squirmed in his seat, reflexively pressing himself against the door. "Relax, Boy. I told Robbie about how you were working at the dealership and that you were really a nice kid and he thought it was a hoot. You'll see, he's a great guy."

"Does he know I'm coming?"

"Doesn't matter. You're my date." Date? And when she saw his obvious distress she added, "Really, it's not a problem. Robbie's a great guy. You just caught him at an awkward moment, is all... but I guess you figured that."

In an irking coincidence Robbie Clark was leaning against the bell pole. He was wearing a pair of dress shorts and a polo shirt. His hair was short and blonde, but full and combed back, neatly parted in the middle. Tommy reckoned himself a good couple inches taller than the Clark kid, but Robbie had a powerful frame, more reminiscent of a chiseled welterweight. In the daylight, it was clear how he was so easily thrown and dragged that night. Clark possessed a bright-eyed baby face with small, attractive features, except for his thick, pinkish lips. His face was tanned and smooth with a clear complexion. And Robert Clark did not have a tupperware container full of ambrosia.

He came to Reggie's side and kissed her. She pushed over against Tommy and Clark gave him the once over before putting the car in gear.

Reggie said, "Robbie, this is Boy."

Robbie said nonchalantly, "Yeah, we met."

Reggie pinched Tommy, secretly this time, and flashed a told-ya-so smile.

"I'm not Boy. My name is Tommy."

Robbie stopped the car, reached across Reggie and extended his hand, "Robbie Clark."

Winding out of the property, Robbie pulled off the driveway and skidded to a stop in front of one of the pastures. Reggie waved her hand at the swirling dust. She demanded, "What are you doing!"

"C'mon, I wanna show you something."

Robbie gestured for Tommy, too. As they stopped on the first rung of the split rail fence, Robbie balanced effortlessly atop the upper rung, surveying the horizon and pointing to a distant pasture.

"What?" Reggie demanded.

"It's an American bison. A buffalo."

"A buffalo? Good God! Why do you have a buffalo?"

"For meat."

Reggie made a face and said, "Sounds disgusting."

"There's another one on the way from South Dakota. My dad's gonna see if there's a market for it, maybe establish a herd. I'm told it tastes pretty much like beef, but leaner."

"Doesn't appeal to me in the least," Reggie said.

Robbie said, "You know, buffalo don't defecate in their water source like cows. Cows just shit wherever, like the world is one big crapper. Buffalo don't stink where they drink. I think that puts them a step up on the evolutionary ladder."

"Well, that's too much buffalo information," Reggie said.

"Really? That bother's you?"

"I wouldn't say bother. It just seems like an awkward conversation to have with your girlfriend."

"How about you, Tommy? Is buffalo shit awkward for you?" Robbie asked undaunted.

"Don't bother me none," Tommy said trying to keep up.

"Must be a guy thing," Reggie concluded.

Robbie was still perched atop the fence, suddenly introspective.

"Robbie," Reggie said loudly, calling him back, as if from a distance.

Parsing the far field, he was transfixed, grasping at universal truths just off his fingertips. Tommy looked up at this privileged little prick and considered the whole of him quite pretentious. He was a caricature of entitled progeny, acting with a sophistication borrowed from a life of rubbing up against it. This boy, his greatest accomplishment being born well. Seriously? Standing up there like some Greek god, while they genuflect in grace. The sun cascading sparks of gold through the tiny blond gaps of his perfect hair.

"Earth to Robbie, we gotta go," Reggie yelled again, breaking the spell.

Robbie jumped down and put his hand on Tommy's shoulder, "All right, Tommy. Let's get our Reggie to the ball."

Tommy considered the whole of it quite odd. Him and them. Why would this couple, from life stations so distant, embrace him in kinship? He couldn't help but feeling used, the charity case from the wrong side of the tracks. But still, at that moment he was a part of them. This whole connection concocted from such delicate circumstance, that ordinarily, they might not even recognize each other. That is, unless one of them was in close erect proximity. Suspicion aside, the happy collection took off for the park; top down and 1520 on the AM dial, buoyed by the influence of a sublime mid-summer day.

# 7
## ✿ Lost in the Maelstrom

Maddy opened the door and signed for the delivery. She brought the bubble pack to her mother in the kitchen where they were working on a jigsaw in the quiet times since her arrival. It was a 1000-piece puzzle of La Sagrada Familia and was spread across the table in the breakfast nook. It was an east view with the Nativity facade, their progress mostly confined to the border, some sky and the top of the Jesus spire.

"Fedex for you. Who's Linda Clark Brighton?" Maddy asked.

Regina's face must have given way to the emotional geyser roiling beneath the surface. She knew these were coming eventually, but wasn't prepared for them now. In hand, contents imbued with her greatest love, her greatest sorrow and secured with the twine of bitter family rivalries; adorned with a ribbon of her deepest secret.

"What's a matter Mom?" Maddy asked, sensing something.

Composing herself, as best she could. "Oh, it's... I think it's some letters. I wasn't expecting them so soon."

"An old lover, Mother?" Maddy teased.

It was a shockingly frank response, "As a matter of fact, yes."

"Oh my God! Does Dad know?"

"They were friends, too."

"Oh my God! You were fooling around with Dad's friend!"

Gee could just manage a smile to hide her guilt. A guilt Madeline would never figure.

"Well, aren't you going to open it?"

"I will."

"Open it," Madeline said hovering.

"Madeline! I will... Alone, if you please."

"Okay, but you're killing me with suspense. You know that right?"

"We'll talk about it later."

"Suit yourself... So I'll just go hang with Dad then?" Madeline threatened, implying a tale to be tattled.

"Fine. Good idea. Go see your father. Fly, fly away, little birdie," she said annoyed. But that was the way it was with her daughter. Prone to the incessant meddling that comes from being an only child. That need to be in the absolute middle of everything. It's surprising how much she didn't know. Well-kept secrets are the ones that really count.

She left the package on the island and plugged in the kettle. Alone with her thoughts, she kept it at arm's length, working the cabinets for a cup, a spoon and a bag of green tea. And she kept her distance at first sip, only then summoning the courage to retire to the bedroom with the envelope and the tea. The tea was set on the nightstand and the envelope on the bed. She curled up at the foot of the bed to where her chin rested between her knees. Her face was in the bureau mirror. How old it seemed. Crows feet about her eyes and lips. Once supple cheeks, now set with lines that mocked her expressions. She had done her best to stay young, but the cruelties of age steal in at moments of weakness.

These letters knew the cruelty of time. No longer white or supple, but tarnished and brittle, frayed at the folds. A psycho-chemical reaction, whereby the tensile strength of the paper is consumed by the message therein; a message discovered in a distant capsule and sharpened with age. Inside were six letters. One letter was sealed and unopened, the rest loose and unfolded, each in its own plastic baggie. The sealed one was addressed to Peanut Donahue. There was a hand-drawn peanut with a smile, long-lashed eyes and a heart on the cheek. One of the letters was one she sent to him, despite a vow to never write.

First she read the note on Linda's personal stationery:

*Dear Regina,*

*I read everything but the letter still sealed and addressed to Debbie. As much as I wanted to read it, I left it - it's for you to decide what should be done. I guess I never really knew Robbie, except that he was a remarkable kid who could make everyone fall in love with him. I never understood why he felt it was necessary to leave us - and still don't. There are days when I scream out loud at him for being so selfish and leaving us in such a mess. It's bad enough that he was so reckless with his own life, but he killed our mother, just as if she was shot right there with him. But mostly I'm angry that we lost such a perfect and beautiful brother - and for what?*

*As for Debbie's letters I think maybe you were right and she should have them. I'm leaving it up to you - Honestly, I wouldn't know where to find her. She has been treated quite uncharitably by my family; by me. I never believed there was anything real between them and even if I accept the notion that her daughter is a Clark, it seems unfair that she should have kept it after a one-night stand, not to mention how young she was. It's clear to me my brother loved you both and I'm not sure what I should do about it. I have been a horrible aunt thus far.*

*My sister and I are planning a memorial for Robbie at the Basilica in May, on his birthday, followed by an internment in the family mausoleum at Forest Lawn. I hope that you, Tommy <u>and Madeline</u> can make it. I'm hoping to make some amends then. I've seen some photos of Madeline on her social media profiles and I know who her father is. I've always known and I understand why you did what you did. I see her father in her eyes. Those big, bright eyes and that square chin. I won't press the issue without your approval, but I'd still like to meet her.*

*And lastly, to complicate things even further, there is yet another surprise. Robbie was being Robbie, no matter how deplorable the conditions. I have a niece in Vietnam, and by logical extension, Madeline has a sister in Vietnam. I am doing what I can on that front and plan on visiting the place where he died in the near future.*

*Affectionately,*
*Linda*

Madeline has a sister in Vietnam? With Robbie Clark, the stew is constantly thickening, long after the pot has cooled.

And, *affectionately, Linda*? When they were dating, Robbie's sisters were mostly absent. Between college and social calendars exposing them to a litany of eligible bachelors, there had been precious few occasions for a connection. The girls did not inherit the gregarious warmth of their brother. In fact, Robbie was completely different from every other member of the Clark family. He was the sun which nourished their emotional pastures.

Reggie had always sensed a polite distance from the Clark women, mom included. They weren't willing to fully commit to a girl who could never be *the one*. While Regina Albach was certainly pretty enough, and her family was marginally respectable, she was however, an older woman. Not to mention, she was a little too wild and a little too ambitious.

What Robbie needed was a refined young woman of impeccable looks. Someone who could run a household and keep things interesting in the bedroom. She should have the benefit of a good post-secondary education – something like Barnard or William Smith – but only to keep up with the rest of the Junior League crowd. She should be a good breeder, capable of spitting out the kids, but always getting back that petite figure. That's what Robbie needed. Not this older woman who embraced the sixties and the sexual revolution with a little too much enthusiasm.

One by one she took the letters from the bags and spread them on the bed. She sorted them, reading only the date and salutation. Those for Deb she put to the left and the others, hers, to the right. Meticulous in this avoidance. Wanting, but not wanting. She had a good life and it was getting better. The years passing through the mist, siphoning off the bitterness of painful memories. The sweetness of life now coming through the pour and the bad times, less so, clumped in fragments on tentacles of wisp.

The first letter to Reggie was dated February 2nd, 1969:

*My Dear Beautiful Forgiving Reg,*

*First off, I want to apologize for our last night together. I'M SORRY, REG! I was so awful, when all you had was love and concern for me. I was selfish in my want. I wanted your body, not advice, or love for that matter. It was selfish of me to want you that way – to take you that way, but I* have always been selfish when it comes to that. I hope you can forgive me and my insatiable wants.

Second, I hope you can forgive me for taking so long to write. I wanted to punish you for telling me we were through over this whole thing. You said you would never write to me, but I didn't believe you and I've already got your first letter (I'm hoping there's more to follow).

I know in my heart that you didn't mean what you said that night. I know that while you didn't say so in your letter, it's clear you still care for me. I guess I hope you still love me, but I know I've disappointed you. But at the same time I can only live the life that's meant for me. This is what's meant for me and no matter what happens, this is what I had to do. I know you don't understand and I do love you for your convictions. What's right for me isn't necessarily right for you - and that's okay.

As for my life over here so far. It's really not so bad. Once I left the States I took a commercial flight to Okinawa where me and the guys waited for deployment. Our station was right on the ocean and I've never seen such crystal clear water and you could see the coral reefs stretching out forever. The island of Okinawa is so beautiful, I can't imagine not coming back again in this life.

Anyways, I officially arrived "in country" on January 8th. I came in on a transport which landed at Chu Lai Air Force base. It's on the South China Sea and it's surrounded by barren hills and it's not nearly as jungly as I had imagined. Once again the ocean is beautiful and I'm beginning to think I could spend my life on an ocean somewhere. Our first night we crashed a short-timers party (Guys who are about to go home). What a wild night of debauchery! The next day I was hurting so bad and our platoon sergeant didn't have an ounce of sympathy – getting us up early and setting us on preparations for moving out. We've been stationed on one of the surrounding hills called FB Rhonda and our job is to be on the lookout for NVA's who look to shell the base at Chu Lai.

I'm with a great bunch of guys and I've been able to hit it off with most of them immediately. It's everything I hoped *for. Guys from everywhere - different backgrounds and races and experiences bonding together like brothers. It really feels that way already. Of course, brothers fight, too. Two of the guys had a knock down, drag out fight in the hooch. Broken crap everywhere! But afterwards everyone calmed down over a smoke and a beer and all seems to be forgotten.*

*We quickly find our routine here. Our days are spent on one detail or another, and at night we take turns on watch and ambushes. So far no real action to speak of... I have to say the worst thing about this place is the food!!! (Help, send cookies and Kool Aid!!!!) Last night we were supposed to be resupplied and supposedly steaks were on the way. It's all anybody talked about the whole day. When the chopper touched down and no steaks were on board, the pilot barely escaped with his life. There was more than one of us that wanted to shoot the messenger. Not to mention the rotor wash set off all the trip flares and the CO made me reset the whole bunch.*

*As for your letter, Reg. You were right to scold me, but not because of my choices. You were right to scold me for being selfish – as I said before I wanted to touch you one last time and that was what I wanted. I didn't care what you needed from me. I know you say you can't forgive me and I can't help but notice that you signed the letter with the cold and distant "Regina". I must say, it was more than a little hurtful not seeing the usual, "A million and one kisses" attached to your signature. I am who I am, Reg. I can't be what my parents want me to be, I can't be what my sisters want me to be, and I can't even be what you want me to be. Could you even love a man who would be someone else, just to please you? I'm not like Tommy and you're not the kind of girl, Reg, who could truly respect a man who changes himself to please you.*

*As I said, I know I was wrong for using you – but I'm not the only one who has used someone. You used Tommy and you used him terribly. In my mind you've been far worse to him than I was to you. The choice he made because of you will eat away at his soul for as long as he lives. At his core he is a warrior and a patriot and you have turned him against himself with your beauty and charm. You have taken his essence, his soul, and taken him from his family. I know he's infatuated with you now, but I believe he will ultimately hate you for this. He has given everything for you and what has he got in return – not even a real kiss as far as I know. Not the kind of kisses I know. Tommy should be here with me, that was his destiny and you have stolen it. I know I will never respect the decision he's made. It is a contemptible weakness which will result in lifelong self-loathing.*

*I don't know what will become of us. I don't know if you'll ever really forgive me (I hope you will) and I don't know if we'll even be together again when I get back. For all I know, maybe I've guilted you into becoming a couple with Tommy. I can see you being with him just to spite me.*

*Anyways, I guess that's it for now. I'll always have a deep emotional attachment to you, Reg – no matter where I am or what I'm doing. It's not a just a physical thing - you are an amazing person in every way and I just don't want you to hate me, Reg.*

*A million and two kisses,*
*Robbie*

As hard as this letter was, the next in the bundle was harder still; the first letter she sent him. She called the big house and got the address from Mrs. Clark. The letter was neatly written on personal stationery given by her parents on her eighteenth birthday. A large "R" flourish at the top on white linen. She can remember sitting stiffly at her father's desk with the study door closed and locked.

She remembers the dream she had about being pregnant the night before she wrote the letter and she remembered how her body echoed this prophecy. How much she wanted to hurt him when he was so far away and vulnerable. She wanted him to wonder if she would ever be his again. His punishment would be time and distance and the curtain she hung between them. It wasn't written as comfort in a time of need. It was written to deepen their collective burdens. A *Dear John* letter with purpose. She spent the years since trying to rationalize its awfulness. She always hoped it never made it before his disappearance.

*Dear Robbie;*

*I wasn't going to write, but I feel there's still things to be said between us and I didn't want to leave it the way it was the last time we were together. We've been friends for a long time and it isn't right we should end it that way.*

*But I am so mad at you. I'm so mad how selfish and impulsive you are. I'm so mad you made me fall in love with you. I'm so mad you think so little of me, that you just don't care what I think. And I'm so mad to think you lied so you could have me one last time.*

*In all the times we spent together, I never took you for a liar. That was one of the things I liked most about you. I liked that you said what you meant and meant what you said. Even if I disagreed, I knew I could always count on you to tell me the truth. That night was the first time in our whole relationship that I felt used by you.*

*Quite honestly, I don't know if I can ever respect you again. You'll always have a place in my heart, but I don't know if we can ever get past this. I suspect that after leaving me, you went to Debbie. Did you tell her what she needed to hear so you could have her, too?*

*Anyways, Tommy has been given space at a house in Toronto and I'm going up to visit him soon. It's been a rough time for him. It took a lot of courage for him to make that decision and I have such great respect for him.*

*Robbie, I hope you find what you're looking for. Obviously my love wasn't enough for you and I'm truly sorry about that. I think that two people in love have a right to reasonable expectations. When those expectations are conflicting and unresolved, then I guess it was never meant to be.*

*Be safe,*
*Regina*

# 8
# ଓଃ The Eternal Flame

South out of Orchard Park, the road lifts along the face of Chestnut Ridge. Before the rise, there's a break in the treeline exposing the sled hill and toboggan chutes, and further, the big stone casino and it's commanding view of distant Lake Erie. Albach's reserved a prime spot at the bottom of the hill. A grass and gravel lane swept down the hill to a grove and large picnic shelter. There were swings and a hobby horse beside a push and pull merry-go-round. Two groomed horseshoe pits would find action all day. Beyond the grove was the spillway for the sled hill; acres of mown lawn, large enough for several playing fields.

Charlie Buck was already there in a pickup loaded with supplies. His last name was some long Polish name, but everyone just called him Charlie Buck. The mechanic was waiting for some muscle to move the big steel grill that would be fired all day, serving up hot dogs and hamburgers. There were two kegs of Simon Pure sunk in a tub of dry ice and some fifty-pound bags of charcoal. Robbie didn't wait for Charlie's permission, shaking his hand then pulling the tailgate pins.

"That's a heavy son of a gun," Charlie said about the grill.

Robbie jumped up on the truck bed and said, "We'll get 'er."

"Probably best wait for some of the guys. That's a heavy son of a gun."

Unchecked, lifting the end to measure its heft, Robbie said, "Sir, why don't you come up here. Tommy, you and I can get underneath and let her down."

When it was mostly off, Robbie took all the weight, telling Tommy to switch ends and help Charlie. It was *a heavy son of gun,* Tommy and Charlie laboring together on their end. After lugging it downwind of the shelter, Robbie threw a bag of charcoal over each shoulder.

Reggie was unloading the car and she set the ambrosia on a table in the shelter. She told the boys to set up the volleyball net and mark out a ball field with some canvas bases.

Tommy set home plate down and Robbie moved it decidedly an arm length's west, as if the grass was absurdly greener there. Her boyfriend then mapped out the rest of the diamond with a certain meticulous deliberation that came across as completely annoying. After, they filled balloons with well water from the iron hand pump. They cut rope lengths for the three-legged race and put knots in the tow rope for the tug of war. Picnic tables were lifted into the sun and Reggie had Tommy walk up the hill to fasten balloons to a signpost. Tommy would disguise secret glances as she arranged and unpacked, nibbling on her lower lip while working. God, she was beautiful.

With things in order, she sat cross-legged on one of the swings, a leather saddle suspended from a long metal chain hooked on a twelve-foot a-frame. She told Tommy, "Push me, Boy."

Tommy started off gently, his heart racing with each touch of her back, touching her hair for the first time, and then touching her lower back. She smelled of vanilla and coriander and sandalwood and this was a tease which ached somewhere beyond his ability to reason. She was as fresh and clean as the puffs of lake breeze edging round the spires of hardwood and pine.

"You call that pushing?" Robbie asked.

Could he be more annoying? Push... what push? This was an exercise in ecstasy. This was a father and the clumsy clutch of a first born. It was a bookmark to be opened and remembered on every sweet summer day. And in older days, it would be a reminder that he, too, was once young and fresh. A push? It was a sexual time stamp. It was deeper than any finger, this was a fantasy come to call. A push?

But then Robbie pressed his will, brushing Tommy aside with that deliberate confidence. The confidence that comes from knowing exactly what you want and how it's yours for the taking. He pushed her with the feverish zeal that was his essence. There was nothing reserved, nothing subtle, nothing timid in the way he handled her. Quickly Reggie was beyond reach, approaching perpendicular. She shrieked and wrapped her arms around the chain, a hand pressing down the hem of her dress. Robbie stepped back to admire his work... *that's how it's done, Tommy,* he must have thought. Reggie weaved a wide, pendulous path, her hair lifting through the air, each pass bringing her closer, back to them. Finally, low enough to jump into Robbie's waiting arms and they kissed completely. But just as suddenly she withdrew, aware of Tommy, and Tommy aware of her restraint.

"It looks like the boys got that tap in. Let's grab a cold one," Robbie said.

Tommy took the cup sheepishly and Robbie encouraged, "It's a picnic, nobody cares. It's just a beer."

After, Reggie began working the assembling crowd of employees and families. She was an accomplished hostess, stopping at each table and introducing Robbie as her boyfriend. Tommy watched the men watching her. When Fred and Marilyn Albach finally arrived the party was rolling.

On his own now, Tommy faded into the landscape and looked for a landing spot, finally hanging his hat at the table with Jesse's family. They walked his daughter up the hill and into the old stone casino. When Jesse refused to carry her, she cajoled Tommy into putting her on his shoulders. Inside she scampered across the fieldstone floor towards the mighty fireplace and its huge pile of unsplit logs, waiting to warm the bones of hearty sledders after the weather turned. It was cool in the casino, stinking of soot and timbers.

"You come here with Reggie Albach?" Jesse asked.

"I wasn't coming and she made me."

"Nice."

"Yeah, except her boyfriend came with us."

"Yeah, that Robbie kid?"

Tommy said, "Yeah, Robbie. As in Robbie Clark. As in *The Clarks.*"

"Oh, wow, a Clark. Kind of tough to compete, huh? Makes sense, though. She's rich kid pretty."

"Rich kid pretty?"

Jesse was a country kid at heart. A simple soul without a lick of pretension. He explained, "Yeah, you know, rich kid pretty. Pretty enough to get any man you want, I guess."

"Yeah, she's so damn pretty," Tommy lamented.

"Remember I told you that first day. I said you should go after her. Guess you'll have to get someone more like Doreen."

"Doreen's pretty," Tommy said with mustered enthusiasm.

"The thing is, she's the best one for me and I know she loves me. Some people think getting her pregnant was a bad thing, but it was the best thing that ever happened to me. Maybe she ain't as nice as Reggie Albach, but she's a really good mom and all. That counts for something, right?"

"Everything, man," Tommy said.

Heading back, Jesse suggested they all roll down the hill and this resulted in giggles and grass stains.

Robbie Clark did not fade into the background. He was a whirlwind of shaking hands, swapping stories and making tap runs. It seemed he always had a hand on the shoulder of one fella or another, emptying his burgeoning bundle of tall tales. Charm came to him as naturally as blossoms to a magnolia in May. He challenged Fred Albach to an arm-wrestling match and controlled the action, finally succumbing as a suitor's courtesy. Later, he grabbed Reggie by the waist and pulled her off to pitch shoes, partnering her with one of the more robust salesman.

At the big softball game, garage versus showroom, Robbie was recruited by the showroom side. In the history of the picnic, garage had never lost to showroom. Tommy did pretty well, reaching base with every up and catching a line drive by Schultzie to end an inning with the bases loaded. A heroic he hoped would not be remembered. But of course, Robbie was a one-man wrecking crew. He broke off rallies with great fielding and with each successive trip to the plate, garage would push the outfield back, and every time he would best them. As showroom emerged victorious, there was much grumbling about *the ringer*.

The day was growing long when Reggie reconnected with him, tapping his shoulder. She had changed from her dress and was now in sneakers and shorts. She said, "C'mon, Boy, we're going for a hike."

Robbie was waiting for them at the top of the hill. Reggie asked, "Where to?"

"Down the hundred steps and up the creek. There's a great little waterfall I wanna show you."

"It's far?" Reggie wondered.

"C'mon, it's definitely worth the trip."

A worn trail led to the hundred steps. Exactly one hundred stone steps leading down to a narrow ravine footed by a gentle slate-bottomed brook. Soon enough on their own, they started along the creek bottom. The couple held hands and Tommy behind them, moving quietly in the shadows of late afternoon. In the places where the water flooded across large slabs of shale, it wasn't much more than inches deep. A turned stone sent crayfish scurrying. When the stream came to a join, they followed the second one upstream. The ravine narrowed and they alternated shorelines pouncing from stone to stone. Robbie said "Awggh, shit" when he got a hotfoot. Reggie moved smooth and certain and without caution, as graceful in nature as society. The waterfall was hidden by a small bend, but it was beautiful when they saw it. The water spilled softly over twenty-five feet of shale, landing in a wide, shallow pool.

"Worth the walk. Definitely," Reggie agreed.

They sat on the bank and Reggie took a baggie from her pocket, a Zippo and a pack of rolling papers.

"Do you get high, Boy?" she asked as she sprinkled the leaves on the paper. "No?"

"That weed'll rot your brain, Tommy," Robbie said. "Gimme your lighter, Reg."

Robbie climbed the bank along the waterfall and there was a flat slate pocket behind the water curtain about ten feet up from the pool. He reached in and sparked the lighter. There was a quick puff and then a long wispy orange-blue flame took hold.

"Oh my God!" Reggie said. "How'd you do that?"

"Magic," Robbie boasted. "It's a natural gas seep. I've been here a few times and sometimes it's going."

"Wow! That's amazing! Doesn't the water put it out?" Reggie wondered.

"It's pretty far back. It must take a big wind pushing up the gully. It's probably been seeping gas since the Indians trapped this creek. Who knows how long it'll keep going. It blows my mind.

What a goddamed place. It's like… I dunno, you could say it's damned spiritual, that's what this is. If I believed in spirits."

Reggie took the lighter back and lit the joint. She passed it to Robbie and he passed it back, after hardly taking a draw.

"Do you wanna hit, Boy?" she asked again.

Tommy had talked about smoking grass with his friends and they were up for it, but nobody had a connection. He took the fat, loose cigarette and sucked in a shallow puff, exhaling quickly.

"You gotta hold it… Hold it in, Boy" Reggie explained, demonstrating for effect. "I remember the first time I smoked… didn't hold it in and didn't do a darned thing. Everybody else was loopy and I'm wondering, what's the deal, you know?"

Tommy took a long drag the second time around and held it as long as he could, letting go with a stifled cough.

"You're corrupting him," Robbie said.

"It's okay, Boy. It's just like booze without the hangover. It's a lot mellower than a beer high. It's such a happy drug."

"What kind of people are we? We need happy drugs? Jeesh!" Robbie pontificated.

"Okay, Mr. Beer."

"I guess," Robbie conceded. "But a man doesn't have to hide behind a beer. He can stand up tall and take a drink right there with the Mayor. That's all I'm saying."

"That's because we live in a puritanical, uptight society. Why should you be able to get your beer in the store and meanwhile, I've got to buy my pot on the streets and smoke it behind closed doors. Our government is such a hypocrite when it comes to pot."

"Maybe so, but more drugs doesn't make us better people. Drugs are just a time-waster. Just an escape, they aren't real."

Reggie passed the joint to Robbie, "Another hit, honey?"

"I'm just keeping you company, darlin'. It doesn't really do that much for me."

"You're such a good boyfriend."

"I'm a swell boyfriend."

Tommy was beginning to feel happy. He asked, "Where do you get this stuff from?"

"I get it at school. It's everywhere in college."

"You're in college?" Tommy figured her a bit older, but supposed she worked full time at the dealership.

Reggie was back on her elbows, leaning against the rock wall. She told him, "I'm taking business management at Buffalo."

"She's gonna take over the dealership from her old man," Robbie added.

"I suppose, someday. If he lets me. I am his only kid."

"Still, you gotta wonder if he's gonna give it all up to some pothead," Robbie said, almost serious.

"You're such a jackass," Reggie said, flipping him the finger. "How about you, Boy? You going to college?"

"I'm just gonna be a senior this year."

"Yeah? Me too," Robbie said.

"I thought you were older," Tommy said.

"My little boys," she said playfully.

"You planning on college?" Robbie asked Tommy.

"I'm enlisting... the Marines."

"Don't be stupid," Reggie said.

"It's not stupid," Robbie defended Tommy. "It's noble. It's what real men do."

"Real men know it's really stupid. It's a stupid time to enlist. Tommy, promise me you're not going to join this stupid war."

"Maybe I'm gonna join up," Robbie said.

"Yeah, right," she said sarcastically, dismissing it as idle talk.

"Maybe. I mean I've been thinkin' about it for a while. I think it's time us Clark's took a turn. I mean, my dad and my grandpa never served. We made millions in these wars, but we never really staked anything."

"Now's not the time for making amends. Believe me, it's an awful war and we should all refuse to take part in it."

Tommy had never seen her so serious about anything. He argued, "Are we just gonna walk away and let the commies take another country?"

"How about we let the Vietnamese people decide for themselves?" Reggie shot back.

"Yeah, but you got China and Russia mixed up in it. They can't decide on their own."

"Well, I've been thinkin' maybe I should join up. Join up and take some responsibility in life. Start bein' a man, you know? Right, Tommy?" Robbie said.

"Go ahead. You just join right up and, while you're at it, you can find yourself another girl."

"You'd really dump me?" Robbie asked seriously.

"You wanna serve your country, how about using your family's influence to get us out of Vietnam. That idiot Johnson just keeps digging us in, deeper and deeper."

"But would you? Would you really leave me?"

"You're not joining," Reggie insisted.

"But if I did, what would you do?"

"It's a hypothetical. It will never happen... First of all, your father would never stand for it. And then your mother, oh my God! Your mother would never let her precious baby go off to war. It would kill her. So I'm not answering things that are never gonna happen."

"That's where you're wrong, Reg."

"You could probably go in for officer training," Tommy offered.

"Nah, if I go, I'm going in as an enlistee. If I wanted to keep away from the action, I'd just go to college. I wanna be there, experience everything, see everything."

"You wanna experience being dead?" Reggie quipped.

"I wanna experience the specter of death, yeah. I wanna know if I can kill another man. To look square across at another fella and decide whether or not to take away everything he was or ever will be. Would I think about what his mother will do when she finds out? Does he have a girl, maybe even a kid at home? Would I need to hate him? Could I just do it and never think about it again? I dunno, it's gotta be the most intense human experience. Sanctioned murder."

"Sounds really great, Robbie. Sounds super. You just run off and join right up."

"There's no reason for you to be scared for me."

"Is that what you think this is? I'm scared for you? Please! It's morally wrong for us to be over there. This is American imperialism at its worst. Who even knows if Vietnam wants to be like us? Do you think the average peasant farmer trying to feed his family gives a shit who's running the country?"

"I think so," Tommy interjected into the spat.

"Scared for you? I wouldn't even pity you if you went over there."

"War is our nature," Robbie said. "I suppose a man needs to experience war to appreciate his own existence... to appreciate peace. To confront our dark side, to live with it as a young man and hopefully come through it. To know you've confronted fear and mortality."

"I wonder if all those kids dying over there appreciate the philosophical advantages of their lost existence?"

"Those aren't kids. Those are men. Those are men putting their lives on the line for their country. Kids run off to Canada, men face their responsibility."

"You're crazy. I guess I shouldn't let you smoke."

"No, Reg. I see everything with complete clarity. And because I do, I know there's no point in aggravating you further, 'cause maybe you won't love me for some whole different reason by then," he said and started back down the creek.

Reggie said, "He's full of it. And don't you go do something stupid either, Tommy. Nobody thinks you're a hero."

On the trip back, Tommy missed a rock and got a hotfoot, too.

It was past midnight coming home. Reggie sat against Tommy, at one point laying her head on his shoulder and closing her eyes. As he climbed the porch steps, Robbie hit the horn twice. Then they were gone.

# 9

# ☙ Peanut Butter & Bananas

Thoughts of Regina Albach. From then on, boyish want, a brume behind which the rest paled. Tommy ached to taste the sweetness of adjacent beauty and plotted those moments their paths would cross at work; only to endure the torment of missed connections.

This aching had led to him to be particularly short-tempered around the house, especially with Peanut. It was Saturday and she was pestering for the television, even though the ball game was on. She flung a pillow and he was about to swat her when footsteps on the porch were followed by the rattle of a knock on the screen door.

"Get it," Tommy ordered.

"You get it," Peanut snapped back.

Tommy started after her. She screeched and ran for the door. She didn't know the boy on their porch. He looked at her forthrightly and she did not shrink. Not so long ago she would have looked away shyly, but she had begun to harness her charms. This newly-forged mettle a gift from the boys at school. These same boys who used to tease her, or worse, ignore her; now finding every gesture, each utterance, an absolute fascination. Tommy was jealous of this acquired confidence and found this sudden sex appeal completely annoying. How easily it came, with a padded bra and a smile. Nothing was easy for Tommy when it came to girls.

The boy at the door was wet from exertion and smudged with engine grease, "Does Tommy Donahue live here?"

"Come in," Peanut held open the door. "Tommy, it's for you!" In the hall he slapped her and she pretended it didn't hurt, laughing out, "My TV now."

"Hello, Tommy."

It was Robbie and Tommy felt poor.

"Sorry, I'm such a damn mess. My jeep died in town. It's air in the fuel line and usually I can get it with a little gas in the carburetor. Not today, though. I need a phone to call for a lift."

Tommy told him, "Come in."

"I'm a bit of a mess," Robbie apologized.

Peanut was on the couch, her legs tucked neatly under her shorts as Robbie Clark followed into the kitchen. Tommy did not see how they fell in that moment of passing, two droplets on a windowpane, funneling down in a collision course of hearts. How her big brown eyes fell like a lasso upon him. The cotton of her cheeks funneling his eyes to the taper of her chin and the gentle expanse of her neckline. How it seemed they decided to inhale at once, sucking from a single strand of air; each tugging on a thread of breath in the still heat of a mid-summer's day.

In the kitchen Tommy asked Robbie, "You wanna Coke?"

"A glass of water sounds great," Robbie said as he helped himself to their sink and scrubbed the grease from his hands with a scouring pad.

"Sit down," Tommy offered.

"I don't suppose your folks want my sweat all over their furniture."

"Don't matter none," Tommy said, but Robbie drank without sitting.

"So you go to school in town?" Robbie said idly.

"The high school, yeah."

"You're lucky, man. My parents got me at Nichols. With all the other stiff necks. Bunch of pretenders, you know? Rich kids who think they got it all. No substance though," the pot mentioned to the kettle, or so Tommy thought.

Robbie's attention turned through the kitchen door and his eyes went back to the second droplet, "Nice place."

Yeah, right, Tommy thought. Then he saw him looking at Peanut as she pretended to watch a cartoon, clutching a pillow to her chest and thinking about the other droplet.

Knowing exactly what he wanted and how it was his for the taking. A confidence beyond money and looks, Robbie abruptly dropped his conversation with Tommy and approached his sister directly, "How are you? I'm Robbie."

"That's Peanut," Tommy answered for her.

"Peanut? Who called you that?"

She said unabashedly, "My dad. 'Cause when I was a baby I liked peanut butter so much."

"It's because she's a nut," Tommy said.

"Ever have it with bananas?" Robbie asked.

"Oh my God, I love it! Peanut butter and banana sandwich, it's *soooo* good," Peanut said.

"So, you're Tommy's little sister?" Robbie asked.

"She's fourteen," Tommy answered again for her.

"I'm almost fifteen," Peanut added for clarification.

"She's fourteen," Tommy reiterated, making it clear she's not to be trifled with. He was uneasy, this direction Regina Albach's fella was heading.

Robbie said, "I'm such a mess. I gotta get a ride home and jump in the pool."

"You got your own pool?" Peanut asked, taking the bait.

"Sure, you wanna go for a swim? You and Tommy?" Robbie said, extending the offer to Tommy for cover.

"Mom told you to clean your room." Tommy tried to dump Peanut from the equation.

"Did already," she said, locking eyes with Robbie again.

"Go get your suit on, we got towels up at the house."

Robbie called the barn and arranged for a lift. Tommy put his swimming trunks on and was back in a flash, his pants rolled up under his arms. It was awkwardly quiet as they waited for Peanut. Tommy knew what he was thinking and it left Robbie compromised. Clark's swagger suddenly tempered and he couldn't even manage a lick of small talk.

Picking up the load, Tommy said, "You should call the garage and let Reggie's guys tow your car. You can still catch'em, I think."

"We got a tow dolly up at the house. I'll have one of our guys help me later. We got a mechanic on the farm."

Of course you do, Tommy thought. And then he asked, "Where's Reggie this weekend?"

"She's with her folks in the Finger Lakes. Her mom's sister has a cabin there, I think. Something like that."

Peanut made an entrance in cut-offs that complimented her legs and a bikini top showing under a white see-through tee. She saved her allowance and bought the swimsuit while shopping with a friend. When her mother discovered it they had a private conversation and came to an understanding that, under no circumstances, would this be seen in the company of her father. As far as Tommy knew, this was the first time she wore it outside her room. She brushed out her hair and pinched her cheeks, too.

"We gotta walk to the circle, my guy'll meet us there."

"Where do you live?" Peanut asked.

"It's not too far," Robbie said modestly.

Peanut stumbled out of untied sneakers coming down the porch steps and giggled. She was mastering the art of turning chagrin to seduction. Tommy wanted to slug her.

The pickup was waiting at the circle and they rode in the back. At the estate, the truck came up using the back way, a short cut along a dirt field path. They bounced along clutching the wheel wells, Peanut wide-eyed passing through the stone wall.

She asked, "Does your dad work here?"

"Yeah, sometimes," Robbie said.

Tommy had enough of this modest suspense and snapped, "This is Robbie Clark. He lives here."

"You don't live here," Peanut scoffed.

"Does too."

"Na-uh."

With a jolt, the truck stuttered up onto pavement again, turning sharply and soon stopping out front the big house. A spotted dog with a hunched back ambled up to meet them, its tail pointing down and wagging with effort. Robbie gathered up the mutt's ears, smothering her with hugs and coos.

"Is that your dog?" Peanut wondered.

"This is Ella. Somebody just dumped her along side the road and I've had her since she was a pup. Can you believe that? Just dumped her out in the big world. She sleeps with me every night and she's my best girl, aren't you, Ella?"

Robbie's mother and sister were reading on loungers by the pool. Having just come from the club, they looked showered and fresh in their tennis skirts; daughter Linda's hem showing inches more thigh. She posed with a *Look* magazine that had Johnny Carson on the cover.

Robbie introduced them as Tommy and Peanut and Mrs. Clark needed clarification, "I'm sorry, dear. Who are your friends?"

Robbie repeated, "This is Tommy Donahue and his sister Peanut."

"My, what a name!" Mrs. Clark said. "That surely can't be your real name."

"Her real name's Deborah. We just call her Peanut," Tommy said formally.

"Debbie," his sister corrected.

"Are you from the city?"

"No, we live here."

Mrs. Clark looked them over and said, "That's odd, I thought I knew all of Robbie's local friends."

"They live in the village," Robbie clarified.

"The village? Oh? How do you know each other, then?" his mother asked Tommy.

"I work at Albach's."

"Oh, I see. A friend of Regina's then?" Mrs. Clark said with a judgmental air, which was her way.

"Yes, ma'am."

"You may call me Mrs. Clark," she corrected him.

"Okay, ma'am," Robbie clucked, pointing out his mother's pretensions.

"Oh, I hate being ma'am. It's what someone in servitude would say out of obligation. Mrs. Clark is what I prefer."

"Yes, ma'am," Robbie said again.

And when Robbie introduced them to Linda, she excused herself in a mood.

In the cabana, they were each given a stall to change and hang their things. Tommy saw the chair, that first portrait of Reggie and the memory became vivid again, the fullness of the towel as it clung and that hair tumbling rich and everywhere. The husky voice still buried in the rafters. The longing had warped his summer and now it was bad again.

They waited in shade of the cabana for Peanut and there was no discretion in Robbie when she pushed open the stall door, a faint blush on her cheeks and crossing her arms to cover herself. The bikini was a clunky thing with loose fitting shorts and a top that covered her completely. Maybe for the first time Tommy saw his sister as a beauty. Not a beauty like Reggie, but slight and proportioned and a woman in waiting.

As Robbie's eyes lingered uncomfortably, she had enough and stomped her foot, saying, "God! Are we gonna swim or what?"

Peanut and Tommy slid timidly into the pool before Robbie took a leaping cannonball into the middle, it's splash causing Mrs. Clark to recoil with a footnote of disapproval. They had an underwater distance competition and raced laps with handicaps, as Robbie was so much faster. At Marco Polo, Peanut and Robbie would find each other with feigned vigor, resulting in handy discoveries. Through it all, Tommy assumed third wheel status, as was his custom. The pool couple had not escaped the veiled attention of Mrs. Clark, who was seen peeking over the rims of her sunglasses.

After sun drying on deck chairs they went in the big house for peanut butter and banana sandwiches. Tommy was put off by the *un-wonderful* wheat bread and settled on just a banana. Standing shoulder-to-shoulder, Robbie slopped on the spread and Peanut giggled at him, slicing and pressing the banana chunks into the goo. All to be followed by a great sucking of fingers.

It was Tommy who suggested they better get home and Robbie took them in one of the barn trucks, Peanut stretched sideways in the back compartment, snuggling with Ella. When Robbie was gone Tommy told his sister, "He's got a girl, you know?"

"So... big deal," she said, dashing upstairs to avoid any chance of being discovered in her bikini.

# 10
# ❧ The Bench Player

Boy knocked on the bedroom door and she turned down the letters.

"Well, our Maddy's in a snit," he said.

"I know. Bad timing, for sure. *Suppose she really knew about these?*" Gee said, the little smile she wore diminished by a certain sadness in her voice.

"Do you need some time alone?"

She realized the distance and came back to him, "No, I want you to hold me. Squeeze me, Boy."

She swept the letters away and he sat beside her. She pulled him close, kissing him with a younger passion and he drew back surprised. "Those letters must be awfully interesting."

"I love you so much, Boy... I do. I love you, Tommy... Do you wanna read them?" she asked earnestly.

"No, those are yours."

She didn't fight him and said half-heartedly, "You sure? I don't want these between us."

He paused and said what had been on his mind since she became his, "You know, it's okay if you loved him first. I'm okay with second place."

"Don't say that? You know you've always been my love."

"You shouldn't lie. You're not very good at it, sweetheart."

"Okay, maybe I didn't know it then. But you were always the right one for me."

"Sure, I had all the looks, but what about the money?" he said trying to lighten the mood. "You missed out on a life of leisure."

She looked at him, sad eyes fighting tears.

"What?" he wondered.

"Nothing... I was glad for a career."

"What?... Tell me."

Looking away, letting her hair fall between them, keeping his eyes from hers, she said regretfully, "Robbie... he had a way... he could see me. I'm not sure you ever could. You wouldn't have wanted me if you really saw me."

"I saw you from the start."

"Sure, my face, my legs... my chest."

"Whatever I saw, it was all I ever wanted. From that first night in the dark, scared and dumb, there was never anyone else... never."

She squeezed him and buried her face on his chest.

He told her, "What I wouldn't give for another lifetime with you."

She spoke into his chest, "In his letter, he said you'd hate me. He said I took you away from your destiny and I drove you from your family. He was right. You should hate me. I've thought it, I swear I have. I've thought there must be times when you honestly blame me, and you should. You must have thought it. Maybe not straight out, but deep down."

"Never."

"It's fine. It's okay if you blamed me. I was a ridiculous little girl who took your life, just like that war took his."

"I never thought that. Not once, Gee."

"Well, I have. I was a stupid, ridiculous little girl. And I took your life because I couldn't have what I really wanted."

They knew it and she said it. She wanted the other one most and they knew it between them.

"I'm sorry," she said.

"For what?"

"For saying that."

Tommy rested his chin on the top of her head, holding tight, "I told you, I've had a great life as a bench player. I know how you feel... how he still haunts you. I know the longing that comes from a true love unsatisfied."

"Yeah? Who's your great unsatisfied love?"

"You know... it was you. It was always you. I was so selfish, Gee. I was glad Robbie never came back. If he came back, I can't imagine my life." She wiped a tear and tried to smile and he continued, "I know you settled, but you doing that... I can't imagine my life otherwise."

"He wouldn't have ever come back to me. No matter what. It was Debbie all along. I know that now. So, I didn't settle, Boy. Having you is the furthest thing from it."

He let his fingers walk lightly upon her neck and said closely, "Sure you settled. But you settling, that made all the difference. Don't you see? To have you; to share everything important with you. Letting me be a father... giving me Maddy. I've had a life of substance and meaning and my only sadness is I wasn't all that for you."

"You think you haven't been everything to me?" she wondered.

"I think there's always going to be some doubt – some *what could've been*. Moments of reflection like this. I don't have that. For me, there was never anyone else. Your feelings about Robbie, they're natural, you know? I suspect most people have feelings for someone before marriage, or they find someone along the way and wonder *what if*? It's never been that way for me. It's always been you, Gee. I've never thought about a life with someone else."

"You're such a liar," she said and punched him playfully on the shoulder.

"What?... You know it, right? You know it's only been you, right?"

And she did know it. It had only been her for him, although she could never dismiss thoughts of Robbie. She often thought of that lost love in those moments alone. She would try to remember his face and she would remember the happy times and intimate moments they shared when Robbie was hers. How she never felt so deeply again. And there were those times when she was making love with Boy and she would shut her eyes and pretend he was Robbie and the sex was sometimes better because of this. Yet, she did love Boy and these thoughts should not be construed as regret. They were, as he said, uncontrollable thoughts of *what if* and nothing more.

"Boy, I've been thinking about Maddy. And now with Robbie found... I don't know."

She wondered if now was time to set the record straight. At the time of her birth, the path of least resistance had become a comfort for each of them. But Maddy has other living blood and her father would be coming home, too.

Being rejected by his daughter was a secret fear he wrestled with through the years; the irrationality of competing with a dead man. Boy said, "I'm not so sure, Gee. Would telling her be a comfort or would it open up a wound that won't heal? It's been so many years and it's too late to change anything. Really change things, anyways."

"She's a tough kid."

"But what if she resents me? How would you feel if you find out your whole existence is a lie?" he worried.

"It's not a lie. You're her dad and I'm her mommy. It's not so much as where the seed comes from, but who tends the field. Nurture over nature. That's what I believe."

"Did you make that up?"

"Yeah."

"Just now?"

"Not just now, but it's something I've thought about... a lot"

"Really? You're awfully deep, sweetheart," he quipped. "Besides, who would she hear it from, if not us? It's been so long since then. This is a secret I'd just as soon take to the grave. You can tell her when I'm gone."

She threw an arm around him. It was a secret she kept for him. It was a deal they made before Madeline's birth. The baby would take his name. She would be a Donohue and he would love her as his own. There was a caveat; if Robbie ever showed up alive, then Maddy would know. But the exception expired with the discovery of PFC Robert Clark's earthly remains. Yet here was Robbie and his interminable presence, both burying the truth and exhuming it, all at once.

"I'm not so sure that's entirely fair to Maddy. This thing with Robbie turning up and all. It is her real father." And she immediately wished she hadn't put it that way. She retraced her steps and said tenderly, "Boy, you're her daddy and always will be. You're her daddy and even if she gets upset, I deserve the blame, not you. You gave her a wonderful life and never held anything back, even if she wasn't your blood."

Boy felt tears about to come. Afraid of losing Maddy, if only by disappointment. He said softly, "I always thought of her as mine. I suppose it was selfish."

"It wasn't selfish, it was completely noble. You've been a wonderful father, but now..."

She stopped and they sat quietly.

"What about Debbie and her daughter? You think she knows?" she asked.

"I suppose. My sister wasn't the type to keep things in like me. I mean, she had to tell her daughter something about a father."

"I'd like to think the two sisters could get to know each other. Let them decide if they want a relationship. I think Maddy might like having a sister."

"I hated having a sister."

"Shut up," Gee scolded playfully. "She's your sister and I can't help thinking, maybe getting our girls together might help bring you two around."

"Is that what this is about? Me and Debbie?"

"I don't know. Maybe. You know, I'm responsible for what happened. I feel awful. You lost your whole family 'cause of me. Really. If I could somehow make it better for you, it would be better for me... It was just a thought, is all."

"Bad thought."

"Bad Boy," she said.

He laid his head upon her lap and shut his eyes while she pet his face, as a young lover might. The act of touching and feeling the warmth of the other, a nest for their collective brood. She took another letter and he kept his eyes closed, happy in ignorance. She took it because she wanted him to know he was part of this. She wasn't hiding things, like with Maddy.

At first blush, it was a letter wrought with angst, the handwriting sloppy, unlike his usual meticulous, almost feminine cursive. It was written over several sheets of ruled paper, the thoughts crossed out and revised between lines. Amendments were scribbled in the margins, pointed at with arrows.

*February 2nd, 1969*
*FSB Rhonda*
*Quang Nam Province, South Vietnam*

*Dear Reg,*

    *My first letter to you snuggles in my pocket, beside your letter, and now I'm already writing again. It's nearly midnight and I should be sleeping, but here I lay, wide awake in a foxhole, a flashlight propped between sandbags and thinking of you – I hope the handwriting isn't too awful! There's been some action here and we're supposed to move out on a little S&D (Search and Destroy) any time now. The thought of real action had my heart racing, but now, as I look up and see these stars strewn across the south Asia sky, somehow they calm me with thoughts of you. It reminds me of times with you on your back porch. The hammock and you asleep and just watching these same old stars and listening to the sound of your body at peace.*

*I don't even know if I'll send that first letter, <u>so if you only get this one</u>, know that I've decided to spare you my cranky side.*

*And through all this rambling I neglect to talk about what really needs to be said. It's cowardice, plain and simple, that's what it is. Even now as I write word upon word and never get to the point. And as sure as this pen doesn't cease its incessant scribbling, it's just as sure that I can't find the words this letter deserves. I never once doubted my love for you. <u>Not once!</u> I could never not love you and what I have to say will make you think that what I just wrote is complete bullshit. But it's not. Hell, when I say it out loud, it even sounds ridiculous.*

*So, here goes...*

*That night, after being together, after the fight and after you hit me (I still can't believe you slugged me – I don't know who's more dangerous. you or the VC), I did go to Tommy's sister. I was so confused at having such deep feelings for two women (I know you don't understand and I don't blame you). Confused at wanting to be true to you, but knowing I had feelings of love for another. While I could always explain my affection for you, I have trouble understanding my feelings for her. Over here the Vietnamese have a word for men who sleep around and they call them "butterflies". I'm not a butterfly, Reg. I know she's young and we don't know each other like you and I - but I love her, too. I'm sorry, Reg, but I can't help myself. It's primal – unlike anything I've ever felt before. I find I want to possess her completely, take care of her, nourish her. I want her to blossom under my care and guidance. Do you understand any of this?*

*You are a completely different person, Reg. You don't need me. You don't need any guy. We were always an equal in every sense of the word. You are a person who knows what she wants and can take care of herself in any situation – and I love this most about you.*

*I swear, there are tears in my eyes right now and I'm smearing the ink with these tears – look at it, Reg. This smudge is my heart ground into every fiber and aching to hold you and make it like it was. Like it was before Vietnam and like it was when we first dated and when every moment apart was a moment of sweet anticipation. I love you so much, but I think she possesses a place somewhere deeper in my soul.*

*It would be easy if I knew you hated me now! I hope you despise me! I hope you are completely done with me! How easy that would be, but I know it's not like that. Is it presumptuous of me to know that when you get this letter it will make you cry and hurt you like the death of a lover? I know you still love me. Your letter, while short and indifferent, can't mask the fact that I'm still the love of your life. I don't know what to do, Reg. We are perfect together. You're the smartest woman I've ever known. You're the most beautiful woman I've ever known - you're an incomparable lover. You're a soul mate in every sense of the word. Why isn't that good enough?*

*Still, I'm bewitched by her. I know it's irrational and I know it could never work and I know what my parents think of me with her. But I think of her more than I care to admit, my dear Reg. I know this is horrible of me to write like this, but being so far away and never knowing what might happen tomorrow...*

*Maybe I'm just writing to myself and maybe I'll never send this. Never tell you of my selfish torment. Spare you such pain when maybe it all becomes pointless. Maybe I'll step on a mine or maybe a bullet will find me, then you can rest knowing I did love you with all my heart - and I do love*

*you. Somehow dying out here suddenly seems appealing –
just kidding.*

*Well, I know this is a horrible situation for us, so far
apart. This whole situation has been eating me up, though.
I love you so much and I never want to lie to you again. I
want to be the man you knew and respected. So, there you
have it. Shitty as it is, there it is. One more reason for you
to hate me. When I come home, I hope we can talk and work
through our true feelings and continue our friendship (our
love?) – maybe you never want to see me again, or maybe we
have a destiny together. I don't know which.*

*Please take good care of yourself and I hope things are
going well at school.*

*A million and two kisses
Robbie*

# 11
# ‿ What's For Lunch

Sometime in August, after the picnic and after the swim in the pool at the big house, Reggie began having lunch with Tommy. On nice days they would sit behind the garage under the sprawling canopy of century trees above them. Their backs against the block wall. The buzz of impact wrenches on lug nuts and Regina's breasts heavy and high in her crew neck tee shirts.

For Tommy, every moment a precursor to that half-hour in the glow of Regina. She would look in his brown bag and make him guess what mom had packed. She thought it pathetic a lunch was made for him.

"Thuringer sandwich?" he guessed.

"Close."

"Baloney."

"That's not close."

"It's really close."

"Thuringer and baloney aren't even on the same planet," she said.

"They're both round."

"So what? All lunch meat is round."

"Not ham," he argued.

"No, ham's are round, too... Go ahead, guess again."

"I give."

"Guess," she said, holding the bag away from him.

"Gimme," he said, reaching to take it back.

She grabbed his arm, holding him off. When she laughed and tried to escape, he pulled her close, by the waist. He was flush with the closeness and there was her mouth and lips and his only instinct at was to touch them. As he lunged, she parried; the bag thrust between them. Her hair flicked up and brushed across his face.

"It's salami. Salami and thuringer are like practically the same thing, Boy."

She composed herself at once and he was frustrated by the awkward advance. There was nothing more made of it, though, at least that afternoon.

A few days later behind the garage she asked him about the swimming day. She said, "I hear your sister made quite an impression up at the pool."

"Whatta ya mean?" he wondered earnestly.

"Just that Robbie seemed quite bug-eyed is all."

"Who said that?" he asked.

"Mrs. Clark. Out of the clear blue, mind you – she says to me like I should know, *Robbie, had the young girl out from the village, the sister of that friend of yours, and they seemed quite involved. I don't like Robbie so involved with such a child,* she said. I don't know if she was trying to make me jealous or what?... And you? Did you think your sister was flirting with Robbie?"

"My sister's just a kid."

"She's cute, I've seen her. And she's old enough to flirt. So, was anything going on?"

"No," he said, even though Robbie did seem a little too familiar with Peanut for his liking. "We just went swimming and we were all fooling around."

"It really doesn't matter. I know he looks at other girls. I see him. I was just wondering if there was anything going on, that's all."

"I didn't see anything," Tommy said getting annoyed.

"I might have to castrate him. Make him a steer and put him out to pasture with the buffalo, you know?" As she said it she made a ball-busting fist.

"It bothers you? He looks at other girls," he said, finding it ridiculous this goddess beside him should feel threatened by his silly little sister.

"No... well, sure."

"You look at other guys."

"Just you, Boy," she said and pinched him. "But seriously, I don't really look at another guy the way he looks at girls. I know he's always thinking about doing them. It's a guy thing. It always come down to sex. I mean, there's plenty of guys I could get, but I don't. I have a boyfriend."

"So you think you can get anyone you want?"

"I could get you."

Tommy blushed and she said, "I know I could get you. I have you. You tried to kiss me, didn't you? I wasn't very nice. After all, I was teasing you. In fact, I was a bitch. Maybe you should try again sometime."

"Maybe I will."

"Maybe I'll kiss you first," she kidded.

"Yeah, right," he dared to dream.

"No, you should do it. I appreciate assertive men. Definitely, you should be the one."

"How about right now?"

"Not now!"

"And what about Robbie?" he wondered.

"You're right. It wouldn't be right... even if it was just a little kiss between us. You must think I'm pretty slutty, huh?"

He wanted to keep this kissing discussion alive, so he decided to push her buttons and said, "Will you kiss me when I go off to Vietnam?"

"Never. I told you, you're not to go."

"What if they draft me?"

"Don't go." she snapped.

"You have to go. They'll put you in jail."

"Jail's better than going. Besides, you could go to Canada. Lots of guys are doing it. At school there's a whole support group for conscientious objectors."

"Conscientious objectors? That's a bunch of garbage."

"So says you."

Then he grabbed her hand and said directly, "But if I were going... and I am going. When I go in the Marines, you won't even give me a goodbye kiss?"

"On the cheek."

Then she kissed her fingers and placed them lightly on his cheek and stood up saying, "So long, Boy. Back to work."

# 12
# ◌ Dear Peanut

Eyes shut, Tommy lay in Regina's lap. A place he adored. Feeling each breath, and if she bent just so, he could pick up a heartbeat. A stethoscope of love, this place reserved for him alone. The solace of her body and how she accommodated his desire. Her entrance below, a moment from his lips, where everything came true. An arm across him and her fingertips lightly on his back. Natural together in a lifetime of closeness.

Linda's letter in her other hand, she read the words again and wondered, "Boy, what do make of this? *To complicate things even further, there is yet another surprise. I have a niece in Vietnam. I* mean, I know what it sounds like."

"Who said that?"

"Robbie's sister. It says here she's got a niece in Vietnam... I mean, really Robbie?"

"That's Robbie. What's new?"

"You would think he could keep it in his pants for a month, especially after the mess he left here."

"Well, we know you girls and how you go for them rich, good-lookin' guys," Tommy said, his eyes still closed. It was a throw-away line, with no intention.

Abruptly, she pushed him away and snapped, "Jerk... You're an asshole, Boy."

She carelessly scooped up the letters and stormed into the bathroom, locking the door. Tommy stood outside and called softly,

"Gee, don't be like that... I didn't mean anything. I really didn't... Gee?"

He turned the handle to check if it was truly locked. It was.

He tried again, "Don't be mad. I'm sorry... Come on out. I've got work in the garage, so you can have the room. Don't lock yourself in there... We can talk about it later."

She came out, alone again, and read a letter addressed to Peanut. A soul-aching pain enveloped her. Nothing she could pinpoint, just a low-grade pain that took her breath away. A fury of heartbreak unleashed by triggered memories; a scab of deception and rivalry picked off. Confirmation of who loved who. She should have just folded it up and put it aside for Debbie. It was written on the night of the mission, placed with hers in his backpack.

*February 2nd, 1969*
*FSB Rhonda*
*Quang Nam Province, South Vietnam*

*Dear Sweet Pea;*

*Tonight we're breaking out from the monotony of our daily routine. Enemy activity has been seen in the valley and I'm going out on my first real mission. It's night and it's real quiet here. I'm just waiting for the platoon sergeant to round us up and head out. We're moving out at night to avoid enemy eyes.*

*If you could see me now in my whole infantry getup I think you'd be proud. Sarge said we may be out for three days, so my pack is fully loaded.*

*- Six quarts of water*
*- Nine C ration meals*
*- A couple of smoke grenades (to direct artillery)*
*- Two frag grenades for killing*
*- A machete for chopping brush*
*- A gas mask*
*- An air mattress and poncho in a roll*
*- Two claymore mines*
*- Two flares*
*- Some C4 for heating our meals.*

*I'm taking the cookies you made and I put them in an empty ammo container along with the picture you sent. I love that picture so much and you look so beautiful. I don't know why you think it isn't good. I doubt you can take anything but a beautiful picture.*

*I haven't strapped on my bandoleers yet, but they're right here in the foxhole. They carry my —16 Ammo and you wear them in an X across your chest. They're heavy, too. Almost 10 pounds fully loaded. I'm going to hang my towel around my neck to wipe the never-ending sweat off. It will be pretty gross by the time we're back. Some of the guys wanted to go out in Boonie hats, but Sarge wasn't having it and I guess I agree with him. I'm wearing my helmet. After all, I have to get back to see my Peanut.*

*Wanting to see you again is ever on my mind. When I signed up all I could think about was getting here and being a part of this big human drama; then you became mine. Now I find that I am constantly thinking about coming home to you. I think about your smile and your face and other things that I won't say in a letter. I think about those other things a lot. I'm so grateful for you on our last night and that you should think me worthy of your innocence and your love. I hope you still feel I'm worthy of your love, because you have all of mine.*

*It seems I get a letter from you every time there's mail call and I'll be so disappointed the day there's not one in the bag. But don't feel like you have to write!... But I hope you do.*

*In my last letter I sent you a photo of me in my Army getup and I hope you like it half as much as I like the photo you sent me.*

*Well, I've still got a few things to do before we head out. Don't know if I can write before we get back. Either way there's no mailbox in the bush.*

*A big squeeze and lots of honey*

*From sunny Vietnam,*
*Bobby Bananas*

Bobby Bananas was in love with *her* and he wasn't in love with *she*. If it had been otherwise, he would have stayed and their collective fate would have jumbled in a different spill of the dice. It was clear he was conflicted only in trying to tell her. Debbie was Robbie's true love and even a lifetime later, this hurt.

# 13
# ᘓ Bully For Him

The waning of summer had come to Tommy with an uncustom-
ary ease. The steady work left him with pockets full of cash... and
self-esteem; the society of colleagues proved a springboard from
the friends of his youth. This new beginning ensconced in an understanding that the world of adolescence was fleeting. Having
tasted snippets of independence, he began to know the future was
this seed sown in a pasture of pubescent rain and nurtured in a
sun of masculinity. And then there was the love of his life. It was
only a game they played at lunch; at work. But oh, such sport! A
sport of soulful depths where scores are kept with points of pain
and envy, lust and desire.

This morphing of worlds created a dichotomy as he passed
through the threshold of public education for one last lesson. For
one more year he would be but a boy, before magically emerging
from this chrysalistic confinement and deemed capable of defend-
ing a nation.

The last Friday of September was a highlight of the school
year... *Freshman Friday*. Much dreaded by the incoming class
and oft recited by veterans of the ritual. The day of reckoning for
newbies in the old building on Main. On this day freshmen faced
the specter of enforced servitude backed by threats of pantings
and pushings (into bathrooms and change rooms of the oppo-
site-sex). There were stories of kids being locked in lockers over-
night and rumors of beatings, more legend than fact.

Tommy really didn't know any freshman, so he was given to gloming on to Will and some of the other guys who had kin or neighbors new to high school. Will had been baiting his cousin Trent at every chance for about a year now. The gang was together as they spotted him moving in a crowd at the far end of the hall. Trent had seen them, too, and was trying to bury himself in the herd moving between classes.

"There's the kid," Will said deliciously. "I'll circle 'round back and you push him my way."

Trent was a frumpy kid, socially awkward and anxious in public. Born with a bully target on his ass, he couldn't even count on blood to spare his dignity. While reveling as much as the next guy in the spirit of the day, at heart Tommy abhorred bullies. And though his friends were not bullies by nature, today they were such by association. This was Freshman Friday and what was all the talk and anticipation if not followed by action. Why, in the years to come, these freshmen would thank them for holding to tradition. One day, they too, could enjoy the ritual of intimidation and pointless torment.

As a freshman, no one had bothered at all with Tommy and this could be attributed to a total lack of distinction in the community. However, he had put considerable effort into scaring Peanut prior to her first year of high school, but she was an unabashed tattle-tale and their father held him personally responsible for her safety. He did manage to string up her locker with enough knots to make her late for gym and send her to the office for a pass. It was a face saving each could live with.

Will had come up fast from the other end of the hall, collaring his cousin with mock affection, "We've been looking for ya, buddy."

The boy's terror scarcely hidden by a crooked smile.

"Thought we told you to meet us outside after third period?" Their original plan had been to lace his Keds together and wrap them around an overhead utility line. But he skipped out on his appointment.

"Where ya' goin', buddy?" they asked.

Weak and easily flushed from the security of the herd, the kill was on. Will took him by the buttons and yanked him into the stairwell.

"Hey guys... Guys... Guys, c'mon... Guys..." He kept saying *guys*, as if by saying it he became one of them. They had him encircled and were pushing him off from one to another. Kids passing up the stairs watched, but kept moving. Girls giggled and guys whooped things like, *Die freshman!* You could tell the other freshmen in the mob, as they passed quiet and swift, avoiding eye contact.

Jenny Pierce passed just as Tommy pushed hard for the first time and Trent's books hit the floor, papers puffing out in all directions. The guys laughed. Tommy looked at the lips he kissed, now contemptuous and dripping disgust from angry corners. There was a perceptible shake of her head as she wound out of sight.

He felt mean and the thrill of the hazing deflated into a moment of self-loathing. It was a bellwether moment he would always remember; the moment of escape from the clique and a confronting of personal truths. The first bloom of sun-moistened masculinity pushing forth from a thicket of buds. He looked at Trent, trapped, fragile and scared. Stilling echoing *guys* as his books were kicked and scattered under the stairwell. At that moment Tommy had enough of the pack and pushed back.

He shouted at his friends, "Knock it off!"

Will, flush with the taste of blood and bereft of reason, continued his prodding. In an out of body experience, Tommy ripped Will's hands from his cousin and pushed him hard enough that Will stumbled to the floor against the wall, "I said let him go!"

Will got up with fists drawn and screamed back, "I'll kill you, you faggot!"

"Whatta ya gonna do, hit me?" Tommy had not taken a defensive posture.

"I'll rip yer damned heart out!"

Will observed the astonished faces of the others, especially Trent.

Tommy turned his back on Will and started to pick up the books, saying, "It just ain't funny anymore. It's stupid, man. He's scared. Why you gotta be so mean? He's just a kid for Chris'sake."

"Awghh, I wasn't gonna do nothin'."

"Ya already did. Ya already messed him up. He's your cousin for Chris'sake!"

Tommy shuffled the books and papers together as neatly as he could before handing them to the boy, "Sorry, man."

Tommy walked off and Will attempted to rein in the pack by yelling, "Always knew you were a damn faggot, Donahue."

"Yeah, guess so."

The rest of that day Tommy felt friendless, yet breathlessly empowered; having dared to strike a true course and damn the consequences. No longer defined by others, but by personal truths. He could've gone along to get along. He always had. He could've rode the drift, taking refuge in the comfort of the pack, just one of the guys; but instead daring to push against the current.

He had Jenny in two afternoon classes. Until then, she had been hinting for a homecoming date, but that afternoon she ignored him completely and understandably so.

After last bell Tommy didn't dawdle, nor did he look for walking companions. He didn't even go to the locker, heading straight for the doors.

He still worked Saturdays at the dealership, but Reggie was back in school and hadn't been seen since August. She continued to occupy his quiet times; giving wings to fantasies and schemes that would make them a couple. And walking through town, a fantasy passed by in a teal blue Camaro SS. The car stopped quickly, nimbly jutting to the curb ahead of him. It had dealer plates and a puff of auburn hair was draped across the seat back.

He strode up to the passenger door as she rolled down the window "Hello, Boy. Wanna ride?"

Of course he wanted a ride, but just played it cool, "It's only a couple blocks. I can walk."

"Let me take you. I haven't seen you for so long!"

He got in. "I remember this car from the lot. You got it now?"

"Until daddy takes it back."

"It's loaded, huh. Power windows, push button AM-FM. This thing is pretty cool."

"It's fast, too. Got a 350 V8. I got pulled over by a state trooper doing eighty-five on the thruway. I swear I thought I was doing, like maybe, sixty."

"You couldn't tell by the fact you were blowing by everybody else on the road?"

"I thought maybe they were all just a bunch of slowpokes or old people, I suppose," she giggled.

"So you get a ticket?"

"Got a warning."

"Got a warning? That's ridiculous."

"What? I just explained I didn't know. I wasn't lying. I didn't know how fast I was going."

"That's garbage! You got a gauge right in front of you. It tells you how fast you're goin'. You think I would have got a warning?" Tommy asked.

"Sure, why not?"

"That's ridiculous. It's because you're a girl and so damn pretty, is all." He meant to say it's because you're the most beautiful girl in the world, but then they were in front of his house.

He asked, "You workin' any Saturdays?"

"Not right now, school and all, you know? How about you?"

"Every Saturday, eight to four."

About to leave she asked, "You busy tonight?"

Not wanting her to suspect he was friendless and a complete loser, he said, "I dunno, I thought I might hang out with the guys..." *These same guys he turned his back on this afternoon?*

"Well, you wanna come into the city and hang out with me?"

"How would I get there?"

"I can take you. They'll be lots of college girls. It could be fun for you, Boy."

"Is Robbie going?"

"He's got a polo match all weekend. Up in Saratoga, I think."

"Like with horses, you mean?"

"Yeah. It's a family thing. Him and his dad are really into it. They have a field on the property." Then she asked him again, "So you wanna hang out later?"

"Yeah, I guess so. That sounds cool."

"Great. I'm heading home and I'll pick you up sometime after dinner, say seven-thirty?"

"Wanna meet at the circle?" he suggested.

"The circle? You sneaking out then?"

He was about to lie, but said, "Yeah, kinda."

"Okay, fine. See you at seven-thirty... at the circle."

# 14
# ❧ A Tuesday Feeling

At school, Peanut was a fine student. She had many friends, including an assembly of boys who thirsted for moments beyond friendship. She was a temptress, for certain, but not intentionally so. She did not lead them in an exercise of ego, as so many other girls did, but treated their admiration with a demure respect. She would distance herself from the most aggressive pursuers. Since the summer she had been in love and her heart was not available to these boys.

They met one time after the swim date. Robbie called the house and by no coincidence she answered. He saw Tommy with his mother in town and raced to put a coin in the pay phone. Straight forward, he asked for her. Could she meet in the park for a bag lunch of peanut butter and bananas?

And so it went, she did meet him alone that day. Many thoughts crowded close as she scurried to the spot Robbie was waiting. It was the Friday before Labor Day and the most beautiful summer day of her young life. She made her way through the side streets of the village and shivered to think about romantic advances. She would reject him, of course, but it couldn't be an absolute rejection; it would have to be a tiny scolding, tempered by a dose of desire. She would show a willingness to move beyond little girl status, given time. She imagined turning her cheek and letting his lips caress her neck as she explained that she was only fifteen and they had been recent acquaintances and she was not ready for more, but... And she thought of his lips on her neck and how this was the first step along their path.

But his lips never came near that day, nor did they touch at all, even in happenstance as he was a perfect gentleman. She was completely at ease as they filled in blanks with stories of their lives, each listening as old friends might, gleaning context and nuance. They laughed and told stories that explored the depth of their private lives and when it was over he drove her close to home and they wished each other well on the school year ahead.

In the days that followed, she found herself floating through life. In love and knowing it was the same for him. So, therefore the boys at school could only be boys and friends and there was no pressure to oblige them, even for ego's sake.

It was many weeks later, on a Tuesday, when he waited for her outside the high school in his old Jeep Willys. She was pleased, but not surprised.

"I get out early on Tuesdays, thought I'd bring you a sandwich." He showed her it was peanut butter and bananas. "Can you go driving?"

"I have to be home by supper," she said.

They parked down an old dirt road that led to an abandoned gravel pit. It was up a hill that looked back toward the city. The fall leaves winking hints of crimson and gold, a reminder of things to come and the gloom of winter they soon would endure.

Robbie took the Jeep off road, tilting it thrillingly up through bumpy field grass, finally positioning it with a wide view of the city and lake. Peanut grabbed his arm and leaned into him until they were there, at the top. He shut the engine and the car wobbled back until he engaged the handbrake. The sandwiches and the chocolate milk were tied in a basket behind them.

"See those smokestacks down by the lake?" he asked. The smoke from the furnaces at Clark Steel cut the distant horizon.

Not knowing, Peanut said, "I think it's ugly, all that pollution."

"That's Clark Steel."

"I'm sorry," she said embarrassed.

"It's okay. It is ugly and dirty. That soot and smoke keeps a lot of people working, though."

"I wouldn't have said, if I knew it was yours."

"First off, it's my dad's... and second, never lie about your feelings. Not with me, anyways."

He unpacked the basket and placed a cloth napkin on her lap. As they ate, he told her, "I like to come up here by myself and just look over the city. Kind of makes you feel like a king in his kingdom. Looking down on thousands of people, just like us, living their lives. People dying, kids being born. People profoundly sad with no way out; thinking about killing themselves right this minute. People making love. It's all happening down there right now, Peanut, and here we are, above it all."

"You're kind of funny," Peanut said.

"Funny how?"

"Funny... you pretending to be a king. I mean you kind of are a king around here, aren't you? You live in that place, have lots of pretty things and you don't have to worry about money and everybody wants to be like you. I bet your dad gives you whatever you want," she said, looking down at his hands, conscious of his eyes on her. His hands were steady and strong, one on the stick and one on the wheel, not given to the nervous fidgeting of her own.

"My dad takes good care of us and we do have a nice place and lots of things, but I don't need things. Things are just stuff without meaning. What's special about having money... the real thing about money is it gives you choices. All paths are open to me, money is never an obstacle. A lot of people are stuck in unhappy lives because of money. I'm never stuck," Robbie said with great consideration. It was his way, to be thoughtful and self-aware. He continued, "But they always say money can't buy happiness and I know that's true. If things are all that matters, there's always someone who has better things, even for us. Some people spend all day worrying about things. Not me. Not one second."

"It's nice to have nice things and I appreciate them. In my house we learn to make due. When we do get clothes, like for Christmas and school, we know it's a sacrifice our parents make."

"Nice clothes don't make nice people."

"It's nice to think I look pretty, like when I wear a dress for the first time."

"Well, you're about the prettiest thing I ever saw and it wouldn't matter to me what your clothes were. The ugliest rag couldn't hide you from me. Even before I saw you in that little bikini, I knew you were so damn pretty. That's what I think."

Blushing, she turned further away, shielding her eyes as she spoke in a timid voice, "What about your girl? I hear you have someone."

"I do. Reggie Albach. She's a great girl and I thought I loved her about as much as I could love anyone. For a while there, I couldn't imagine anything coming between us, but then we're both young and things change fast when you're young. You know that, right? When you're young like us, things change fast."

He watched her until she looked at him, obliging him, "Yup, things change fast."

He continued earnestly, "You never know what's gonna happen. We've been together since last year on June fifteenth, me and Reggie. I know it almost to the minute when we first met. We had a two o'clock tee time and she came running up all fabulous at the last second, looking about pretty as anything I had ever seen... *up 'til then*. It was at the club, she was playing with her dad and I was playing with mine. Just the luck of the draw, us getting put together as a foursome that day. Life's funny, how it puts two people together, don't you think? Fate or chance?"

"Fate, plain and simple. God has a plan for us," Peanut said, looking into his eyes now.

"I figured you for a fate girl. You're a Catholic, right? I'm a chance guy myself. I'm not so sure there's a God, and if there is a God, it seems like he'd be way too busy to care about who goes with who."

"I believe in God. I know he cares about us and he answers our prayers."

"Yeah, you got prayers he answered for you, Peanut?"

"Yes... and none of your business," she cut off his question. "That girl is still your girl, though."

"She is and I'm not sure what I'm gonna do about that. She's my girlfriend and this is a bad situation. I guess I just say to myself that you and I are just friends, that's all. And we are, Peanut. Just secret friends who like peanut butter and bananas and I'm gonna just keep bringing you sandwiches and chocolate milk and being your friend. That's all I can do because I have a girlfriend and it isn't fair to fall in love when you're already in love. It should be impossible to fall in love when you're already in love, don't you think?"

"I don't know. I've never been in love." And she did not say *until now*.

"Never?"

"I'm still fifteen, you know?"

"I was in love way before fifteen."

Surprised, she smiled and challenged him, "Yeah? How many times have you been in love, then?"

"I dunno. Too many times, I suppose. I suppose it wasn't really love. A lot of it was lust, I guess. Love has to have some permanence. Even with Reggie, is it love if you've been together for a year and a half? Is it love like what our folks have, lasting years and years together? I don't know. How can I know?"

Peanut liked how he sought her opinion and explained, "Love is just a feeling and I guess you know when it happens. I mean, feelings are just that, something you feel and something that happens. Like when something bad happens and you're sad. It's not something you're taught or something you decide. It just is. When you're happy, you're happy and it's not something you do or don't do. You just are."

"Well, are you happy?"

"Are you?" she countered.

"I think I'm really happy."

"With your secret friend?" she said, perhaps accusingly.

"Yes, with my secret friend. Does that bother you, being a secret?"

She did not think about it and responded truthfully, "I don't mind being a secret friend. I understand what people would say, you with me. What your parents would say. What Reggie Albach would say. I guess it has to be secret for me, too. After all, my dad would kill me if he knew I was up here with a boy."

"I don't want it to be secret always. I hope that someday everyone knows. Everyone down in our secret kingdom. I hope we can just let them know all about us."

"Someday?"

"That's right. Someday."

# 15
# ଓ The Pot Party

He told his mother not to worry, he'd stay at Jesse's and hitch a ride to work in the morning. Jesse had been to supper and his mother liked him. He didn't know Reggie's plans, but if this turned into a sleepover, the lie was in place. There was a chill in the air and she was late to the circle, coming after dim streetlights fashioned muted shadows.

"Sorry, my mom was in a super chatty mood. Couldn't get away, you know?"

"No problem," he said.

"Now that I'm back in school, she misses me, you know? I think she gets lonely. Me being her only kid and all."

"You're lucky, being the only kid."

"How's that?" she wondered.

"I bet you're a spoiled brat."

"Am not," she said laughing. "Sure, I suppose they do spoil me, but I think I'm a pretty respectful daughter. Just because I get all the love and attention, it doesn't mean I'm a brat. My dad, he was tough on me growing up."

"You're just lucky you don't have a sister."

"And how is your sister?" she said, more prying than curious.

"Her? She's just so... she thinks she's so damn cool. All these guys at school are in love with her, so now she thinks she's special. I don't get it."

"That's all?" she pressed.

"What else?"

"Just that somebody said they saw her and Robbie, that's all."

News to him, he said, "I told you about the swimming."

"No, this was recently. Someone saw him driving around town with a girl and I figured it was your sister from the sound of it. I thought maybe you heard about it."

"Who said that?"

"Just someone. Not important."

"Well, nobody told me. Debbie didn't say nuthin' about it, either. I suppose I'd know if she was riding around with Robbie."

"Okay," she said.

She headed north past the Clark estate, towards the city. It was a quiet road, remnant farms speckled with mom and pop businesses. Gas at the Sinclair station was twenty-seven, nine. She had one eye on the road and one on him, a half smile, portending of a pinch or a statement ending with the endearing, *Boy*. But she left it to him.

And he finally said, "What?"

"What?" she answered.

"What're ya lookin' at?"

"You. You're not a bad-lookin' guy. At first I didn't think you were much. Especially that night, you know… well, neither here nor there, but you're not a bad-lookin' guy. I definitely like you with shorter hair. You've really matured since the first time we met. I think so, anyways."

"So, you're saying I'm good looking, then?"

"Yeah, you're not a bad-lookin' kid."

"So, you think I'm just a kid. I'm old as Robbie."

"Yeah, I suppose… You'll always be a boy to me," she said matter-of-factly.

"I don't wanna be a kid tonight. Not with all those college girls."

"Oh, you'll be the kid, all right, but you'll be fine. My roommate is jealous I got a younger boyfriend. I told her about you and she digs younger guys. Especially virgins. She wants to meet you."

Tommy reddened. "You don't know."

She gave him the look again, "Oh, Boy is embarrassed. I simply love when you blush for me! I'm not criticizing you. It's just that you're a shy guy and I think that's cool. Guys who mess around with a bunch of different chicks, yuck! Guys think us girls don't care about a guy's virginity, but they do. Some of us anyways."

"You're not one," he said.

"I'm not what?"

"A virgin."

"Well, I'm not telling you if I am or if I'm not," she said smugly.

"I saw you and Robbie."

"Yeah? What did you see?"

"I saw you."

She laughed, "Well, if you saw, then was I doing it?"

"He was naked and..."

"And what?" she teased.

"I know what he was. He was more than just naked." Tommy remembered that thing so close to his face.

"There's lots of different things you can do... naked. There's plenty of things you can do with your clothes off. You're not necessarily... *doing it*."

He didn't like this conversation. He didn't like thinking about her doing anything with anybody else naked. And he didn't like this teasing that revealed delicate personal truths.

"Well I don't believe that you're still one."

"I told you, none of your business."

"But it's okay for you to say about me?" Tommy said facing her. The flushness in his cheeks transitioning from embarrassment to anger.

"Yes. It's okay for me to tease, because that's our thing."

"I don't like it."

"Sure you do. You like it when I tease and I like to see your rosy red cheeks when I get you all flustered. You're so shy and cute and naive. You're my adorable little boy."

He was furious and she sensed it was time to pull back, "Don't be mad at me, Boy. I'm sorry. I don't want us to be this way tonight. I wanna show you my place and introduce you to my friends and I just wanna have some fun tonight. If you're gonna be mad at me it's gonna be a drag."

He still said nothing.

She pulled off to the side and faced him, "Do you wanna go home?"

It was a power move. She held all the power and this was a reminder. He was in her sights, the hammer was cocked and a finger on the trigger. Dignity was in the crosshairs and time had come for him to behave. Just remember who's the alpha dog here.

"Tommy, should I take you home?" she repeated, the hammer cracked and the bullet flew.

"No, I wanna go. I just don't wanna be teased all night, is all."

She sighed, and then, "Well, can I at least tease you until we get there? After all, Thomas, it's just you and me now and if it's not your thing, at least can it be mine?"

She leaned over and put her chin on his turned shoulder and did a quick tickle causing a squirm.

"All right!" he giggled as she did it again.

"Good."

And that was settled. She didn't even tease on the way there. Her house was off Bailey near the Main Street campus and it was shared with five other coeds. It was a girly place with colorful things covering the tenant drab walls and a heap of petite shoes stacked on a rack in the foyer. Remnant furniture dotted the downstairs living space, surfaces covered conspicuously with beer cans, a bottle of Haig and another of Seven Crown. Large button tacks pinned up posters, the transient art of youth; anti-war ones, concert dates, Hendrix and Dylan. Another of Ricky Nelson, campy and out of place with the counter culture of the rest.

The console stereo was spinning *Surrealistic Pillow* - specifically *Today* - and Grace Slick on that song would always remind him of his epiphany; a vivid recall of that time when doctrine became questioned. A scented candle, an elixir to doubt, and over that, the smell from the day at the eternal flame.

The couches were full with boys and girls sitting close, familiar and comfortable; completely contrary to the mixed socials at the Boys and Girls Club, where the anxious airs of desperate yearnings were confined to postures of cool from the farthest walls; waiting and hoping to be noticed, or not. At Reggie's house they fancied tattered jeans and frilly vests. Cool came in beaded headbands and tie-dye wrap skirts.

One fella stood to greet Reggie with a hug and kiss and she told everyone, "This is a friend of mine, Boy."

"Your name is Boy?" A girl sitting cross-legged on the floor in bell bottoms giggled.

"Oh, I mean Tommy. Don't anyone dare call him that. I'm the only one who can call him that. Boy, I mean. You guys call him Tommy," Reggie corrected.

She took him by the hand up the side staircase to her room and someone clucked, *See ya later, Boy... I mean, Tommy.* She shut the door behind them. There were two beds in her room. He sat on the other one and she told him it was Karen's.

"She's the one on the floor by the stereo with dangly earrings. The one with the peace sign necklace and bell bottoms. She's the jealous one who digs virgins. Not that you're one," Reggie said smiling, and teasing just a little.

Reggie's desk had an open book on statistics with a half-written assignment. In the side drawer she had a baggie with pot and rolling papers. Her fingers elegantly working the papers, the cigarette moistened and sucked through her lips before letting him light it. He took a draw and passed it, comfortably holding back the smoke this time. She let it burn under her nose, looking at it, and only then taking a long draw; after a while letting it out in an easy blow. When it got short she took a roach clip from the drawer and attached it.

"Got a buzz?" she asked.

"I'm soooo... holy cow, I dunno, man," he said.

"It's good, right?"

After, they went downstairs. Reggie made seven and sevens and they sat on the floor with pillows against the wall. Karen held up the Mamas and Papas album that had all of them in the tub, but a guy with a stubbly beard on the couch said that was shit. Karen shuffled further down the crooked stack on the floor and pulled out an album with the three band members fish-eyed and air brushed on a psychedelic background. The Jimi Hendrix Experience written in neon purple on a lemon background. The record jacket was worn and cracked. The dead space at the beginning of side one popped with a scratch that carried into the first track. Karen turned it up as Hendrix chopped out the alternating high and low chords that soon slid into the signature riff of *Purple Haze.*

A *Free Martin Sostre* poster over the couch sat uneasily with Tommy. His father had been articulating with increasing vile about this nigger and the goddam commies who came to the city to cause more trouble. It was hard for Tommy to understand why anyone would want to free Martin Sostre. The door to the shelter of his life had been busted down and a different world howled under the same moon.

Reggie made proper introductions. The guy with the scruffy beard was Harold and his fingers were playing in Elaine's hair. He asked, "So, Boy. Are you a student here?"

"Me, no."

"I told you, please don't call him, Boy," Reggie persisted. "I told you. His name is Tommy."

"You go to school?"

"He works at the dealership," Reggie answered, deflecting the question.

"So you work for Reggie's old man?"

"Yeah."

"Is her old man just like her? If he is, I bet he's a son of a bitch."

"He's a good guy," Tommy answered.

"Oh, she must get it from her mother, then. One bitch to another."

"My mother's a peach. I'm just a bitch to you, Harry," Reggie said.

"And to me," Karen added.

"It takes one to know one," Reggie spat back.

The conversation was politics and music and school and protests and ever so cool. Tommy was no part of it, but eagerly digested the feast of notions foreign to small town boys everywhere. He was sitting on the floor with her, close enough to touch with a lean or shimmy or even a deep breath and each time it happened he would linger longer in the softness of her. The kids spoke with convictions about making a new world, of seizing power from the establishment and that's what they called it, *the establishment*. The only establishment he knew were places where his father might go for a drink.

Sometime later another housemate arrived and brushed through the room, she had been crying. Reggie told Tommy she better see what's up. She assured him he'd be fine by himself for a little while.

Alone, Karen scooted up beside him. She whispered, her lips tickling his ears, "Reggie told me all about you, Boy. You're just some kid in high school. You are just *a boy*."

"So what?"

"So, nothing. So I know about you, that's all." And she got close again. "Don't worry I won't bust your cover."

"I'm not trying to cover anything."

"Promise, I won't bust your cover. My lips are sealed," she said, nuzzling in again. She nuzzled up in a sexy, suggestive way, her lips brushing against his neck and ears, moving even after the words were done.

"Where's Reggie?" he asked.

"She's up with Jen. Jen's got boyfriend problems and she's bit of a mess. You wanna go up and smoke?"

"What about Reggie and that girl? I don't wanna interrupt."

"It's okay. Let's go upstairs and check it out. C'mon."

The door to the room was shut. Karen knocked and from inside Reggie asked for a minute. When the door opened Jen, with the boyfriend problems, was sitting on the bed and an obvious wreck.

"Me and Tommy, we're gonna smoke. You guys in?"

Reggie gave her the pot and said, "Maybe later. We got something pretty heavy goin' on. You can use Jen's room, if you want."

He felt anxious when Reggie shut the door again and Karen pulled him across the hall to another room with a single bed. It was a small room with no window, a glorified closet with a sharp slanted ceiling that followed the roofline. The bed was tucked under the slant and you could only sit up from the inner edge. Insecurity heightened as she locked the door. There was a little table full of burn marks and she lit the candle on it. It was their only light and she was sitting against him as she rolled the joint.

Tommy said, "Are you all hippy chicks or what?"

"You think?"

"You look like hippy chicks."

"You're funny, Boy. We're just college girls," Karen said, her tongue painting the glue on the wrapping paper.

"You look like hippy chicks. And what's with the free Sostre poster?"

"Martin Sostre? Guy was framed. The pigs needed a scapegoat for the riots. Somebody to pin it on. Can't arrest society, so they go after the scariest colored guy they can find and arrest him. Problem solved."

"He's the guy who got the niggers going. Even they said so," Tommy said.

"Got the *niggers* going?"

He had been so used to hearing it at home, it was second nature and he was embarrassed now.

She confronted him with a smile and her pretty face glowing in the dim of the candle, "What are you, Boy? Are you from Alabama? Are you an old southern racist; one of them good 'ol boys with their sheets and hoods maybe?"

"No, it's just that those guys who are doing the rioting and stuff, that's what they are," he squirmed.

"'Cause I'm a Jew, you know. I don't want to wake up to some ol' cross burning in the yard."

He couldn't be sure that he actually ever met a Jew before. There was a Jehovah's Witness girl in his class and he quite honestly didn't know the difference. This day he was far from life in the little village of East Aurora.

"I'm not a racist. I wouldn't care if you were colored Jewish," he lied.

"Colored Jewish?" she giggled. These college girls sure liked exposing inadequacies.

"You know what I mean."

"Yes, Boy, you're toking up with a genuine Long Island JAP."

"What's that mean?"

"JAP... Jewish American princess. Privileged, spoiled and entitled little Jewish girls."

"So I guess that makes your mom a queen, then?"

She spit out a laugh and said, "You're a funny guy, Boy... Hey, you know how you can tell if a Jewish American princess has an orgasm?.. She drops her emery board."

He smiled, but didn't get it. So she tried another, "Or, you know how to get a Jewish American princess to stop having sex?"

Quite stoned he said emphatically, "I have no idea!"

"Marry her."

He got that one and laughed a hearty laugh of intoxication.

As they smoked, she told him she was a psych major. Buffalo wasn't her first choice, but she definitely wanted to go away to school and they were the first to send a letter of acceptance. A bird in hand, she took it. She really didn't like the winters here. And she really didn't know what she was going to do with her major, but thought maybe she could work as a school counselor.

Then she said, "You wanna shotgun?"

"Shotgun?"

"Okay, blow all the air out of your lungs... Now come here, Boy," she commanded.

She took a long draw on the joint and pulled him tight to her mouth. She led him with her lips, opening his mouth and filling him with a strapping dose of narcotic breath. After, when the smoke was gone, it was just them on the bed. Primitive and instinctual, he pointed the way and she assisted capably in the short, awkward journey to experience.

"Oh, you're not done, are you? Don't be done! Are you done?" she gasped.

"Yeah," he whimpered.

She was still longing and clutching as he retreated. He was embarrassed for leaving her wanting and he was afraid of what Reggie would think.

Shuffling around for his shorts she grabbed what was left and said, "What's your hurry, honey? I think there might be some permanent damage here. I think we should hang out and make sure it grows back."

"I should go see if Reggie's looking for me."

And having come to terms with the disappointment, she felt around the wet spot on the bed and said blithely, "Sorry, Jen. I should probably wash this. Probably won't, though."

# 16
# ◌ℨ The Sibling Reunion

It was a trip he would have surely avoided, but his wife's insistence had drawn a line in the sand. Gee said she would go it alone, if necessary, and Tommy imagined the trouble this could start. Of course, the trouble started long before this, but he felt certain a physical confrontation was imminent if Gee showed up unannounced at Debbie's door. At their mother's wake, Debbie had to be restrained from going after Regina in the parking lot. The rest of the viewing and service was complicated with schemes to keep the two women away from each other. Tommy and Gee did not attend his father's funeral, years before that. His father's life had fallen apart when things went south in a hurry, ending up a full-time drunk living in a trailer, they found him dead on the floor in a pile of vomit.

Boy and Gee made the trip silently. By the park they strained to see the numbers on steps and porch posts. She parked on the street.

"Sure you don't want me to come?" Gee asked as he took the envelope.

"No, it should be me. I don't think she'd open the door for you."

"Don't get emotional," she told him.

"I'll be fine."

"Well, just don't get emotional," she said a second time, driving home her point.

There were two names on the front door; none were his. Wandering down the side, along a broken asphalt laneway and there were two more names, Ryan and Donahue. He pushed the bell and heard footsteps creaking in the stairwell. She looked even older than the last time they met, but it was her. Did he look as distant from the boy she once knew? But she knew him at once. Her face became detached and impenetrable.

"Peanut?" he asked.

"Debbie. Nobody calls me Peanut anymore," she said back coldly.

"I brought the letters."

"Okay," she held out her hand to receive them, and nothing more.

He handed them over and asked, "Can I come in? Can't I at least talk to you?"

"I don't have anything for you, Tommy."

"Can't you at least talk to me? Debbie, I swear, I can't figure how it ever got like this?"

"If you can't figure that out, what's there to talk about?" Her rigid exterior had come to her over the years, finding toughness to survive as a woman in her circumstance. There was little left of the shy, sweet girl he remembered.

"Sure, I know you're mad at Regina, but she isn't the only one to blame. He was her boyfriend, you know? You were fooling around with her boyfriend. Did you expect her to be gracious?"

Her face went blank, "He came to me on his own. You have no idea what we had."

"You knew what you were doing," Tommy said, unable to hide his anger.

Debbie took a moment to reflect, convinced there was no reconciliation coming, "You're right. I did know what I was doing, and so did he. We did it together and now I've carried the burden, alone, all these years. Who helped me? Where would I be if he lived? If Robbie lived?"

"Life's a two-way street, Deb. We're ready to make amends. We want a relationship with you and your daughter. Whatever it takes."

She tried to shut the door, but he wedged a shoe tip in, a crevice of communication.

"Debbie, I didn't have to come. I didn't even have to tell you about these letters."

"I didn't ask you for these, Tommy. I really didn't."

"Don't you understand, I wanted you to have them. Gee wanted you to have them. She thought it was important. These letters are all that's left of him. Of Robbie. That's not important to you?... I came because I wanted to see you." His insides roiled with emotion and he remembered his wife's words of caution.

She widened the door, bent down and moved his foot back, shooing a bug that had blown in by mistake. And while shutting the door for a second time, she said, "I gotta go... And do me a favor, tell that bitch that called me, never to call my house again. Ever... Got it?"

He pounded on the glass and shouted after her, "She wants to make it better, Debbie. She feels bad about things. She's sorry as hell... Can't you just talk to us, for cris'sake?... And one other thing, you know Roberta's got a sister! How about that?" And even louder, "Roberta has a sister, you know!" And shouting now, "And she has an uncle, too!"

As his face pressed against the glass, he heard the door at the top of the landing shut and the clunk of a lock latching.

Debbie peeked around the drapes, watching as her brother left with the woman she blamed for her lot in life. A woman she had often referred to as a bitter and jealous witch who lied specifically to ruin her. Regina Albach was the one person alive, besides herself, who knew that Robbie loved her. The one person who knew the truth and refused to tell it when it mattered most. To tell it now would change nothing, the damage had been done.

At her kitchen table Peanut reread what she had written to her true love, in delicate handwriting, a tattered lifetime ago;

*January 14th, 1969*

*Hi Bobby Bananas;*

    *These last two weeks without you has been simply awful. I can't stand you're so far away and I pray to God for your safe return every night. I find myself sleepwalking through school and only imagine you on a plane coming home to me. I'm trying to do better, but my grades are suffering because all that matters now is you. I'm writing this letter in science class and the teacher thinks I'm writing up my lab. I'll try to do better, honey, but all I want is you. I want to be in your arms again. Do you want me too, baby?*

    *When I told you before how much I missed you, you asked me, "How do you think I feel?" You feel with your hands, honey. You feel me with your hands, just the way we've always done it. Me in your hands, just the way it has always been and my arms around you and our lips together, honey. That's how we feel. We feel together and everything is all right when we're together. My only happiness is you and my whole being is you.*

*I'm sending you this picture, but it's not very good. I looked and couldn't find any good pictures of me, the way I want to be for you. This was taken in the booth at Vidler's and it isn't very good, but it's the best I could do. I tried to smile for you, honey, though I'm hurting without you. I swear this is the best that I could do right now, but I'm going to do better. I'm going to try and last the whole year. I swear I'm going to be strong for you. I'm such a baby, back here in the safety of these United States and you so far away and with people who want to kill you. I don't care if we win or if we lose. I only care that you come back to me and I continue to pray to God that you will. I pray for you and then I pray that there is a God who cares about us.*

*I'm just repeating the same shit over and over and now the teacher's walking around so I should hide this letter, but I can't. Know that I love you, honey. Know that I'm praying for you right now and in 11 months we'll be together again. If there's anything that you want, know I will give it to you. I'm yours completely and I feel there's already part of you in me now. I shouldn't even think that, but it could be true or it could be false, but I don't care. I only care about us.*

*I baked the cookies and I hope they aren't too stale when you get them. I kissed every one, so they're just for you and not for sharing. Each cookie had my lips on them - just a little kiss. Eat each and every one of my kisses, honey.*

*Write back as soon as you can. I miss you so much, baby!!!!!*

*Kissing you like mad,*
*Sweet Pea*


Reggie read it too, a voyeur; a fly on the wall. Her love was real and strong, but by expression alone, it paled in comparison to the passion of Debbie. Words of raw and unadulterated passion; words she was incapable of. Who would blame the man who took it? It was innocence and purity and fresh sensuality. Debbie had known then, too, just as she had known. If nothing else, their bond was in knowing about fresh life.

# 17
# ❧ The Flogging of the Lately Chaste

Reggie was down with the rest when he hatched from his tryst and Tommy sheepishly cuddled into a nearby nook. She greeted him with a sagacious smile. Karen was down shortly after completely waveless, ignoring him but for a sideways glance while lighting a cigarette. She flung herself on Harold's lap, throwing a cozy arm around him, as if nothing happened. In contrast, Tommy sat stiff and stoned, paralyzed from the shock of her body and its easy extraction of innocence. In those precious seconds where everything was lost. How he became so pleasurably unconscious in just the feel of her. How simply she took him and how willing he was to have it. And now after, contrite beside the girl he wished for.

Another seven and seven and Captain Beefheart and *Safe As Milk* and what was, was gone. Softly, the music and the night and nothing before and now beside her. He floated as laughter and emergence and closeness swirled round, innocence lost and innocence found. He and she, Tommy and Reggie, they were singing along with *I'm Glad* and the girl of his dreams sang close, swaying, *so sad, baby... so, sad, baby... so, glad, girl.*

And later she asked him, "Tell me... did you and Karen have some fun together?"

"We just got high is all," he said.

"Hmmm, that's all?" she asked, already knowing. "Guess I can't tease you about being a virgin anymore."

"I didn't even want to with her. I wish it were you," he said quite honestly.

"Oh, Boy, you're such a sweetie."

"I am your sweetie, you know that. Still, you wouldn't have wanted to be with me," he said impetuously.

"I am with you, Boy."

"I mean upstairs. You wouldn't have wanted to be with me upstairs?"

"But we were upstairs? Remember?"

"Yeah, but, you know."

"Oh yeah, of course... *upstairs.*"

"You know, upstairs. Upstairs and your top off. You know what I want. And besides, you said you wouldn't tease me," he reminded.

"Sorry, you're right. I did say I wouldn't tease, didn't I? But you know I have a boyfriend."

"Yeah, but what if you didn't?" he pressed.

"But I do. It's all hypothetical shit, this talk, Tommy. I don't deal well with hypothetical shit, you know that. I've got a boyfriend and I love him very much. And who knows what a year from now brings? Who knows where I'll be, where he'll be or where you'll be for that matter? I mean, who really knows, right?"

"So in a year, then. What happens if you're not in love next year?"

He was just staring at her, with a longing, and she continued with a push in her attitude, "I mean, you and Robbie, you're the tough guys. You say you're going off to Vietnam. Maybe you'll both be dead, for all I know... Sorry, that was a pretty awful thing to say. Maybe I'll be dead, who knows?" She could see he wasn't satisfied and added, "Besides, you have a girlfriend." And she spoke above the whir at Karen, who was still wrapped around Harold, "Right, Karen? Isn't that right, Tommy's got a girl?"

Karen gave Tommy a dull stare and replied cruelly, detached and without emotion, "How should I know? I barely know him."

"Oh, that's not what I hear."

Karen said to him, "Boy, didn't anyone ever tell you it's not polite to kiss and tell?"

They were in between records, so it was the conversation of the room; all hands on deck to witness the flogging of the lately chaste from the strap of the virginity thief.

Harold said, "Karen loves Boy."

"For God's sake, I was just babysitting the guy. He's just a high school kid. Think I'm a cradle robber or what? And besides, so what if I did?"

He wanted to run. Tiny smirks and innocent snickers gashed his tender pride with a dagger's swath and even he couldn't believe it when he blurted out, "Well, at least I'm not a damn slut."

Everyone did laugh now, including Karen; she refusing to relinquish the power and easily deflecting the joke right back at him, "So, okay, maybe I took advantage of him. I always wanted to do a virgin, so shoot me."

"Well, he may be a kid, but he's got you nailed," Harold said playfully.

"Literally," someone else said.

Tommy sat red in the face, flush with the bitter trivialization of his most intimate historical experience. He felt small... no, microscopic; he felt an uncommon rage puffing through his veins. Fight or flight? He had fought and been gored by the horns of derision. Time to fly.

.

# 18
# ०३ Enid's Treasure

Robbie stretched on the wool rug in front of his mother's bed reading a *National Geographic*. His sisters, Judy and Linda, were parsing through the opulence of jewel boxes collected by their mother through a lifetime of plenty. They had been hinting, and in fact she had promised, the time had come for her to forfeit some of the loot; that clinker which seldom left the felt-lined jewel boxes. Except for the good stuff, her most prized possessions, most of it remained neatly hidden and seldom worn.

There were those pieces of great intrinsic value and those pieces of great sentimental value. Those things which would only pass on after death; her grandmother's diamond, the anniversary pendants and earrings from father, and the rose garnet ring from a first beau. As she took each piece from the box she would tell its story; stories that bookmarked events in her life. Stories she hoped would last in the memory of daughters and grand- daughters. Generations recalling her life, just as she did with Aunt Enid's necklace.

Holding the necklace against her blouse she began, "Enid was widowed in the first world war, you know, and Uncle Marcus was her second husband. A lot of people don't know Enid was married before Marcus. The necklace itself is pretty, but the diamond is small and flawed. Her first husband, Albert, came from very little and it was the best he could do on a tradesman's wage. He was killed in the battle of Blanc Mont Ridge."

"Oh, how horrible," Linda said.

"Albert had come from poor immigrant parents and he met Enid while doing work in my grandmother's house... I've shown you that place; you know, the one by the park with the carriage house."

"Enid and Grandma Bea were sisters, right?" Linda asked.

"That's right. Their father, your great-grandfather, owned a shipping company that carried cargo from Buffalo to Chicago and all across the lakes. They were quite wealthy at the time, but eventually lost it all in the depression... Anyways, Enid would watch Albert as he worked, and it was the same for him, each had secretly fallen in love at first sight, or so Enid would say. Of course, Albert never suspected there was a chance a girl of Enid's station would ever fall for a simple carpenter."

"Who could ever love a carpenter? A question that haunts Christians everywhere, don't you think?" Robbie clucked.

"Don't be blasphemous, Robbie," his mother scolded. "But Enid did love Albert and because her parents would never accept Albert, they were secretly married just nights before he shipped out. Since a ring would give away their secret marriage, Albert saw the necklace in the pawn shop and gave it to Enid in their room on their wedding night. He promised a ring from Paris when he got back from the war, but fate would leave Enid with only the necklace."

"Why would she give this to you?" Judy wondered.

"Well, when she was dying in the sanatorium - she had TB, you know - Grandma Bea thought it would be a grand idea for me to correspond with Enid and keep her spirits up. It was a chore I would have surely avoided had your grandmother not shamed me into it. One letter led to another and Enid opened up about her secret love affair and marriage. It must have been quite scandalous at the time and the secret must have been a burden she didn't want to take to her grave. Grandmother knew of Albert and the wedding, but she never understood the depth of their love affair the way it was written to me. Anyways, Enid and I wrote quite often as she was able. I began to look forward to her letters. It's funny to think this woman, who knew her days were numbered, was preoccupied by this momentary love affair."

"It's so romantic, Mother," Judy said.

"I find it completely sad. I mean, Enid's second husband was very well to do and he was a good man who treated her like a queen; Enid ruled that roost and Uncle Marcus catered to her every whim. Anyways, at her funeral, my cousin Lou comes to me with a jewelry case and a note. The note just said, *For Helen, from Enid via Albert.* Of course, I knew right away this was Albert's necklace and I asked my cousin if he knew why I was getting it. He just said his mother wanted me to have it because I was kind enough to write. And then he said quite innocently, *I have no idea who Albert is. Must have been an old beau.* So I guess Enid never even told her only son about Albert and the secret marriage. Strange, isn't it?"

She held the necklace up to the light and let it twirl in her fingers, contemplating its material value, saying, "Of course, this is a piece I would never wear out, but the chain is delicate and I suppose you could replace the stone, though it would seem a shame to do that to poor Albert. Dear man's time on earth cut short. Oh, life. Cherish it girls."

"It would be sinful to replace the stone," Robbie said.

"Well, of course, that's why I don't. So this poor little jewel never sees the light of day."

"I remember Aunt Enid," Robbie said.

"Really? You were just a child when she died," their mother said.

"I remember her, before she was sick, too. She was a jolly woman and she loved to tell jokes."

"I'm quite surprised you remember Enid. I mean, you couldn't have been three years old when she got the consumption."

"I remember her and she would always be telling me to do something silly, like make a face or run around like a chicken and flap my wings."

His mother frowned as she recalled Enid, saying, "I always thought she was terribly sarcastic; quite gruff really. Enid would always tell you what she thought, right to your face. Tact was not in her vocabulary."

"So you prefer people talk poorly *behind your back?*" Robbie accused his mother.

"I just think tact was a skill found lacking in Enid. Tact lets us behave civilly, even in situations with others who we don't necessarily agree with. It's prudent for ladies and gentlemen to act with discretion, at all times, in social situations. What would this world come to if we all just said whatever we thought, no matter what the circumstance, right girls?" she sought allegiance with desirous ears.

"I don't know, Mother, but I prefer a world of Aunt Enid's over these phonies we call friends."

"That's so harsh. We have wonderful friends. Who, specifically, are you referring to?"

"I'm talking about the snobby, pretentious privileged assholes we associate with." Robbie grabbed one of his father's dinner jackets from the coat rack and stood on a stool in the corner, acting like quite the snob, "Oh, yes Monte, we just returned from a week in Mallorca," intentionally mispronouncing the Catalan with the hard *Ma-lor-ka*, "Quite nice, really, but the yachts in the harbor were quite puny. Nothing like the yachts at Monte Carlo and Cannes, and of course, there were far too many Spaniards in Mallorca... Quite right, old chap. Couldn't agree more about the glut of Spaniards."

"That's not fair, Robbie," his mother said.

"I'm not saying we're better than them, because we're not. We're just the same. We're all show and pretension and... *tact*."

"What a grand-stander you are, Brother. You love being as pretentious as the rest of us," Judy said.

"I'm not pretentious. Pretension assumes putting on airs. I don't put on airs. With me you get what you see... Pretension? That's all you, Judy."

Robbie threw down the magazine, jumped up feet first on the bed and grabbed Judy's hair pulling it up in a bun, her protests ignored. Robbie said, "Let's get mother's tiara and put it on pretentious old Judy. Mother, do you have your crown? Judy wants to be a princess, too." Judy giggled as he fussed with her hair.

"Oh, for heaven's sake, the only time I've ever worn the thing is the day I married your father. It's not pretentious to wear a tiara on your wedding day," his mother said, smiling at his frivolity.

"No, Princess Judy deserves her crown. She needs her crown before she goes off to clean her horse's stall. Princess Judy needs her crown so she can go shovel poop."

"Stop it, Robbie!" Judy yelled with mock indignation.

"Still and all Mother, can I have Aunt Enid's necklace?" Robbie asked, surprising his mother.

"Who for? Reggie?"

"Not necessarily."

"Sad as it may be, it's still a family heirloom."

"You said yourself the stone was nothing to write home about."

"Sentimentality, Robbie. Aunt Enid gave it to me on her death bed and she wanted me to remember Albert and about how she once married for love, not money."

"I'll only give it to the woman I'm going to marry and I wouldn't marry anyone who couldn't appreciate the family credo; love over money."

"Now that does sound like Enid," his mother said.

Linda said, "It's not really Reggie's style."

"Oh, Linda, you don't know a thing about Reggie," Robbie snapped.

"Reggie is more of a beads and bracelet girl," their mother said. "I have plenty of nice bracelets I can see Reggie wearing. She's much more Bohemian in style."

"Bohemian?" Robbie mocked.

"Perhaps not Bohemian, but mod and counter culture, outside of the ordinary if you will. Of course, it's not a criticism, Reggie's a lovely girl. A bit old for you, perhaps."

"You think she's too old for me?"

Linda piped in, "I think it's absolutely creepy for a college girl to be dating a guy in high school."

"You're creepy, and those snobby stiff necks you frolic with."

"Mother thinks she's too old for you. She just said so."

"Mother said she's a lovely girl."

"But too old. She was using tact," Linda said.

"Was that it, Mother? Were you a practitioner of tact right then?"

"Well I do find it a bit odd such a pretty girl would fall for someone still in high school," his mother affirmed.

"Oh, I see. You think she's a social climber then?"

Judy teased, "I think she's just using him for his body."

"Well, I guess I won't hold that against her," Robbie mocked, pressing affectionately all over Judy.

"Get off me, Robbie! You stink!"

"You stink, Judy. You smell just like your stupid horse."

"Well, you smell like Ella."

"I love the way Ella smells."

"You would."

"I do... Besides, you're all gonna miss my stink around here when I join the Army."

They all stopped. They knew him and they knew his way. Idle threats not his style. What they saw was what they got. Snippets of truth like distilled droplets collecting in an oak cask, aging for consumption. Their mother frozen, a frail spirit clenched with fear. The girls paralyzed betwixt.

And then unfrozen, but still clenched, his mother said reasoning against the tide, "Your father has expectations for you."

"Of course, but I have my own expectations. Besides, I've spoke to him about it and he didn't say no," Robbie said.

Their mother quietly left the room, without the strength to protect them from the weakness of her own spirit. Disappointment and fear upon her, they had seen it before.

Linda said, "Nice going."

"I know. It was stupid. Telling her like this. When she's done pouting, I'll go and talk to her," Robbie said, Enid's necklace in his hands and thoughts of stories untold.

"Dad won't let you, you do know that? Especially after Mom gets at him."

"Well some things... they just don't need anyone's permission."

# 19
# ∽ The First Part of Her Story

Christmas time was generally a happy time in the Donohue home. It was traveling to mother's side on the eve and entertaining father's folks on the day. Mother would make a ham and a turkey. Aunts would bring casseroles, breads and pies. Tommy would go with his dad to cut the tree from a farm, just outside of town. There were Santa's gifts in the morning; mostly necessities, but always a luxury item or two. In 1967 Tommy and Peanut each got a Timex watch. Their uncle held court with a penny ante poker game on the folding table. When it was his turn to deal Tommy would always call for *follow the queens*, a stud game where the card following an upturned queen was wild, unless another queen changed it. All their games had wild cards and gimmicks and at the end of the night, Uncle Jack would see to it the kids went home winners. He had to be cheating.

After dinner, mother questioned Peanut about a necklace peeking out from inside her sweater. She grabbed it and remarked about how it looked so real you'd think it was gold, and my, didn't that stone look just like a diamond; intimating, of course it couldn't be. Peanut withdrew smoothly saying it was from a friend and just costume jewelry. Their mother, understanding the innocence and discretion of a first beau, did not press the issue. Tommy found himself supposing its origin.

By chance, he saw the two of them in the village waiting for tickets outside the movie house some weeks before. Seeing him, they mocked enthusiasm and wasn't it funny they should all meet so coincidentally? Robbie was slick enough, but her face told truths;

not to mention, if Peanut wasn't with him, then who? It wasn't plausible she came alone and there was no lying around that.

He did not like him with his sister. And even though Tommy could let this slip with Reggie to his own benefit, he wouldn't hurt her that way. How could a fella in possession of a goddess prefer this kid, this plain little girl of no particular consequence? This was not just sibling prejudice, surely anyone could see this. Yet here they were, a secret couple.

Tommy sloughed off the suggestion they all sit together, as he was with his own friends, not to mention he was no third wheel on the road to his sister's party. It was Audrey Hepburn and *Wait Until Dark*. The couple sat inconspicuous in the corner of the last row, and afterwards discreetly exited the side doors, tracing a separate path into the dark. Peanut was up in her room, when Tommy got home.

Tommy was in his pajamas, under the covers, reading a Louie L'Amour when she knocked on his door. She stood away in the shadows and said meekly, "You're not gonna tell dad are you?"

Tommy answered coolly, "What are you doing with that guy, anyways? You know he has a girl?"

"We're just friends, is all."

"Yeah, right."

It wasn't so long ago she would barge in his room at bedtime and pester for attention. He would grab her by the neck and knuckle the top of her head or tickle the bottom of her feet. Back then, she begged him to read aloud, whatever he chose. She would fall asleep and he would have to nudge her awake and back to her own bed. When she was a child, Tommy was her everything. In those days she worshiped him. Lately, their distance was a gulf of envy and secrets.

She retreated to the doorway, steadying herself with the handle. When she asked, it came out almost breathless, "You're not gonna tell Reggie Albach, are you? I know you like her."

"I don't like her," Tommy scoffed defensively.

"Are you gonna tell her?"

"I suppose you'd like that?"

"No... But are you gonna?"

She waited, clinging to the handle, steadying her breaths with her back to him. She looked broken and suddenly he hated it. He hated she thought he might hurt her. And he hated being replaced by Robbie Clark. Him, of all people. The boy who had Regina Albach, and now his sister, too. But still, he wouldn't be the one to spirit painful truths and reassured her quietly, "Don't worry, I'm not gonna tell nobody nuthin'."

"Good night, then."

"Night, Peanut," he said, but she was already gone.

Tommy spent the last night of nineteen 1967 at home with his parents and some of their close friends. His mother spent much of the evening trying to distract his father from drinking too much. They watched Guy Lombardo and his Royal Canadians in black and white from the Waldorf Astoria. Peanut arrived before midnight, she had been at Michelle's house; supposedly. All the kids joined in toasting the arrival of 1968 with a glass of Pink Catawba, hugs and kisses. Debbie neither toasted her brother, nor obliged him with a perfunctory kiss; already intoxicated from an evening of first kisses.

Reggie was on winter break and working part-time. She didn't work Saturdays, but her hand writing was on his last pay envelope. It snowed pretty much every day and working outside was a brutal chore. Brushing and shoveling between the cars all day long in the cold and damp. Each pass of the plow meant another trip to clear the driveway aprons, lifting higher to place the snow atop ever-growing piles. He was grateful when asked to warm up the test drives and park them at the showroom door. While delivering a new Caprice wagon he saw her for the first time since he was no longer pure. She was with her father, still bundled up in winter clothes. As their eyes met, he looked away and retreated. She followed him.

"Hey, you. How's it going?"

"Fine."

"Come inside. I wanna talk to you," she prodded.

"Can't. I gotta get another car ready."

"Okay," she said perturbed. "Come after you get the car."

"Can't. I gotta shovel the front after that."

"Are you gonna make me come out? Do I have to come out and shovel? Is that how it's gonna be?"

"It's your place. I can't stop you from shoveling," Tommy said.

"It's my dad's place, but okay, then."

When Tommy got around to shoveling, she had already been at it, leaning over the handle to catch her breath.

"Tommy, I don't know how you do this all day. This is awfully hard work."

"I'm fine," he said, starting to shovel, without looking at her.

"Are you still mad at me?"

"I ain't mad."

"Because I'm sorry about the way things went. I'm really sorry. I shouldn't have let Karen take advantage of you like that."

"I'm not angry."

"Well, I am. I'm really mad at you. You know, I went looking for you. I drove around for hours, just looking for you. For hours, Tommy... And I was really scared. What the hell were you thinking?"

Tommy started pushing snow; ignoring her.

She took the shovel from his hand, "What the hell were you thinking, Tommy Boy?"

"I wasn't thinking anything."

"Well, what happened? Where'd you go?"

"Home. I ran home."

"Tommy, that's gotta be fifteen miles," she said incredulously.

"I showed up for work, too."

"I know. I called to make sure you made it," she said again. "Well, it was stupid. I know you were mad or embarrassed. I get it. I was mad at Karen, too. For what she said."

"Mad and embarrassed? I suppose so. But you don't care," he pouted.

"I get it. So, you're saying you didn't have fun with me. Sorry."

"With you. Not with her."

She sat in the snow pile, exasperated. "Well, now I guess I feel really crappy. I thought I was doing something nice. I mean, I thought you were so sensitive about being a virgin and all. I thought... I just thought guys really wanted to get that over with and it was something... I dunno... I'm an idiot, I guess. I thought it didn't have to mean anything."

He took back the shovel and she laid back in the snow bank, hair falling out from under her cap, a soft red fan in the sooty white snow. She said, "Okay, since I know all about you, I'm going to tell you something. I'm going to tell about my first time and about how I felt after. It was a lot different for me and I should have understood that's what you'd want, too... Why wouldn't you want it to be something really special with someone you had feelings for? I'm such an idiot." Sitting up, she took his hand and pulled him down with her, "Sit... What I'm telling you I've never told anyone. Not even Robbie. You can't ever repeat it. Promise?"

"This must be bad or something."

"I need you to promise. I know you'll keep your promise to me. If I'm gonna tell this, I need you to *promise*. It could create some big problems for someone."

"Yeah, sure, I promise," he said blankly, trying to hold back his enthusiasm for this gossip.

She bit her lip and seemed to reconsider, before finally beginning, "I started working for my dad when I was very young. At first he had me in the office filing and he would have me help the bookkeeper doing deposits, entering sales in the ledger and stuff like that. I was like fourteen or fifteen back then... Anyways there was this salesman who I had a little girl crush on. He was really good looking and seemed so cool and fun and he was one of the younger guys in the showroom. He always took time to talk to me and he treated me like an equal. Like a woman, even though I was just a kid. And he drove this motorcycle in the summer and he seemed so cool and he was really good looking..."

"You already said he was good looking," Tommy noted.

"Well, he was really good looking. Still is."

Tommy sat up and looked at her. He thought about which salesman might be good looking and he couldn't think of anyone that rode a motorcycle. She started again, "Anyways, I was only about fifteen, but I loved this guy more than anything in the world. It was my first real puppy love crush and he sensed it and over time I knew that he was looking at me in way which meant more than just friends. Anyways, this went on for a couple years and I'm seventeen now and it's the summer and I'm pretty well working full time in the summer. I wanted to work as much as I could, just so I could get chances to be with him. Then one day he tells me he's taking his bike down to Allegany for the day and how great a ride it was. Then, umm... he said he wouldn't mind some company. You know, like would I be interested?"

Having a crush on someone at work and longing to be close, Tommy could relate.

She continued, "Of course, there's no way my parents are letting me go biking to Allegany, let alone with a guy almost twice my age and he knew that, too. But being a selfish, manipulative little bitch, I made up some lie and he picked me up... *by the circle*. Funny, huh?" she commented, for his benefit. "He never asked if I had permission. And I never asked about what his wife might think, either..." She bit her lip and paused for effect at that juicy morsel. "It was an Indian motorcycle and it was beautiful and there was no seat back and so I had to wrap myself around this guy and I had never felt anything as wonderful as being wrapped around this gorgeous guy and flying down the roads to Allegany. It was just the most perfect day ever. I remember it was hot and it's funny, but I can remember being so afraid of sweating and smelling of sweat. I remember I was just wearing a headband and my hair was flying out behind me and I was clinging to him, not for safety, but because I just wanted to be all over him; be completely a part of him. It was the first time I remember being truly... well, *truly hot* for any guy. I mean, I thought about being with a guy, and I wanted to be touched, but it was exciting and scary at the same time, you know? I don't know what it's like for guys or what it was like for you."

Just then Mr. Albach called from the door, "Regina. Gotta go."

"Be right there, dad."

"Let's go, we're late!" he barked.

They pushed up from the snow pile and she brushed fresh snowflakes from his coat, "God, sorry, I gotta go. I wanna tell you this story, though. I really do. Crap! I'll have to finish this later. Sorry. This is my life, just when you get to the good part and I gotta go."

Tommy asked, "So, this guy, is he still around?"

She bit her lip and the answer was clear, "I'll tell you the rest later."

"Promise."

"I hate making promises I might not keep," she said and started running.

# 20
# ℭℨ Waiting on a Bastard

Maddy's time on Willardshire was thin. Years and time skewing affection between friends, so the nights burnt faster than they once did. Catching up done in shorter installments. The last week spent muddling in the home of her youth, under the dote and care of her most fervent admirers. So, a restless nerve had twitched; a need to transition back to the life she lived mostly, and apart. Not so much a yearning to leave, but an understanding of an independent life and the beckoning back to the every day. The life that would be hers when they were gone for good.

During this restless time the letters and their unanswered questions troubled her like a windfall of forbidden fruit. She had tried to pry some information from her mother, but was told they were too personal and in time she would know. This only heightened the intrigue. They were out with errands and she inspected the bedroom, finding the envelope in her mother's underwear drawer, hardly disguised at all beneath a veneer of panties.

She read the letters and the dates and recalled the sense of turmoil alluded to during those times. Half-told tales of estrangement; delinquent grandpas and aunties. The family history deflected and obfuscated about the time of her mother's pregnancy. Stories of strange meetings and burgeoning romance.

She knew she was born a bastard, but despite the shroud of implied shame, Maddy never suspected anything except mommy was mommy and married to daddy. A daddy who loved and nurtured her in all and everything, but who had lent nothing of flesh and structure. The complexity of human biology answer enough, but deeper, previously unanswered truths coveted attention, barely hidden in the broken seal of a cardboard Fedex pocket.

She read and reread Robbie's letters, stringing up timelines and decoding mysteries. *Nine months from when?* You lied so you could have me one last time. She looked at the dates again. You lied so you could have me one last time. She read other letters about Tommy and Peanut and she ran through timelines. You lied so you could have me one last time. *Nine months from when?* Where in this narrative was the romance between Tommy and Reggie that wrote the story of Madeline. *Nine months from when* and being had for one last time? You lied so you could have me one last time. *Nine months from when* and a thousand and two kisses?

Shaking and wilting under short heavy breaths, intoxicated with truths exposed and unwanted, Madeline left the letters exposed in their discovered state, unable to proceed. This falsehood. This denial of her most intimate truths... who perpetuates lies as these? Not parents who claim to love her as life itself. And as much as she wanted to take it back and have another day of ten-eleven eggs, she couldn't. It was a mistake on the highway. That moment of distraction survivors carry through consciously, forever. Wishing over and over for just a few seconds back and the attention to keep from crossing the line into oncoming traffic. Wishing for just a few seconds and a do-over. The moment of crowning difference; the moment between contentment and despair. The moment most never confront, be it through luck or fate. Maddy wanted her moment back, but moments of regret are non-refundable.

Madeline hastily packed and called a cab. She told them to hurry, there was an emergency and a plane was waiting. There was an empty apartment in Pensacola waiting on a bastard.

# 21
# ∽ His Father's Agenda

Robbie took the skyway from Nichols to the mill in Lackawanna. The road rising up over the city and looking out over the
lake towards Canada, vistas of grain silos and industrial fallout.
The Clark Steel company was perched on the edge of the lake, rail
lines and inlets bunching amidst the stacks and blast furnaces of
the iron works.

His dad's secretary kept him outside the office, as if he were a
salesman come to call, explaining Mr. Clark was in a production
meeting until four-thirty. The old man was not one of those admin-
istrators who allowed meetings to linger. The agenda was gospel;
all meat, no gravy. He believed in making time count and had told
his son this many times. Make time count. A mantra accepted and
practiced. Like now, his father would arrive as scheduled and their
time was crafted with purpose and meaning. This was not a frivo-
lous excuse for a father and son's pleasure, it was a business
meeting at work, during the week and the agenda had been set.

Just after four-thirty the old man walked in briskly and put a
hand on Robbie's back as they entered the office. He took his place
behind the big desk perched on a riser and Robbie sat in a leather
chesterfield wing back across from him. The office was quite aus-
tere, less impressive than the other executive suites in the plant.
His father believed in function over style. It was clean, but the
carpet was worn and the furniture was purchased when grandpa
ran the place. The window provided a shabby view of the lake and
the piles of iron ore pellets offloaded from lake steamers. Beside
that the mounds of slag, fertilizer and cement slag. And still more

piles, the piles of snow after a long winter, brown and craggy, gritty against the gray spring sky.

"I thought we should meet here. Keep your mother out of it. Settle this thing man to man. You know she's pretty worked up about this Army idea. You've got to let her know you're reconsidering this scheme. Not for always, but at least until this war is finished."

"I wouldn't want to join a peacetime army. Kind of defeats the point," Robbie said. "And besides we discussed it."

"I know we discussed it, but discussion and action are two different things. I was wrong to lead you on, but honestly, I didn't know how serious you were at the time. You've got your mother pretty upset and you know she's not a strong woman. Now, you certainly understand there's no need to upset her unnecessarily, is there?"

"Of course not, Father."

"Good, then you'll tell her you've reconsidered and that'll be that."

Robbie sat forward and said, "I don't want to lie, Dad."

"What about officer training? You've got the grades and I've made a couple calls, so West Point is certainly an option. At least as an officer you'd have specific duties, important duties. You'd be a part of it, but not necessarily in the line of fire. I could sell that to your mother."

"You mean I could pat the men on the back as they marched into battle."

"Certainly, you might see it that way. But I see it as important work and a chance to really make a difference. Lives are lost and saved based on decisions made by leaders. A good officer can be worth a hundred lives, maybe more."

Robbie smiled at his father and replied philosophically, "It's funny, but I've got this friend and he's gonna be a Marine. His family couldn't be prouder. It's what his father wants for him. They don't have much in life beyond their children, but they think it's important their son serve his country. You and Mom, you have everything, yet you're prepared to sacrifice nothing."

For the first time, Mr. Clark lost his cool, "Don't give me that bullshit, Robbie. This isn't about doing your duty for your country. This is about you doing your duty to the family. Haven't we given you a good life? God knows we've given you more than enough room to make all your own decisions... *and mistakes*. I can't remember the last time I've said no to you about anything. What about Clark? I'm counting on you to carry on. Go to college, learn how to run a business like this. A man can't just walk into this business and run it. You've got to learn it from the ground up and that takes years. Grandpa had me sweeping floors when I was ten-years-old and I've been here ever since. That's something I never made you do."

"You've been wonderful parents and I think I've turned out pretty well. That freedom you've given me; the freedom to succeed... the freedom to fail. It's made all the difference. You've given me the freedom to think for myself. This is my choice. This is my decision and you've given me the strength, and courage, to act on my convictions."

"You're not going to disappoint your mother, Robbie. Not on this you're not. You go to school, like we talked about. There's no room for compromise here. You're too important to this business; to us. You go to school, become a man there, then if you still feel the same, well okay, that's a different story."

"You mean, buy time? Change my mind?"

The old man sensed a chance to reason here and said with conviction, "Sure. Of course. People change. It's called growing up. We all do it. What you think is right at eighteen, what you think you know... well, at twenty-two you realize maybe you didn't know it all. Maybe you'll see your parents were right all along."

Robbie looked at his father directly, conveying a seriousness normally reserved between peers and equals, "I won't turn eighteen until May, so I can't do anything until then. Like I said, I don't want to lie, but for now I promise I'll consider all my options. I won't withdraw any of my college applications. We'll tell Mom, that at least for now, I'm not sure what I'm going to do, but you should prepare yourself, Father. In May I turn eighteen."

"Well, you know where I stand."

"I do. And I know Mom is weak, she worries, and it's not my intention to scare her. I knew I made a mistake when I said it. I don't want her to be worried, but let's be clear, most guys come back from 'Nam just fine. There's a hell of a lot better chance that I'll come home in one piece then I'll be killed or wounded. I'm not trying to get killed. I've just been feeling it's important for the

Clark family to serve the country for once. No one's benefitted more from the American dream than us. I love this country, Dad, and I can't stand that all the kids at my school just want to take the benefits and expect someone else to pick up the tab. Father, you've always said there is no free ride in life, someone always picks up the tab. Well, why should those with the least have to pick up this tab for us? I'm sorry, but that's how I feel and I've been feeling this need to stand up. I've been feeling it more and more lately. Is that wrong?"

"So you've got a guilty conscience, is that it? You think we were given everything? Nobody gave us anything, pal. Your family. Your grandfather. Me. We've worked twelve hours a day, seven days a week. Nobody handed us anything. We pay more taxes than ninety-nine point nine percent of the country. We provide a living for thousands of people. You don't think that matters? You don't think that's worth something?"

"Of course. It's worth something for you. What does it mean to me, though? I didn't work those hours. I didn't invent those patents. I was born well. So what? How does that exempt me from anything?"

Now, the old man sat up in his chair and his fist was clenched on the desk as he raised his voice, "It exempts you, because I've fucking earned it for you! I earned it for you, you ungrateful shit! And this is how you reward me? This is how you repay your mother?"

In a reversal of roles, will as his only buckshot, the dependent upbraiding the provider. Before him now, his maker stumbling away his omnipresent cool and control. This man who ran everything, now cornered. Seldom rebuked by powerful businessman or politicians alike, now cornered by the one to whom gratitude should be unyielding. His father, always self-assured and on point, now off topic. The agenda, so carefully crafted eighteen years before, so easily shredded with disregard.

His father broke his stare, his brash assuredness pegged down. He pleaded, "Goddammit, Robbie. You know, this is going to kill your mother?"

Robbie didn't shrink, but said calmly, "I'm sure she'll survive. I'll write every day and I'll only tell her I'm completely safe. Believe me, when it's all said and done, you'll both look back at this decision with pride. I know you will. Take a step back and realize it's only a couple of years and it's going to be the most valuable life experience I can ever get. It will make me more of a man than any ivy league diploma and way more of a man than riding your coattails could make me. I'm absolutely certain you and Mom will be proud of me. And don't worry, nothing's gonna happen. I've always been lucky, Dad, and this is no different. In a couple years I'll come home and then we can talk about school and business and getting on with things. It's two years and then I'll get on with it. I swear, I'm not trying to hurt anyone. I hope you'll be as proud of me as I am of myself."

And at that moment, the realization of what he had made, it did make him proud. Pride reflected in the face of his boy's determination and obstinance. "You don't have to serve your country to make us proud. We are proud of what you've become. Nothing will change that."

"I know you're scared too, Dad. But I tell you I'm not. I'll be back and there's plenty of living left to do. I don't plan on missing a minute of it." And they took this in, man to man, at once coming to a quiet understanding between men.

When their silent consideration became uncomfortable, his father broke from the agenda, "One other thing I need to discuss with you, Robbie. I've been getting some reports about you with some young girl from the village. I'm not going to tell you what friends you can and can't have, but I'm told she's very young and it seems to your mother - *and to me* - that nothing good can come from an affair like this."

"It's not an affair, Father. She's just a friend."

"There's nothing romantic then, because that's not what I've heard?"

"She's a nice kid. She makes me happy when we're together. God, I'm like a big brother to her. Who's telling you this stuff? Whoever it is, is completely full of it."

"I've got my sources."

"Well, that's very secret service of you, Father."

"Just be careful, is all I'm saying. Young girl, she meets a handsome young boy who comes from money. She sees an opportunity for some advantage... happens all the time. That's all I'm saying."

Robbie laughed a belly laugh at his father's sensibilities, the elder not knowing the depths of his son's desire. Desires so palpable, a daily tussle to control his want ensues the moment his eyes open and she envelops his conscious being. The father so ig-norant of his son's struggle to keep from using his position and natural charm to take advantage of a girl so pure and true as Pea-nut Donahue. The irony was delectable.

His father continued, "All I'm saying is a young man in your po-sition has to be aware of young women looking for a way out. A girl who might tempt you into a bad situation for more benefit than love."

"Not to worry, Dad, Reggie's not that young anyways," Robbie teased.

"Yes, well Regina is another situation entirely. She may break your heart, but I'm reasonably sure she's not using you for your money."

"You mean, your money."

"Well, for now, I suppose," his father said.

# 22
# ༀ Abandoned on the Road to Grace

Bertie checked on the little ones, askew in the single bed. She would usually scoop them up quietly and carry them down to the car, one at a time, skinny arms ragged around her neck. Debbie would be asleep on the couch and blurry-eyed, anticipating the five o'clock alarm of postal work, but not tonight; instead slouching at the kitchen table, empty beer cans in a line, open letters in a pile.

"Can't sleep, Mom?" The sister-like daughter said.

"You wanna beer?" The sister-like mother said.

"I'm beat, Mom. These doubles kick my ass."

"I know honey, but have a beer. Have a beer with your old mum," Debbie requested.

"Are we celebrating?"

"I'm celebrating you."

"Celebrating me? You're drunk, Mom."

"Just a little."

"What about work? Little late for a buzz, ain't it?"

"I called in."

"What's goin' on, Mom?"

"Have a beer with me."

Bertie had the soft pouty lips of her father and the bull-like strength, too. Had she been nurtured by the privilege of her birthright, she would have been an undoubted beauty, but she grew up on tough streets with too much freedom and too little example.

Sexuality exercised for convenience from an early age with low-born men who, without conscience, robbed from her the charm and allure of chastity; or at the very least, the discretion of middle class sensibility. Bred uptown and raised downtown, abandoned by circumstance on the road to grace. Not from lack of love or care, for her mother loved her as wholly as she was able, but economics and ignorance derail the best intentions. Her mother, a child herself, forced to reckon a path of necessity with the cold truths of social services her only parachute. Even this she was loath to rely on. Debbie took pride in having won the heart of nobility and from his convictions fashioned a rite of self-reliance, inner truths and stubborn independence. As he cut a path against the thickets of expectations, so she took his seed and spirit to carry on.

"Sure, gimme a beer. Maybe I'll just crash on the couch," Bertie said.

"You can sleep with me."

"You snore."

"I don't snore, you're the one that snores… like a lumberjack."

Bertie twisted the cap off and swigged comfortably like a working man, "So what's going on, Mom?"

"I got news. They found your father."

"They found the Clark kid? Wow, after all these years."

"What was left of him, anyways. They found a grave in Vietnam. I got some letters, too." Debbie spread out the letters across the table for her daughter to see. "They found these letters when they found him. You can read them. You can see how much we were in love. You can see I was telling you the truth."

"I know you loved him, Mom… Man, these are some old freakin' letters."

"If you read these letters you can see how much we were in love, Robbie and me. You can see how your life would have been different. You can see I wasn't lying. He loved me."

"I believe you, Mom."

"I told you how you look like him. He was your father and you're whole life could have been something better. You could have had such a great life."

"Don't, Mom," Bertie said taking a hold of her mother's hand.

"No, Roberta. You had a tough life. I was a rotten mother and it would have been so much different if you had your father. He would have loved you to pieces. I know that. You would have had nice things, good schools. You would have had a chance to be whatever you wanted. You still could've if that family didn't deny us."

"Mom, you always say you can't beat yourself up over the past. I made my own mistakes. My mistakes, not yours."

"Honey, you never had a chance. You were trapped in your life just like I was. I was too damn stubborn. I should have gotten you a dad. There were plenty of good guys who would have loved us, but I was too damn stubborn."

"Mom, you're drunk," Bertie told her.

"I am drunk. I'm sorry. I'm sorry about everything and there's nothing I can do about it now. I'm drunk and you're trapped just like me and now I worry about your kids. I mean, what could Brandy do but join the Army? She was trapped."

"My kids are good, Mom. They have a loving home, plenty to eat, nice clothes, friends... what else do they need? They have plenty of opportunity. Just like I did. I didn't need you to fuck up my life. I did that all by myself."

"Honey, you didn't have a chance. And Brandy, God love her, we did the right thing there. We didn't need another teenage baby."

"Are you saying I should have had an abortion?" Bertie said directly.

"You would have had a chance."

"Just like you, right? You could have had a chance if you had me taken care of."

Debbie reached across the table and clutched her daughter's wrist, "No, honey, it was totally different with you. You're a gift of the truest love there ever was. Never forget that. I may have screwed you up and I may be drunk, but you were a blessing and you were a gift of love. You never forget that. Read the letters and you'll know I'm not lying. Nobody believed me, not even you, but read the letters."

"I believe you, mom."

"Read the letters and you'll see. We were in love."

"I don't need to read those. Those are your letters."

Debbie said desperately, this last chance to prove a point, "No, you have to read them. You have to see your life wasn't a lie. See how much we were loved by a beautiful boy. You're dad, he was a perfect human being and we were the stuff of that love. He was brave and he was kind and he was a lover and I won that love. Me. Nobody believed me, but I was his love. Read the letters."

The letters thrust upon the daughter, and a heavy heart watchful, hopeful; hoping the girl would understand the burden of a love denied. Now she would understand about true love and understand the prevarications that led them to ruin. If only she could understand, now that would be something; almost enough.

And then... the daughter did understand. Tears dotting cheeks that had become arid; products of emotional climate change. And the mother cried at seeing this. They did not make a sound as they cried, a volley of tears on arid cheeks and the mother was no longer lonely in understanding.

After, Debbie went to the cupboard and took another letter, the one in the envelope with the hand-drawn peanut, still unopened. She set it down in the middle of the table along with the picture he sent from before, in his fatigues, from the keeper box in the special drawer.

"I remember you used to show me this picture. You used to tell me *that's your dad* and I used to believe it when I was little." And now she understood.

"That's your dad. That's the man in those letters who I loved with all my heart. Look at him, and you'll see yourself. You didn't get his golden hair, but you got his cheeks, those full pink lips and your beautiful eyes. I see him and you have no idea what it's been like for me to see him there. Sometimes it makes me cry just to look at you. Caleb's got his hair."

"Caleb's dad was a blondie."

"No, that's Robbie hair. I see it in Caleb, just as if Robbie was standing here. I know that hair."

"And what's this one?" Bertie asked about the last letter.

"I don't know. It's never been opened and I wanted to open it together. It's probably the last letter he ever wrote to me. Maybe the last he wrote to anyone. That letter's over forty years old."

"Wow, you guys at the post office don't even take that long to get a letter somewhere," Bertie joked. "He didn't even know about me, did he, Mom?"

"I don't know, honey. I tried to tell him, but I made it hard for him to know… he had to read between the lines. I like to think he did, but I can't say for sure."

Looking at the picture, and seeing it for the first time as a mirror, Bertie said, "I remember you telling me about how my daddy was a war hero and he died in Vietnam. I always figured he knew about me and missed me and I figured he would be so sad dying and knowing he would never see me again."

"I think that must be true. I believe he did know about you, in his heart. If he did, maybe knowing he lived on inside me, maybe that was a comfort for him in the end. I dunno."

"How did you even meet this guy?"

"I met him through my brother. We went swimming at his house."

"I bet it was nice place, huh? Rich guy like him."

"It was like nothing I ever saw. The big house up on the farm. Beautiful place and a big pool. By the time we got out of that pool we were in love. I knew I loved him right then and he told me the same later. We both liked peanut butter and banana sandwiches and that was our little excuse to be together."

Bertie laughed, "Peanut butter and bananas."

"Yep, that's the truth. He came to find me and I always knew he would. Of course, he went to Nichols, and I went to the high school in town. But on Tuesdays he'd wait for me with a peanut butter and banana sandwich. He was a senior and I was a sophomore… We'd just drive someplace quiet and we'd laugh and talk and eat our sandwiches."

"Been there, done that," Bertie said wryly.

"It wasn't like that. I mean, he had a girlfriend and he respected how young I was. At first we kept it like friends, but we both knew it was way more and we knew we had to hide it. God, I never thought I could love a Tuesday as much as then. I lived the whole week for just an hour on Tuesday. We just talked and laughed and looked into each other's eyes. We were both too damn scared to do what we really wanted. He didn't even kiss me until much later, it was on New Year's Eve in 1967 and it was my first real kiss."

"Open mouth and tongue, Mom?"

"Oh yeah, it was all that and more. But it was exactly a year later before we actually made love and we were only together once."

"No shit!"

"It's true."

"You got pregnant on your first try?"

Debbie smiled, lifting this burden from her shoulders, "It's true. It was my first time ever; and the only time with Robbie Clark. The next day he went off to war and that was the last time I saw him. Best night of my life."

"God, I remember my first time. Hurt like hell and I couldn't wait for it to end. Thought I'd never do that again."

"I don't remember it hurting much, but Robbie was so gentle and a very careful lover with me. I just wanted him so bad it all seemed right to me. It never got better than that."

"Awghh, poor Mom. Your love life, all downhill from the very start. I can't imagine. Think of what you've missed."

"Exactly the opposite. I had it all. The best there could ever be and okay, it was only for one night, but I'm grateful for that night and for you. It was only once with him, but I got you forever."

"Should we open it?" Bertie wondered about the letter.

"Let's have another drink," her mother said; one more for the read.

# 23
# ✂ Under Protest

Robbie had gone and done it. He crossed his father, terrified his mother and infuriated Regina. But it was Regina who drove him to the station, as he shipped out to boot camp. Her arms wrapped tightly around him, sending him off with remembrance tears pressed upon his shirt. But this was to Tommy's benefit, as she spent more time hanging out with him; even if his romantic fantasies never gained traction. He even went to an anti-war protest just to be with her.

It was mid-August and the lawn outside the Unitarian Church was packed with kids. Inside were draft-refusers Tim Jenkins and Bruce Freed surrounded by an assembly of combat veterans and high-profile anti-war activists. The standoff had gone on for ten days. Jenkins ignored three requests for induction, burning the last notice on the church steps. The church granted him symbolic sanctuary. Protestors on both sides clogged the sidewalk and fanned into the street, carrying signs and breaking into chants. Eric Burden on *Sky Pilot* was pumping through a loud speaker mixing over a girl singing Judy Collins songs with her guitar under a tree. It was practically festive.

Reggie was there almost every day. Tommy came just once, on her invitation. Robbie's enlistment in the Army had hardened her resolve. What was once mostly talk was galvanized by action. The loss of her boyfriend was replaced with anti-war vigor. Tommy hardly considered himself an activist, but he could see her point. He really just came so he could sit close and feel her skin as she would grab his arm and look in his eyes with her passions aroused; even if it wasn't a passion for him. Those touches and those serious eyes, now that was reason enough. His resolve for soldiering was wearing thin and in such a glorious way.

The kids on the lawn were in tie-dies and beads. They were mocking the cluster of Catholics carrying signs proclaiming *Keep Marx out of the Church*. There was a sturdy contingent of Buffalo cops, their numbers growing as the day progressed. Vets spoke into megaphones on the church steps in fiery pleas to end the war. Among the speakers were men who fought in wars as far back as the second World War.

He saw Carol, Will's Carol, looking the part of a flower child. Her arms were wrapped around an older guy wearing camouflage. Her great ass showing through skin-tight bell bottoms. There was a ribbon of bangs cut through that blond, arrow-straight hair just above her eyes. She saw Tommy and smiled.

Reggie called a guy over and introduced him to Tommy, explaining, "Joe's a Vietnam vet. He can tell you all about it, 'cause he's been there."

Tommy stood up and shook the soldier's hand. Joe didn't look much like a soldier, what with the long wild hair and bushy beard.

Reggie said, "Tommy wants to be a Marine. He wants to go off to Vietnam and get with the program."

Tommy rolled his eyes and Joe asked him, "A Marine, huh? That's some serious shit, there."

Tommy said, "I dunno. I always thought I'd be a Marine. My dad was a Marine."

"I met plenty of Marines in 'Nam. Man, those were some scary mothers. Never met a Marine who was right in the head," Joe said without a hint of hyperbole. "And I know what you're thinking. What's a good Army-boy like me doing here with all these freaks and hippies? I used to think so, too. I get you, man."

"Tommy thinks it's all fun and games, don't you, Boy?" Reggie said.

Tommy told Joe, "She likes to tease me."

And Joe said, "I don't know about fun and games. For me, it was an unadulterated shit show, pure and simple. Nobody wants us there. Half the people you're fighting for would put a bullet in your back, if they had the guts and the opportunity. You can't tell the good guys from the bad guys. Hell, half the time we were the bad guys, killing civilians and abusing women. Being over there, it makes you crazy. You learn to hate like it's a disease, man. All the while you smile at the people, but you just wanna blow their heads off. Kids, women… there's times you just wanna kill 'em all."

"You said they wanna kill you, too," Tommy reasoned.

"Okay, so if we're over there fighting for them, and they don't want us there, then what the hell are we doing? It makes no sense."

"What about Russia and China? Vietnam, what next?" Tommy said with conviction.

Joe pulled at his beard and looked thoughtfully at Tommy. The elder searching for the right words to convince the young buck. He said, "So, we're just fighting a proxy war against Russia in Vietnam? The way I see it, we're dying… the Vietnamese, they're sure as hell dying. Sounds to me like Russia and China are winning and they don't have to lift a finger. You know, Ho Chi Minh would've been an American ally. He was begging for our help. Help, so they could get their independence, but we just turned our back on him."

"Yeah, right," Tommy scoffed.

"It's true, Uncle Ho used to admire America. He admired that we fought for our independence and that's all he wanted was independence for the people of Vietnam. It's basic knowledge, man. You can look it up."

"Independence? What, so he can be appointed dictator for life?"

Reggie but in, "So what? How's your life gonna change if Ho Chi Minh becomes a dictator?" Then she gave him the serious look, grabbing a hold of him, and added, "Don't you see, Tommy? Joe's been there. He knows this war is bullshit 'cause he's been on the ground. Okay, you don't have to believe me, just listen to him."

Tommy said snarkily, "So, you see any combat while you were over there?"

Joe's eyes went to a faraway place, like he was being deep. It seemed like an act and after some time he said mysteriously, "Yeah, I've seen some things. I've done some things, too. I guess I just gotta live with that. I gotta live with the hate. That's with me forever, man."

Reggie was almost gleeful as she took his arm and confronted him again, "Is that what you want Tommy? You just wanna go fill your heart with hate? Have to live with hate the rest of your life?"

Joe said wryly, "Of course, you could be one of the lucky ones. You could die over there. I suppose the hate dies then, too. You come back wrapped in a flag and the folks couldn't be prouder."

Reggie hugged Joe before he climbed the steps and entered the church. Tommy couldn't help feeling it was a bit of a show; a cry for attention by some guy who couldn't cut it as a soldier.

Tommy told Reggie, "I don't buy that guy, Reg."

"Yeah? How come?" Reggie was put out. She was that way whenever he challenged her.

"I've seen plenty of guys who don't feel that way."

"And I know plenty of guys who do," she said and walked away, like the brat she was when he dared to correct her.

As he sat alone on the lawn, Carol came up to him. "Tommy, right? Didn't think I'd see you at one of these."

"I'm not really part of this. I'm just hanging out with a friend. You know Regina Albach?"

"Reggie, sure. She's a cool chick."

It seemed Carol was trying a little too hard to be cool herself. She pulled her man over for introductions, "Nick, this is Tommy. We went to high school together. Nick was in the Marines. That's what you were gonna be, right?"

Another one. It seems like they rounded up every disenchanted vet in the county.

"I still am. I turn eighteen in October," he told Carol.

Nick said, "Big mistake."

"I guess I'll find out."

"I was just like you once. All I can say is don't do it, man. You don't wanna go there."

Tommy didn't want to hear it, so he deflected by asking Carol, "You seen Will, lately."

She giggled and said, "Oh, God no."

She was too cool for his friends, even though the summer before she and Will had been like a couple of bunnies on overdrive. Of course, Tommy hadn't seen much of Will lately, either.

Almost unnoticed a white van rolled up and blocked the street. The back opened and a contingent of men carrying guns and clubs rolled out. About half the cops working crowd control broke off and followed them, while the rest started ordering the protesters back. There were at least 30 cops and federal agents who walked directly up to the steps of the church. As they went a murmur belched up through the crowd.

Nick said, "They're goin' in. It's the FBI and they're goin' in."

Carol said, "They can't do that. It's a sanctuary."

"They can do whatever they want. They're goin' in," Nick said as Carol held his arm dissuading him from joining the fray.

A cop armed with his night stick started ordering the kids on the lawn to disperse. Tommy saw Reggie on the steps. There was a scuffle breaking out between the cops and the protesters who were trying to block the door. Reggie was mixed up in it, shouting at the police. It wasn't long before fists were swung and people were hitting the deck. Reggie looked frightened after the first swing of a billy club connected with a guy beside her, sending him cascading down the steps, his head bouncing off the railing.

Tommy rushed the steps, calling to her. Before he could reach her, a cop locked an arm around his neck and wrestled him to the ground. Reggie was struggling with an officer of her own, attempting to pull him from the guy on the ground. She was swearing and crying. It was supposed to be peaceful resistance, but it had devolved into a brawl.

Tommy broke free and when Reggie saw him she yelled, "Get out of here, Tommy!"

"Not without you," he said.

Then the cop caught him again and put on a choke hold on with his night stick. Tommy thought his neck was about to break. On the steps of the church, another cop grabbed Reggie by they hair and dragged her down the stairs, throwing her to the lawn. She ran to Tommy.

"What the fuck are you doing?" she yelled at the cop who was choking Tommy.

"Get out of here," he commanded.

"He can't breathe," she yelled while pulling on the cop's arm.

"He's resisting the lawful command of an officer," the cop said.

"He's not part of this. He was just coming to get me. We'll go. He can't breathe. Jesus Christ, let him go!" Reggie pleaded.

The cop released Tommy and raised his club like he was about to strike him, threatening, "Then get the fuck out of here, you punks! Get outta here when I tell ya."

Tommy let out a gasp and partially collapsed trying to catch his breath. Reggie put her arms around him and the cop slapped her yelling, "I said get outta here!"

Tommy got up and raised his fist, but Reggie pulled him close and said, "Let's go, Tommy. Let's go."

Tommy said to the cop, "Hit a fuckin' girl? You think your tough, you hit a girl?"

This time the officer came full and hard on Tommy's head with the club, Reggie's arm catching part of it, too.

She implored Tommy, "It's not worth it! Let's go! Tommy, it's not worth it!"

"Fucking coward! Hit a girl?" Tommy said, holding his head where blood was beginning to blot in his hair.

Tommy still wanted a piece of the cop, but Reggie frantically pulled him away. He couldn't escape her arms and concern. She was scared for him and this was not a small thing. By now the church was breached and the commotion moved inside. Reggie just kept Tommy moving. He noticed a scratch on her forehead and blood smeared with tears across her cheek. Then outside the police perimeter, she went limp against him. He took up the slack, two strong arms locked around her trembling body.

# 24
# ෪ The Rest of Her Story

Twelve days after his eighteenth birthday in October of 1968, Tommy's father took him to the post office to register for the selective service. Jimmy Donohue was not a patient man and eighteen years was long enough to wait, so the extra twelve days of excuses were wearing thin. They went downtown to the Ellicott Square building where he was given a physical. Given a 1-A designation, it was off to visit with the Marine recruiter.

All four branches of the military had offices on the same floor and the Army recruiter was kibitzing in the Marine office when they arrived. He teased Tommy, "You look like a bright kid. Too smart for the Marines. Why don't you come on over to where the real soldiers are?"

The Marine recruiter countered, "Yeah, them Army boys are real smart. Good at math, too. Their specialty is following us in and counting the bodies."

After, they went to the Bar Bill where working men stopped for a couple of pops before heading home. The old man ordered them each a Genny and announced to the rabble about how Tommy was a leatherneck.

"Yes, sir, today my boy becomes a man. We just got him his draft card and Tommy's decided on the Marines," his father announced proudly.

"Just what this world needs, another jarhead," one fella said. They toasted him and the bartender gave him a shot to go with the beer.

They cheered as he downed the shot and banged it on the bar. "Good for you, Tommy. He's a good kid, God love 'em."

"Hell of a kid. I couldn't be prouder," the old man said.

"The country needs more like 'em. Good for you, Jimmy."

"He's his old man's kid. A real American. Here's to Tommy! Drink up, kid!"

The adulation he had been starving a lifetime for, arriving rich and plentiful, belching up in wafts of rancid discontent. So late in coming, its sweetness gone sour to a palate sated by a diet of question, discontent and yearning.

He was no longer a sponge of old rites, but congregating in the temple of Regina Albach. Having made amends, she put their friendship on equal footing, so long as he was prepared to submit to the care of the shepherd. With Robbie at boot camp, she sought to equal the score by saving the other. And Tommy was agog exploring the doctrines of the fabulously brunette, his paradise always in sight, faith an implicit promise to salvation. A faith rewarded with innocent cuddles and pecks; friends at ease in open affection. Though Regina still answered to a higher authority, the fella wearing fatigues and carrying a gun. It irked Tommy she sought to deny him the path to glory her sweetheart, Robbie, walked.

At the bar his old man reminisced about his time in the Marines and the men rancored over the politics of the day; the red menace at home and the hippy freaks, too. They told Tommy he'd never have friends like the ones you go to battle with; not before or after. A lifetime spent yearning for the days of paternal camaraderie and now here it was, yet he felt nothing but conflicted. This new admiration squeezed by a future in flux. He was now a soul between promise and betrayal; torn between familial and romantic love. Switch the sides and the remains are the same.

Reggie had immersed him in a world apart. The day at the Unitarian Church and the mark the cop branded upon his head left an ineffaceable blemish upon his perceptions of right and wrong. He was twisted tight now, waiting to unravel, and when all was said and done, he had no sense of which direction he would face.

Two weeks previous she wanted him to protest Nixon's campaign stop at the Aud and he refused. His father was for Nixon and so was he. Skirting presidential politics with her had been a regular pastime, but now she knew. A rabid McCarthyite, she had no love for either Humphrey or Nixon, but Nixon took aim at the SDS and ran on a law and order platform that openly declared war on the student movement. When informed he supported Nixon, she was astonished. She furiously fired off a litany of wrong doings and character failings of one Richard Millhouse Nixon. He stood his ground and was glad about it. They hadn't spoken since, but he was going to drive down to the Urban Action office where Reggie spent most evenings. He was sick of not being her boyfriend and he was going to press the issue. An enlisted man now, enough of being Regina Albach's lapdog. Enough of the work without the pay. Always catering, never a guest.

He never hid his intentions to become a soldier, but she thought the situation was under control day-by-day. She never considered he would just do it and not discuss it; not give her a chance to wrap him like a string around her little finger. It had always worked that way. Wait and see, she had said. Just wait and see. Wait and see what the draft number would be. Wait and see if they come for you. Wait and see if your father lets you wait and see. You can apply to college, or go to Canada if it came down to it. In fact, she had taken to counseling conscientious objectors at the Urban Action office.

One night the office was raided and she got picked up and booked. Her father had to post bail. Even though the trumped up charges were dropped, the arrest was a bitter pill to a respected business person in a conservative community. At the dinner table he supported Regina in her convictions. He was a Rockefellar republican, against the war and a civil rights proponent; at least in his heart.

Tonight Tommy would make a stand. She would have to more than infer, more than cajole, more than press with cheap cuddles. Vietnam or her; and if that was the ultimatum, the time had come for lines to be drawn. It's one... two... three... four, what are we waiting for? His convictions rested on a rail and let the engine push it hither or yon, this was a dilemma she alone could solve. The time for playing was over and no longer would he yield to intimations of future desires satisfied.

He left the old man at the Bar Bill and walked home, getting the '62 Nova Reggie's dad sold him at cost, no doubt on her advice. He had full-time hours since graduation and Albach took payments from his paycheck. The beer and the cheers had built his confidence and today there would be confrontation and resolution.

His confidence stuttered when she coldly ignored him as he walked in, still sore about Nixon, but at the same time a heat of defiance brewed in his belly. Before the Nixon thing she might have thrown an arm around him and smooched him closed-lipped on the mouth, but what had been burning before was now cold wax, hard and tacky. She was in conversation with the others and he didn't really care.

"Let's take a walk," he told her.

"Can't, I'm busy," she said coolly. Even though, it was obvious the only thing going on was the relentless political grumble stewed in the office on long nights of pot and protest.

"Busy? Yeah, right. I gotta tell you something. It's important."

"Okay, tell me."

Everyone stopped and was watching. It hearkened back to the night of virginity lost, but stronger now with lessons learned and emotions in check, he said, "Just forget it, then. I'm done with this."

"Okay, I'll bite... Done with what?" she asked, faltering for the first time to him; ever.

"I'm done with this. With everything, here. I'm done being your little puppy. You, me, everything. I'm done being treated like some kind of an asshole who does whatever you say... and what do I get? Dick all."

"Cut the soap opera, Boy. If I make you feel like an asshole, then that's on you."

"You're right. Only I can make me feel like an asshole," he said and walked out.

Right out the door.

Now suddenly, the prey in pursuit. His lapdog days done. Tables turned, and the other cheek, too; last laughs best. She caught him, already in the car. She knocked on the window and said, "I'm sorry, Boy. What is it?"

He paused for effect before pushing the door open. She got in and he drove. She would be waited out. The silence only hers to break.

"Okay, what is it?"

"I enlisted today. I joined up. I'm a Marine."

"Why did you do that?" she panicked.

"It was time."

"Why did you do that?" she said almost frantically, sensing the loss for a second time.

"Because, my father. Don't you understand?"

"I thought you decided to wait… at least see if you get drafted. I thought you were going to wait?"

"I did it because he's my father and it means everything to him."

"So what? It's not his life, Boy. Don't live his life, live yours."

"I don't know what my life is, what I want… outside of you," he told her. She turned away knowing exactly what he wanted and he continued, "I know I want you, but you're just the same as the old man. You use me and at least he loves me. He's proud of me and I know I'll always belong with him. With you, I know that you'll always play with me and use me and I'll always be second best. I don't blame you. I blame me. I let you do it and I suppose I liked it… being used by you and I let you do it. No more. No more, Reggie. I'm done being whatever you want me to be."

"So that's what you think?" she asked meekly.

"It's what I know. I know how I feel and I know you don't feel the same for me."

"I have feelings for you, Boy."

"Your feelings aren't my feelings. You treat me like your little dog; a little thing you play with when no one else is around."

"What about Robbie?" she asked.

"What about him? You said yourself you can't love a man who fights this war. Is that bullshit?"

"I dunno," she said honestly. "I do love him."

"How about him? Does he love you? Are you his only girl?" Here the truth of the sister no longer unspoken. And now her exterior broken, they drove the parkway; then up along the river and stopping in the lot at the pier where the lake squeezes into the Niagara. The bridge spanned overhead and the lights of Canada's Fort Erie sparkled off the white caps, breaking where the water picks up speed.

They parked away in the shadows, under some trees and away from the places where the fishermen parked. For once she did not fight his advances and for once he did not couch them. Locking equally in desire; tonight he was her man. No longer closing her mouth to his open lips and his arm around her. The other hand down between her legs, she lightly caressing back through his jeans. He unzipped her and felt the damp of the evening and in a moment more, her legs firmly squeezed his hand from further inspection.

"I love you, Boy, but I just can't." He tried once again and she squeezed tighter. "It's not that we can't ever. I just can't now, okay?"

"And now that I've enlisted, if I go?"

"And if you go, what am I supposed to do? It's Robbie all over again. Don't do this to me, Boy."

"And if I stay with you, what then?"

"If you stay with me, then we'll be together."

"Together how I want it?"

"I can't say that. If you need me to say that, I just can't. Don't make me say what I can't, Boy."

"Say it. Say it now and I'll be with you forever," and they kissed for a good while longer and he did not press beyond that. An unprecedented progression in his relationship, come to a stalemate and moment of reflection.

Some time later as she lay on his shoulder and he played with her hair, lost in its luxury as he always wanted, he asked her, "Tell me about that story you never told me. You said you would."

"What story?"

"About that time on the motorcycle, when you were young."

"Oh yeah, that. I was kind of hoping you forgot."

"I've been thinking about that and I figure I know who the guy is."

"You think, huh?" she smiled into his eyes.

"It's Bill Fromm. I'm pretty sure."

"I'll never tell," she said without saying.

"I asked around and he had a bike and the age fits and he's been around for long enough."

"Okay, so what if I say you're right."

"So tell me."

"I said you're right, but you can't ever tell, you know? You're the only person who knows outside of me and him."

"Of course. It's a secret. Who am I going to tell? Tell me about how it happened?... Did it feel good the first time?... Did it... I hear it hurts for girls?... Did you think it was forever and was that the only time?"

"So many questions."

"For the first time ever, Reggie, I've got you cornered. I've never had you cornered before. I've never had the upper hand with anything about you and I like it. I want to know you in every way and this is what I want now and other things can come later. But now I have you, and it's for the first time."

"It's true, you have me tonight. You have me for the first time," she said.

"And that's something I never figured on."

"Me neither."

"Well?"

As she told it, her eyes darted to the light of memories, her husky voice sighing out the start of sentences, "Well, I told you we snuck away on a Sunday. It was the first Sunday in August and it was a hot, sweaty day."

"You said you were worried you smelled?"

"I was... but I doubt he cared. He knew what he wanted and he knew he was going to get it, but I wanted it, too. I wanted to be wanted. I wanted to be touched. I developed early and had been having those feelings for quite some time. And boys and men were always hinting at it, even though I was just a girl."

"Did you go to a motel or do it outside?"

"We drove down to the park and hiked up the bear caves. He kept helping me climb the rocks and we did a lot of touching and he kissed me there. On the way back he said a friend of his had a hunting cabin and he said he wanted to show it to me. It was up in the hills, back in the woods. Of course, he conveniently had a key. I remember it smelled of wood and was musty and dim. It was a single room with metal cots and worn old mattresses. No linens or anything. He half pushed me, half carried me to one of the cots and got on top of me. I had been thinking about it all day and now it was going to happen and suddenly I was scared as hell and I just squeezed my legs tight."

"Like with me?"

"Exactly, only I'm not afraid of you. At least not the same kind of afraid."

"Did you say no?"

"I said I had to pee... There was an outhouse and even though it didn't smell the best, I sat there and took the longest pee ever. When I went back in, he was, well, he was there in all his excited glory and I remember thinking how is that thing ever going to fit?"

"Were you freaked out?"

"I dunno. Maybe. I thought he looked good, though, and it made me feel desired, I guess."

"You liked that?" he asked.

"Sure. I like being desired by people I desire, don't you?"

"I like being desired by anyone."

"Well, I bet Karen still wants you."

"Very funny," he said and squeezed her.

"I yelled at her that night. She's such a bitch. I still can't believe what she did to you."

"Finish," he said.

"Well, you can figure out what happens next, right?"

"Did he get on top of you? Did it hurt?"

"Yes and yes. He wasn't a gentle lover, that's for sure, and he kept telling me it would feel better the next time."

"Did you bleed?"

"A little, but it was his finger that did that I think."

"Did he say he loved you?"

"I said I loved him the next time we were together and that was in a motel."

"So you did it again?"

"Well, yeah. We did."

"How many times?"

"So curious? It was just sex, you know," she said. "I don't really care much about people's sexual past. I mean unless it's just chronic, meaningless sex. I really don't think it defines us. It's just a moment of bliss and then you go back to your real life. Sex is just a moment in a relationship and there's so much more to relationships and love, don't you know that, Boy?"

He sternly corrected her, "It's just sex for you because it comes so easily to you. To me, it's everything. It's the moment of bliss that defines your love for me. That's why I hated it with Karen. It was nothing to her and I was nothing to her. Sometimes I can't stand that I gave myself to her and if I told it to the guys they'd call me a faggot. If I ever get to be with you I'm sure it will be the most important moment in my life. Do you understand that?"

"It's just sex, Boy. Everyone does it. It doesn't last. Fucking is just a moment and then there's everything in between."

"How can you say that? That's like saying the atomic bomb was just a moment and then there's everything in between."

"It's just a moment," she said, kissing him softly.

He broke from her lips and continued, "A defining moment for everyone, before and after. That's what this means to me. It's a defining moment in my life. Tonight is a defining moment in my life. It's not for you, but for me it is. I know you hate me for making it like that, but I don't care. It is what it is for me and just like it was in that cabin and even though we haven't done anything, just holding you and talking about possibilities, it defines me going forward."

"Well, if you really feel that way, then don't go. Stay with me."

"But I've already gone."

She grabbed the bottom of his chin and pointed it across the river, "It's just a river and there's a bridge and you can be there in five minutes."

"A draft dodger? I can't run like some chicken. My dad would never forgive me. Never."

"It's not draft dodging, it's being a conscientious objector. Do you think this war is right? In your heart do you think what we're doing, what America's doing, is right? Do you think all the lives lost are worth it? Is it worth your life?"

"I don't know what's right. The only thing that's ever been right to me is this moment right now. This is the most right thing in my entire life. Holding you. Kissing you."

"Now you are scaring me, Boy." And she pushed him away.

"Good. I like that you're frightened. I like that you know I'm real and I'm dead serious and my feelings are raw and exposed. I'm like a skinned knee on a gym floor. It's real now, Reggie. No more jokes."

"Stop it, Boy... Just stay, okay?"

"Well, I guess you've taught me that there's a lot more to the war than I once thought. I suppose it's not the best war, but there's justice in serving your country, even if it seems wrong in our eyes."

"An unjust cause does not make a country great. What makes a country great, what makes this country great is we have the right to stand up and say this is wrong," she said, her political passions now usurping the physical one. "This is a revolution, Tommy, and you need to be on the right side. Do you think I'm on the right side of the revolution?"

At this he stopped to consider the sides. Considered his father and his life with his family and he thought about personal truths against larger truths, then answered truthfully, "You are on the right side, Reg. You truly are."

"Well then. You need to decide to do what's right for you, for your country. You want to prove you're a man? Well, be a real man and stand up for what's right. You can be the tough guy and go over there and make daddy happy, or you can go over there..." She grabbed him by the chin and pointed him towards Canada again. "...and make me happy. If only you didn't let your father bully you into this, you could have just waited it out, refused to enlist. We could have fought that here. Together."

"Real men don't run," he said miserably.

"When do you have to report?"

"I don't know. They'll tell me. They said it would probably be two or three months."

"Well, we have time to make a plan, then." And she climbed into his lap and they kissed for a while longer under the bare branches of the elm trees at the end of the pier.

# 25

# cos Bobby Bananas Last Stand

Together Bertie and her mom opened the envelope, his last letter. They tried steaming the flap, but ended up carving a slit in the top with a sharp knife. The letter was composed on a Cong propaganda leaflet torn in half. Debbie's half, the top, depicted a young child with arms flung around its mother's neck and a gun strapped around the woman's other arm, the barrel of the rifle poking out above her shoulder. The child lay comfortably asleep as the mother looks ahead with a determined smile. Robbie started on the back and carried over to the front, scribbling across the picture, in black ink.

*Late March, 1969*
*Somewhere, Vietnam?*

*Dear Peanut;*

And Debbie turned the letter down, emotionally spent.
"Read it, Peanut," her daughter said. She took the letter from her mother's hand and read aloud.

*Dear Peanut;*
   *Love and light. Love for then. Love for now. Love for all times. Your love sustains me and sometimes I think I've lost it.*

*It's been almost two months since I've been shot and captured, (Though I've lost track of time). I took a bullet in the leg and it's not much of a wound, but it refuses to mend. It doesn't help that I've been kept in this cow pen with chains and ropes. I keep thinking maybe they'll find me and I'll get out of here. When it first happened I was sure help was coming - I could hear the choppers circling above, but they've taken me far from where I was shot and I'm not so sure they'll ever find me. Even if they don't, as soon as this leg gets a little better I think I could escape. I won't say how, in case someone finds this letter.*

*My present condition is my own fault. I wasn't careful enough, Peanut. I just assumed I was the last guy on earth who would walk into an ambush. It was ignorance... ignorance and bravado, plain and simple. I'm so sorry to do this to you. I didn't have to take point. I could have kept my head down and stayed in the rear. I volunteered because I thought I was invincible. It seemed I was hit almost as soon as I heard the first shot. In fact, I wasn't even sure I was hit. My leg felt hot, almost burning and it felt like somebody whacked me with a bat, but it seemed I couldn't have been shot, because I ran for about 20 yards and felt almost no pain in the leg. It was only when I took cover behind a dirt embankment I felt warm liquid running down my leg and looked at the hole in my pants. I put a finger into the hole and I could feel bone, but it didn't hurt. I guess I was in shock.*

*The next thing I knew three Viet Cong were crouched beside me and pointing guns at my head. They took my weapon and beat me hard with fists and gun stocks. They wanted me to walk and it was only then, knowing how bad my leg was, that the pain hit home. The brain has a funny way of dealing with stress. I would try to walk and then they would hit me, for no reason, until in the end they were dragging me behind them. At one point there were over a dozen guys taking turns hitting and dragging me. When I couldn't stand the pain I would scream and they hit me harder. Eventually I felt nothing and I remembered nothing. I don't know how long they dragged me, but there came a time I regained my senses and I was chained in a* cow pen. I was in leg irons and my hands were tied behind my back. That's where I am today, and thankfully, things have gotten better for me.

There's a girl here who takes care of me. She's not the enemy, but just a poor farm girl who does what they tell her. She reminds me of you. She comforts me and we have developed a certain affection for each other. She feeds me, cleans my wound and is often by my side. Sometimes I think she worries more about me than I do myself. I don't think I would have survived without her. She has given me the paper and pen. Her kindness comes at great personal risk and she will be in certain danger if this letter falls into the hands of the wrong person. She doesn't speak English, but we communicate as best we can and I've made it clear she needs to hide this. I think she understands and she knows she has to get this to you in case I don't make it. Her name is Tien.

I've got your letters with me. Tien keeps them safe and lets me read them when it's only us together. I keep looking at the photo strip from Vidler's. Your hair pushed back by the white bandana and kind of mussed and you trying to smile for me and your big dark eyes and your neckline and Aunt Enid's necklace and if there's a heaven it must look like this. I want to come home to you and I want to get lost in your hair and I want you to take care of me and make me completely better.

I find my mind slips back to New Year's Day. Always back to you, darling. The days are long and the nights even longer and I relive our last night together over and over. In my mind, I've lived that night a thousand times and I long for a thousand times more with you by my side. A world away and I can still taste your lips and feel the luxury of your body as it holds me, keeping me warm and safe. I love you, Peanut.

The only paper Tien had was this piece of war propaganda and you'll notice there's a baby on the front. It made me think of you. I worry about you, darling. I worry that I've put you in a bad situation and if it's true, I can't imagine how you are coping. I think this because of the way you wrote some things... saying but not saying. If it's true, *just hang in there and I'll take care of everything when I get home. If it's true and you decide not to go through with it, I understand. I can't imagine what it would be like to go through that alone. But no matter what you decide, I'll be with you every step of the way. I'll marry you when I get home. I want to marry you, Peanut. I want to spend my life with you, Debbie. So there you have it. With the second half of this paper I have written my parents and told them about us, so you can turn to them for help if you need it.*

*But here is the reality of our situation. If you are reading this, then I didn't make it. It sounds so strange to say that - I didn't make it - writing as if this were my last will and testament, but it is Peanut. When you get this you will know I am dead. Of course, my real plan is to bring this letter home with me and when we're old and married and you're mad at me for something stupid I've done - only then I'll show it to you. Then when you read how much I love you, you won't be able to stay mad at me. And that is my hope. I love you so much and for that reason alone, I can't let this end.*

He had run out of space, so he drew an arrow to the edge of the page and wrote sideways along the margin, almost imperceptible;

*You said you were a fate girl, Peanut. Is this our fate? If this is our fate as planned by God, then no matter what, I'll see you again. Bobby Bananas.*

"He knew he wasn't going to make it," Bertie said.

Debbie tried to speak and her daughter massaged her troubled shoulders, speaking for her "You really were the love of his life. He told you so. It was the last thing he wanted to tell the world. And he knew about me. He said he knew you were in trouble." Then snidely, "I wonder what his family would say, now? Let's see them deny us now."

When Debbie composed herself, she said, "I always knew there was a God and now I need to find him."

# 26
# ෬ A Stable Relationship

Debbie and Michelle were close as kin since their days as camp-fire girls. They shared everything, almost. But this secret was kept until the last of '68. Then she had to tell.

"I need you to do something for me. Something really important," Debbie told her friend.

"Of course. What is it?" Michelle asked without hesitation.

"I need you to cover for me... tonight. Tell my mom I'm sleeping at your house." Debbie felt the muscles in her jawbone tighten as she said it.

"You can stay over. My mom won't care," Michelle said half listening. They were in Debbie's room, thumbing through the latest *Tiger Beat* with Davy's picture on the cover.

"I'm not staying with you. Leave with me and tell my mom I'm staying at your house," Debbie said without looking.

"Whatta ya mean?"

"Remember I told you about Robbie Clark?"

"Yeah?" she said, fully attentive now.

"He's going to Vietnam and I have to see him. Before he goes."

"Yeah?" Michelle repeated for clarification.

"Well, the only time we have is tonight. He's going tomorrow and there's no way my mom will let me out."

"You're gonna be together all night or what?"

"The night. The whole night."

Michelle sat up and said with tones of accusation, "You're not doing it, are you?"

"No. Of course not. It's not like that, but I have to see him. He's going and I have to see him."

"Well, where exactly are you two gonna meet?"

"His house. His folks are out at some party and it's just us."

"So just you two? Alone all night? Not doing anything?"

"Yeah," Debbie said quietly.

She and Michelle had long exposed their little crushes, curled up in quiet spots together; giggling about boy's bodies and their own budding maturity. But love and adult relationships still seemed a distant passage.

Michelle said with some annoyance, "Why don't I know about this? You just tell me now?"

"I didn't tell anybody, and neither did he. Nobody would like us together. Not his parents. Not mine, for sure. And besides, we hardly ever see each other. But it's different now. He's going to Vietnam."

"And maybe he'll get shot."

"Don't say that," Debbie said, resenting the echo of private fears.

"What if he asks you to do something?"

"He won't."

"What if he does?"

"If he does, he does."

But Debbie was planning on this. It had been her constant companion; her lust, even before boot camp. If he doesn't ask, that was her dilemma.

She and Robbie met secretly earlier that day. For minutes, it's all they could manage. They met at the plaza and he parked around back, where the trucks would come with deliveries. At once a clutch of one, desperate for the moment.

He pushed the hair back from her face and said, "I'm leaving tomorrow and there's a family thing tonight. A New Year's party."

Debbie said, "I'm going to miss you so much. Write to me."

"I need to see you, but I'm busy with this party and I have to go in the morning."

"I'll really miss you. I miss you already," she said again.

"I wish we could see each other. Afterwards. But there's probably no way for you."

"Nope. No way," she said and put her lips once more on his. Their voices were soft and discreet, as if secreting something in the middle of a crowd.

"Can you sneak out?"

"It would be hard. It's New Year's and everybody's up."

"Yeah, I know," Robbie said, the hair's-breadth of his lips a whirlpool, sucking in her desire. "I just want to see you before I go. Just you and I, someplace warm and together. Not this car."

"I'd really like that," she said. Daring to hope and hoping to dare. Scheme and she would scheme with him.

"Can you say you're staying someplace, like a friend's or something, and I'll meet you?"

And so they plotted.

A good and reliable daughter, her mother did not question her motives for sleeping at Michelle's. And then down to the circle, that place of meetings; where roads diverge and horizons expand. He was already there waiting, in a white Chrysler Imperial. She sat across from him, restraining from kisses soon to be portioned. They held hands across the seat as they drove, not looking at each other; not wanting to chance this chance.

She asked if she should duck down as they entered the estate. No, his family had gone and the farm help keeps to themselves. The stockmen were gone and they would be late tomorrow, because of the holiday. It would be just her and the horses.

It was an apartment used by the groom, but he just recently rented a place of his own in the village, so it was empty. It was above the horse stalls. Robbie called the horses by name and had them take oats from her hand. She held a girl's fascination with horses and it was just the first thrill of that night.

Up a circular metal stairway wrapped around a pole. He took her coat. A peanut butter and banana sandwich and some chocolate milk were in the fridge; for her. There was a bottle of wine. He said they would open it together and toast the new year. When he got back.

They were standing, in each other's arms and he told her, "I'm going with Reggie tonight. I want you to know, that's all."

"I can't do anything about that," she said without letting go.

"I'm going to tell her. Tonight. I can't just leave without telling her."

"I guess," she said, holding tighter.

"Are you mad?"

"No. I feel bad is all. She loves you, too."

"She does," he said sadly. And then, "You'll be okay, by yourself? I won't be back for hours."

"I'll be okay. I can nap. I want to be awake for you. I want to be completely awake."

"Don't forget about the sandwich."

"I won't," she said. "See you next year."

"You bet. Next year, Sweet Pea."

And they kissed the kiss of lovers anticipating the rest. There, in the glisten of the lie and the secret and the thing to come, she had never felt so right, right then.

# 27
# ❧ Regina's Levy

Clark Steel New Year's balls were notoriously well-attended by Buffalo's patricians. The year before, while the rest of his family frolicked away the last of '67, Reggie came late to his house. They drank gin and made love on the floor in front of the fireplace. That was the first time she sensed a change between them. He wasn't so fervent to undo her and then he was slow to come; this despite the feral atmosphere of the floor and the fire and the woody gun room his father used as a retreat. They scrambled to compose themselves at the sound of car doors and voices.

Robbie asked her to be his escort this year in a letter from boot camp. She spent too much on a dress from L.L. Berger's downtown. It was a black, ankle-length a-line dress with beads and lace that flattered her breasts and waist. It wasn't something she would customarily wear, ever, but it was their last night together. The last chance to settle things.

She fussed over her makeup, going hard on her eyes. She even put on a ridiculous set of long Twiggy lashes before laughing out loud, ripping them off and tossing them in the trash. Reggie's eyes were natural daggers without accoutrements. She pinned her hair in a half updo, a delicate bun of savage auburn hair, with bangs across her forehead and plenty of curl flooding her shoulders and bleeding down her back.

She wanted him to desire her. She wanted him aroused and begging for it. That's what she was planning as she preened in front of the mirror; this society dress had just the right dose of naughty. She wanted him to remember the night. She wanted him to long; to swoon; to beg; to miss. She wasn't going to be easy, but she was going to be... but not without concessions.

She had already come to terms. His terms. Nothing could be done about it now, but she wanted him to say he might have been wrong. She wanted a step in her direction. That's all. Just concede a modest point and she would be the dutiful and chaste sweetheart; writing and worrying and waiting. In her mind, the night had been etched.

While his father hired a car to transport the family to the Century Club, including dates, Robbie showed up alone in the Imperial that was used for toting his sisters around town. Ordinarily he hated the pretension of the thing, with its tail fins and gaudy whitewalls, but there was a glut of play space in the front and back. A feature not lost on the daughter of a car salesman. She was peeking through the curtains as he parked in the snow.

She was ready, but made him wait; busying herself with unnecessary adjustments and admiring her work. Confident in beauty and her ability to showcase it. He was with her father when she made her entrance. Their eyes met and she bent to tug on a heel, for him.

Robbie declined an invitation to drink and Fred Albach noted, "If a man is old enough to serve his country, he's old enough to have a drink. At least that's what I think."

"I agree with you, sir," Robbie said.

"You know what I think?" Reggie interjected. "I think if a guy is dumb enough to join this war, he's probably not mature enough to drink."

After she said it, she wished she could change her nature. Since he left for basic, she had spent too much time in the acrid confines of the student movement. She reminded herself, *don't be such an angry, bitter bitch. Not tonight, Reg.*

Robbie just cupped her lightly on the waist and planted a soft kiss on her cheek, "Good to see you too, Reg."

"Look at you," she said, brushing a hand down the shoulder of his tailored tuxedo. It was hard to believe he looked even better than the last time she saw him.

"Yeah, I was going to wear my class A's for you, but my mom thought it was a bad idea. She thought it was too controversial.

You never know who might get offended by the sight of a soldier in uniform these days."

"Smart mommy," Reg said. Again wishing she could bridle her thoughts.

Fred spoke up, "Yeah, it's a damn shame. A man who serves his country can't even show his pride anymore. Back in my day, a man in uniform never had to pay for a drink at any bar in this town. You could stick a thumb out on the side of the road and the first car would pick you up. It's a damn shame, I say."

"Well, you know, we're just baby killers now," Robbie said dryly and smiled at Reg.

She put an arm around him and shut up for once. Her mother came in with the Polaroid and had them pose for a picture by the big Christmas tree in front of the bay window. She made them wait until it developed, blowing on the paper and flicking it through the air with delicate fingers. Reggie found it decades later, while helping her mother clean out before the move to Florida. She took it and kept it secretly, but never looked at it.

In the car he told her, "You look spectacular tonight, Reg. Thank you for coming."

"Of course. Thanks for asking me."

"I was worried... thought you'd say no."

"Me too. Thought I'd say no. But we've been friends for a long time and that hasn't changed, right?" she said.

"Just friends?"

Reggie blushed and thought about where they'd be after Auld Lang Syne, "More than friends."

"Still?" he wondered.

"I guess we'll see about that."

"I suppose we will," he said without enthusiasm. Like she was a chore; an obligation.

She didn't like it. It wasn't what she counted on. Not so long ago he would have already pulled off into a field, behind a barn, or parked in the far corner of some grocery lot. Her dress would have been lifted and wrinkled, beads on the floor. He would have put her hand on him and asked for her mouth. Now they were on opposite ends of the upholstery. Two vagabonds sharing a lift.

"I guess you've been busy since you got home?" Regina accused.

"I've only been back for three days."

"Yeah, three days," she pouted.

"You think I was avoiding you?"

"I wonder?"

He didn't look at her as they drove, "I'm home for less than a week. My mother's a mess. You know the holidays. I called you first thing."

"Wow. A telephone call. Special me." She let the sarcasm ooze across the space and she watched him watch the road, feigning concentration. "How about Tommy's little sis. You call her?"

"What?"

"What's her name? Debbie? You make any time for her?"

"That's funny."

"What's funny about it?"

"I guess I could say the same. You make any time for Tommy?"

She thought about the night by the river, there had been nothing more. But there was the night by the river. It was true.

"Tommy's a good kid. I like him. That's all," she lied. She regretted not keeping it simple with Tommy.

The second floor ballroom of the Century Club was decked out in linens. Tables were set with china and silver. Streamers and noise makers surrounded the floral centerpieces. Servers in banquet jackets and white gloves patrolled the room with trays of hors d'oeuvres and drinks, while men smoked stogies in the loggia overlooking the snow-covered garden. A sultry middle-aged singer fronted the seventeen-piece swing band. A large banner was strung across the room that read *So Long '68*. At midnight a cord would be pulled and a second banner proclaimed *Hello '69*.

The dance floor was already full by the time they arrived. Robbie knew many of the guests. People who had been to the house or families of the Nichols school kids. And there were the men who held executive positions in the company. The trip to their table was slow and full of introductions for Reggie. She didn't remember any of them, though the list was a registry of local society-types. Names you would have read in the paper or heard mentioned at a philanthropic event. Robbie pointed out two members of congress and some state politicians who sat together, center stage, under the dome. She smiled and shook hands, but her eyes and thoughts were only on Robbie.

A table had been reserved specifically for the children and their dates. Linda and Judy were there with their beaus, sitting with rum drinks.

As they found their spot, Judy said to Robbie, "Always fashionably late, Brother."

"Oh, we know what they've been up to," Linda laughed, already too many drinks ahead of them.

Robbie said, "And just what is this we've been up to, Sister?"

Linda looked coolly to Regina. Her look was complimented by an equally chilly return. Linda stopped herself, saying, "I have no idea."

"Okay then," Robbie said and rolled his eyes.

Mrs. Clark stopped at their table and told Reggie, "That gown is lovely, Regina."

Then she whispered in Robbie's ear before painting another smile at Reggie.

After she left, Reggie whispered, "What secrets is Mumsie telling you?"

"She just told me I better be careful is all. She thought your dress might make me do something stupid."

"She thinks it's a slutty dress, then?" Regina smiled at him.

"No, she thought the dress was great. She thought perhaps the girl's a little slutty."

"Very funny, honey."

He nuzzled into her and said softly, "What's more important is that I want you to be slutty. Be slutty for me tonight, Reg."

Before dinner Robbie took her on the dance floor. He had been formally trained and was quite good. Regina could do a competent box step and she knew he would lead her carefully. Keeping things tight and controlled, gallantly pulling her close for a kiss when she lost the tempo.

It was after eleven when the last of the dessert plates had been cleared and fresh champagne flutes were set in place. Each guest received a box of truffles with the Clark company logo foiled on the lid. They were dancing again as the last song before the countdown played. She cried on his vest as the band got contemporary with Presley's, *I Can't Help Falling in Love with You.*

"Let's get outta here," he suggested.

"It's not midnight."

"Another year, another tear." He wiped her cheek with his thumb.

"You're such an asshole," she said quietly.

"I know."

"I wanna hate you so much."

"No, you don't."

"Oh, I do. I really want to, but I can't. You're such an asshole and I wanna hate you. But I can't."

"Well, stop trying then. Be my girl tonight. Don't hate me to-night. You'll have plenty of time for that later," he said.

They could hear the horn section blowing Auld Lang Syne as they descended the stairway and exited into the sharp cool of a winter night. He had skipped the valet and parked on the street. They moved briskly, she tight in his arms and his coat around her. He petted the edge of her breast and drove her forward, pirating her away. Muted cries and hoots softly ricocheted off the crusted snow from cracked windows and open doorways.

She was drunk and thought he was, too. He drove fast. Onto the highway and out of the city. She slid under his arm and he held her so tight it was hard to breathe. The tighter he held, the more distant she felt. It was a frantic, silent drive. He took her back to his home; the farm. She thought they might revisit the previous year's escapades in the gun room.

Instead he drove past the stables, and past the barn where they parked the horse trailers and farm equipment. There was an old caretaker's house that hadn't been used in years. The driveway wasn't plowed and they got stuck before reaching the house. He left her behind as he pushed up a window for entry. Unlocking the door from inside, he came back for her.

"C'mon," he said, pulling her into the snow.

"Robbie! I don't have any boots," Reggie protested.

He lifted her up over his shoulder and she began to laugh as he carried her through the snow, like a Viking raider with the prized damsel. The house was cold; real cold. He carried her up the stair-way into a room with a bed and flung her upon the barren mattress. She could tell he had been here before. He rummaged through the chest of drawers and pulled out some blankets. Old, musty covers that didn't match.

"Robbie, it's freezing. Can't we just stay in the car and keep the engine running?" she half-giggled.

"It'll be fine," he said, forcing her onto the muddle of blankets.

She pressed back against him and they shifted awkwardly to become undone. She was both aroused and conflicted, the spitting image of a virgin's want.

She was pulling and pushing all at once and spoke in gasps, "Whoa... whoa... whoa... Hold on... Sweetie, hold on."

Robbie was panting, too. He hunched up over her, half-undressed, his hair in tangles.

"What?" he wondered.

"I don't want to do this just 'cause you're leaving. I don't want this to be just one last fuck for you."

"Whatta ya mean?"

"I mean, I have to know what this is. What is this?... What are we?"

"It wasn't me who changed things. That was you, Reg. I told you my plan. My life plan. It was you who made it a problem. I'm the same. I haven't changed."

"Not just the army," she said.

"Then what?"

She bit her lip and let go of him.

"What?" he said again.

"Debbie. Do you have feelings for her?"

"Tommy's sister?"

"Yeah, Tommy's sister. Are you two a thing?"

"I don't know where this is coming from," he said and rolled off her.

"C'mon," she said. "Word gets around. Robbie Clark can't hang out in the village and not be noticed. Someone said they saw you today."

"She was walking home from town. Yeah, I gave her a lift. Does that make us a thing?"

"I think so."

He snuggled next to her on his back. The panting of lust distant now. He told her, "How is it you can hang out with Tommy all the time, and I know you do, and I don't doubt you at all?"

"I have lots of guy friends and I'm not screwing any of them."

He sighed deeply and turned to her, looking straight into her eyes just inches away. There was enough moonlight kicking off the snow for them to see each other plainly. She felt his breath on her cheeks, warm and sweet with alcohol. His perfect eyes melting away the cold, bringing her to where she always wanted to be.

"You're my girl, Reg. Just be my girl. That's all," he said.

She told him to use protection, but neither liked it. He said he would pull out and spend himself on her belly, beyond the reach of instinct and cycles of the moon. Beyond that for which desire commands. Beyond the laws of nature and God. He would spend himself there to be washed away and off to war he would go. The future ignorant of what was lost. That was the plan.

And inside, the laws of nature and God could not coexist with the plan. His feeble attempt to escape thundered away by a sixth force of nature. He let go. She could not.

# 28
# ⚬₃ Tommy's Devotion

Another year and virtually alone. The joy of the holidays a whip lashing upon the lesions of heartbreak. This was especially tough when the one you love is cavorting with the one she loves. Tommy spent the last night of 1968 by the television with his mother. His father was supposed to be there, too. But often his best intentions were waylaid by the call of one more drink at the Bar Bill; just one more drink, Jimmy. Debbie was spending the night at a girl-friend's house. She had told her mother so. She had always been a good and reliable daughter and there was no reason to doubt this.

Self-absorbed as he was, he did not recognize the pain sitting across the room. It was right there with him as the ball dropped in Times Square. Mother's are naturally attuned to the sorrows of children and she had absorbed his burden into hers.

Her burden? That of a love gone stale. Married to a man who had come to love drink as much as himself. Jimmy Donohue was a man of hard truths. Sharp edges defined his view of the world. No curves with hopes of a bright horizon. Yes, he provided for them as a good man would. With limited opportunities, he made his way to the plant everyday, taking his place in the machine and pulling his weight with no hope for something better. His life had gone stale, too. But they continued to break bread and say it was good.

Then ten minutes after midnight, alone in his room. The desk lamp, a beacon on his dispatch from Uncle Sam: *You are hereby ordered to report for induction into the Marines Corps of the United States on **January 5, 1969 at 7 AM** at **The Connecticut Street***

*Armory, Room 1265 for forwarding to an induction station.* The time and place hand-stamped in black ink and block letters. He wanted Reggie there with him, seeing the letter and telling him she was his. *Just stay, darling,* she would say. *Stay with me and we'll be together.* Together they would face this. She had told him so.

But she was not with him. The one to whom the glory would go, that's who she was with. All her sermons and high ideals and still she was with him, her love. In the shadows of the desk lamp, January fifth beckoned to him. The devotion of father and country whispering softly. *Carry on, soldier.* Follow the footsteps of Jimmy Donohue and heartache be gone. This love is but a conjuring; a crook of souls. The yearnings of lust and flesh and nothing more. The world is a sea of flesh and Regina Albach but one purveyor.

He fell into a restless sleep atop his covers and the lamp still beckoned his fate. He woke when Jimmy Donohue slammed the front door closed and stumbled off the walls into the front room where his mother had been sleeping poorly.

"Happy New Year's to you, too," he announced loudly in a slurred voice which had been a frequent visitor of late.

He heard his mother say angrily, "Drunk again. You promised not tonight. Not tonight, Jimmy."

"I'm not fuckin' drunk and so what if I am?"

"You promised, Jimmy. Not tonight, you said."

The house shook as Jimmy Donohue punched a hole in the plaster walls while bellowing, "So what if I fuckin' am? Goddam it all to hell! So what if I am? I earn the money here. You don't tell me what to do around here!"

It was a hole he would have to fix and it would not be his first patch job. Tommy came into the room to find his mother cowering and blood on his father's knuckles.

"What're you looking at?" his father menaced.

When Tommy couldn't find the right words, his father beat him with an ugly glare and repeated, "Huh? What're you looking at? You got something you wanna say?"

"Go to bed, Tommy. He's not fit to talk to," his mother said.

"Shut your mouth," Jimmy told his wife.

Tommy said, "You shut your mouth. Go to bed, old man. You're drunk."

"Why you fucking punk. Who're you telling to shut up? I'll kick you're goddam ass, that's what I'll do for you."

His mother got between them as fighting poses were struck.

"How dare you raise a fist to me?" the old man slurred. "You're lucky you're going into the service, 'cause I'd throw your ass out of this house."

"Don't worry. I'm leaving. I can't wait to go."

"Well good. That goes double for me, sonny boy."

"Good."

"Tommy, don't. Go to bed now," his mother pleaded. "Jimmy, you too. Tomorrow's another day."

He saw his father's face, sad and drawn, the staleness of life crusted over. And the pain in his mother's eyes from that night would always stay with him, coming to him in dark moments of reflection, even after she was gone.

He packed quietly, stuffing what clothes he could into a couple backpacks and his father's Marine Corps duffle; a gift for boot camp. His father tossed it in his lap one evening and said it was ready for action.

He put in his watch and his sneakers and a pair of Sunday shoes. He left his baseball cards and coin collection; most of his summer clothes. He wrapped the money he kept hidden into a towel. And he folded the induction letter into his pocket. He snuck out past his parents' room, moving slowly and avoiding the places where the floorboards creaked. He put the Nova in neutral and let it roll into the street.

Driving towards Reggie's, he pulled the induction letter from his pocket and crushed it. He rolled down the window, the cold of winter washing over his face. Somewhere between here and there, he tossed out the directive. Black and white gone. White as the snow. Black as the night. Gone with the wind.

# 29
## ☙ Deborah's Levy

Reggie rocked the Imperial hoping to reverse it out, the way they came. Robbie was pushing. His coat and vest draped over the hood. The top buttons of his shirt undone and the bow tie loose around his neck. The dress shoes were useless, his feet slipping away as he shoved.

Reggie's hair no longer in place, angry tears dotting the lace of her bodice. She would gun the engine and send the whitewalls spinning and Robbie would implore her to go easy. With each press of the pedal she wanted to take off; evaporate.

She had run out on their rendezvous, into the snow. Just running. Cold against her ankles and shins. Snow crumbling into the edge of her heels. Robbie caught her by the waist and carried her back. She struggled, but he wasn't having it.

Moments before they had been soft and warm under the covers.

"I just wanna make love all night. Like before," she told him. "I don't want this to end. I can't stand that you're going, but it's okay. I'm at peace."

And Robbie let go of her, turning away.

"Come over here," Reggie whispered, reaching around for him. "Don't forget I'm your slut tonight. You can have anything you want. Tell me what Dick Clark wants."

He pulled her hand away from that part and placed it back at her side. Now facing her. Eyes serious and fixed.

"What?" she said.

And he looked at her, his confidence shaken.

"Tell me," she whispered, trepidation creeping in.

"When you asked about Tommy's sister..."

As he stumbled for words, it was already known. No need to finish.

"You go to hell," she said and sprang naked from the bed.

She sent the covers flying, looking for the clothes so carefully chosen and so carelessly discarded. Tricot and lace haphazard in the blankets and poured upon the floor. He caressed the flesh on her back and she whirled around with a closed fist. Had she meant to hurt him, it could not have been more precise; a welt forming in the corner of his eye.

"You go to hell, Robbie," she said again.

"I didn't mean for this."

"Just what does that mean?" she said, pulling on her panties and wiping the last of him into her leg.

"I wasn't looking for someone else. I care for you, Reg."

"It's called love. Care? Go care for your dog."

"Don't go like this. I do love you... but she has me, too."

Robbie tried to pull her close in comfort, but she just flung him away. "That's not the way it works. This love is exclusive."

"I don't know how it works. I just know I want you both."

"Yeah, you want. What Robbie wants. What Robbie needs. That's the way things work, right?"

"I know. I'm selfish. I can be better. Give me a chance and I'll work this out. I'll be gone for a year, let me work it out."

She fixed herself in the small mirror on the bureau. She could see him reflected, naked on the bedside. His head in his hands, looking broken and helpless. For once, the golden boy down on his luck and in need of some tenderness.

"Go to war, Robbie. That's what you really want. You have my permission. Not that you ever cared about that. Go to war and go fuck yourself," she said heartlessly.

They couldn't get the Imperial out of the drift, so he went to the big house for the Jeep. He only agreed to stop pushing when she promised to wait. She watched in the rear view mirror as he fled along the driveway, slipping and struggling to stay upright, a wounded animal on the run. He disappeared around a bend and she put her head on the wheel and wept.

On the ride home, she tolerated no apologies, nor explanations. He said he would write and she told him, "Don't expect me to write back. You're just a liar, and not a very good one."

*That was the last time they spoke.*

He revved the engine on the way out of Reggie's driveway, fishtailing down Willardshire. The car acting out.

When he got to the stables, Debbie was lying sleepy-eyed under the covers. She smiled and noticed the mark by his eye.

"Something happened?" Peanut asked, understanding.

"Yeah. We're finished... Reggie and I, we're through." He didn't hide his disappointment.

She ran her hand along the bruise, a demure smile sketching her face. She knew it was her face that held him. It was always her face that brought him close. Wide brown eyes that smiled with her lips. A pouting lower lip topped by a thin and balanced cupid's bow; dimples her arrows, and luscious dark hair her sights. Hair that rode down mounded cheeks and fanned out to frame a perfect chin and silky neck; falling tenderly upon the curves of a blossoming breast. Her smokey pure complexion blurring the edges between hair and skin, purity and sin. She could always see his eyes when they met, coming first to her face.

He was transfixed on her face as he dropped his shoes and crawled in with her, asking, "Did you eat your sandwich?"

"Nope. And I couldn't sleep. I could hear the horses," she told him, her arms naturally around his neck. Him leaning in.

"You heard the horses?"

"I could hear them moving and neighing."

"They knew you were here. They were begging for apples. They didn't scare you?"

"I liked hearing them."

He noticed the chain around her neck. Aunt Enid's necklace. He took it in his mouth and sucked along the ridges of the metal, following it down into her fitted sweater, stretching the neckline and down to her breast; reaching a hand up from underneath. A move further and her top was off. She unhooked her bra as he took off his shirt. Aunt Enid's necklace perfectly centered and completely modeled, as it must have been when Enid was young, with Albert the first time.

She ran her hands upon his chest and felt him breathing deeply, the muscles stretching and contracting. the warmth of a body alive.

When he kissed her breast, she arched her back and said, "They're not very big. Not like Regina Albach's."

And he latched there, in desire's spell. Answering her desires. Knowing they would soon be one, a place she had never been. As his lips played with her, the hint of adolescent yearnings becoming crystal. A feeling of being made for him and him for her. Together as one. If there had been fears, a wanting replaced them. Her body calling to him, draping him in permission.

But he asked permission, stating, "It's okay if we don't."

And breathless she replied, "You want me, don't you?"

"If it hurts, we can stop," his response.

But he was slow and soft, not forcing. Letting her come to him. Letting her dictate the pace until she had him. There was nothing rushed. They took the long way, laying the groundwork. Plucking the grass from the field where it grew, and licking the dew from the stalks. Then finding their destination with no inconvenience; no glitch, not one wrong turn. The room was prepared and the key had been turned. He lifted her across the threshold and his joy was immediate. She took his happiness and made it her own, cradling it and tending it; securing it and blessing it.

And after he asked, "Are you okay?"

She answered with one of her smiles and a kiss on his chest.

"Did you bleed?"

"Maybe. There's a lot going on down there."

Later, she asked, "What was it like for you? The first time."

"Really? You wanna know?"

"It's okay if you don't wanna say."

"It was in the hay barn. Right behind here. I was fourteen."

"How old was she?"

"About the same. It seemed like it anyways. We were both virgins."

She teased him to continue, her tongue dancing along his chest.

"Her dad was our mechanic and handyman. He fixed everything. They lived in the old house down past the tractor barn." And he didn't say, *the house of an hour before.*

"Is she still here?"

"I don't know where she is. Her dad was let go by our farm boss. It was because of me. It was because we got caught, so he lost his job."

"Oh, wow. You guys got caught?"

"Not the first time, but we got caught together, later in my room. It was my mom. She caught us and they let him go. It was ridiculous. I don't think he had any idea why he was fired."

Peanut considered them together and thought, what if they were caught? A secret no longer. She pressed, "Well, how did it happen? The first time."

"She was a tomboy and we were always goofing around. We were fooling around in the haymow, jumping from the loft into the broken bales. Throwing handfuls of straw at each other. Sizing each other up. At one point I just grabbed her breast. I can't say why, but I was close and I wanted them."

"Her boobs?"

"Yeah, I just wanted them and we were close and playing close with little touches and I just grabbed one."

"And she wanted you?"

"I suppose, but first she kicked me and told me I better not do that again. But all the while she was laughing. She was laughing and she climbed up onto the hay stack. Just laughing. The stack was fresh and tall, they had just put up the last cut of the year."

As he remembered, he took to Debbie's lips. Sucking her lower lip between his, tasting her, and she teased it out, pulling back on his upper lip. Then releasing him and running her face along his cheek and down his neck. Keeping him on point, she whispered into his ear, "And then?"

"I climbed up after and she was trying to get away, but I got a hold of her leg and all the while she was cussing at me, but laughing too. I climbed up on her and we just started kissing right there in the hay. I remember spitting out pieces of straw as we kissed. Her hair was full of straw. From then it was a blur, almost primitive, our pants were off and it was raw and I was inside and it was over. That's how it happened. I don't think it was much fun for either of us. I saw blood in the straw."

"But it got better?"

"Practice makes perfect."

Debbie sighed and said, "I can't imagine anything better."

"Tell me about your first time," he said.

"You should know," she said, surprised.

"I mean, tell me how it felt. Was it okay? Was I good to you?"

"It was the most perfect thing ever. I'm not lying, either."

"I didn't hurt you?"

She took his face in her hands and made him see her, past the glow of her face and into her soul and when she was sure he was seeing, she said, "It was the best thing ever and I'm not kidding. I thank God for you and for this night."

"We've still got time if you want."

"Yes, it's all I want." And as he touched her, she said playfully, "I'm just glad my dad doesn't work for you."

Then he told her, "Now I know, I've never been in love before."

Later he bundled the bed clothes into a burlap feed sack and threw them in the garbage. He took her home, before the sun. Parking away, so she might sneak into the darkened house; retracing the steps of an older brother who had skipped out, hours before.

She told him, "I'm going to miss you so much. I don't know how I'll manage, especially after tonight. I'm so proud of you, though. I'm so proud to know you and I'll pray for you to come back safe. Every day and every night."

"Can prayers change our fate, Peanut?" he wondered.

"I don't know... but I can't chance it."

*That was the last time they spoke.*

30

## ೦3 The Eternal Flame
## (Revisited)

Madeline's disappearance was explained by the pilfered letters strewn across the bed. Her own note scribbled and scattered in the muck... *FUCK THIS SHIT*. The missing part of her uncovered. No more wondering why all that was her dad could not be found in those parts of her. Not hair, nor eyes, nor cheeks, nor nose. Not complexion, nor ears, nor stature and temperament. She was a biological anomaly and the only similarity she could reckon was they were both white. She and her father, whom she loved so dearly.

The fact he wasn't present at her birth, well that was explainable; a fugitive from his country and living in Toronto. It was grandma by her mother's side at Children's Hospital. The thirteen hours of sheer hell. While it was her first refusal to make a timely appearance, it was not her last. Something her mother would tease on all those occasions she made them wait; like when she went hiking in the hills the morning of her wedding. She hit the church an hour late and still in her Timberlands. The wedding her Grandpa Jimmy and Aunt Debbie didn't attend. The marriage that was slow to start and quick to finish.

They called Madeline and left messages that went unanswered. It was Gee who was getting hot, unable to contain her anger in the last message. Boy softly chided her and said they needed to make the trip. This explanation required a personal visit; this decision to obfuscate their daughter's life.

"She still needs to return my calls. I'm still her mother," Gee said.

"And I'm her father, like you said," Boy added. Life's regrets perched upon his shoulder.

Not just the deception of Madeline, but of all things from those days. His dismissal of Jimmy Donohue. His wife's denial of Peanut Donohue. How what was said in Robbie's letter, and thought by Gee, bore some truth. Though he made his owns truths and regrets, Gee had been the life he chose without regret. But there are those times when one is reminded about the consequences of choice and the construction of designer realities to hide hard truths.

They were too late for flying that night and Boy took Gee for a ride. He didn't tell her where, but put her in the car and explained it was important for them. They drove the same way, the route traveled so long ago on another perfect summer day. And now, like then, the shadows were stretching through the trees as they went down the hundred steps and back in time to that place so many decades before. The three of them had gone this way back when life was vast and untouched, a prairie of discovery before them. Back to their youth and back before choices were made and destinies forged.

Down the hundred steps and up the creek in the lingering grip of a perfect summer day.

"This is a bad idea," Gee told him as they descended into the ravine. "As if I couldn't feel any shittier."

"C'mon," Boy summoned, as Robbie had those many years before.

They moved without pause, taking no notice of the maples and oaks, cherry and white pines that clumped along the walls. Many of them just wisps of bark and leaves the last time they passed.

They paid no particular attention to the trickling sounds of a summer stream waiting for a good rain to wash away the debris collected on dry slate banks. The washing that comes to everything and removes those things along the edge, sending them downstream. Ever downstream to settle and become a piece of someplace. And the things unsettled, continuing onward through streams and lakes and rivers before washing out to sea. The insignificant bits that wash beyond understanding and collect unnoticed in the entirety of the whole.

The path was worn over the years, the flame's reputation blossoming. But this late afternoon they were alone as it was before, and when they rounded the bend, the flame was lit and quivering. The eternal flame burning orange and blue behind the narrow curtain of crystal water; splashing down upon the shale and pooling quietly, before surely rambling onward.

And suddenly it was then. It was 1967, the day that Robbie took the lighter and sparked the flame that brought them here. The echoes of politics and choices and the smell of pot bristling above the water. And in the shadows upon the edges of the ravine was Robbie, bright-eyed and confident. Holding court and leading them. Leading them to this place, this time in their life. Boy knew it and Gee, too. If not for Robbie, this place would be an afternoon jaunt with different lovers and different children and other lives of fate or chance.

The eternal flame calling them back. And the understanding of how it was he, who sacrificed for them. How it was his life that created their's and how it was here the lives they shared began in earnest. It was here the first flicker of choices crested above the bow and splashed upon their breast, cold and daunting.

When he would tell the story about how they met, to friends and acquaintances, Boy would recite a tale about a bell and a beautiful girl in a darkened cabana, and about a young man's erection. They would all laugh as he told it and Boy would look at Gee, completely in love, as he had been then. And though they met as awkward strangers that night, it was here, in the late afternoon shadows of a narrow ravine, their lives became bound. It was here under the spell of the eternal flame that Robbie gave them life. It was here, together, he led them.

"It hasn't changed much," Boy said to Gee.

"No, just everything else has," she answered.

Together Reggie and Tommy stood before the flame, echoes playing in concert. His echoes tumbling from above and cascading down the walls of time. Reminding them of what has been... and what never was.

# 31
# ❧ The Bridge

Tommy parked in a cutout where the road crews turned the plows, inconspicuous behind the snowbank. A sightline to her driveway and the Jeep as it came and went; leaving abruptly and tires spinning, the rear-end fishtailing. Something was up. Her lover didn't linger in contemplation of a long separation. Tommy was pleased.

He left the car and footed it up to the house, shoulders hunched. He knew where her bedroom was. There was another time he had been there. Back when it was warm and he was lonely and he hid in the little poplar grove beyond the edge of the lawn. The grove where they carved out a spot for a garden shed after buying the place from her parents. Then he was desperate to glimpse her; to know she was home and alone. Alone like him. He saw her draw the curtains and then her shadow behind them. He stayed even after the light was shut, sitting against a tree and watching her window, imagining her asleep by him. He has never confessed this.

This night, though, he would tap on the window and beckon her. She would be obliged to produce the promise of comfort. His feet cut through the crust and sank beyond his ankles, carving a path to her window. A dim light set an ethereal scene. There was a crack in the pleated drapes and he could see through the sheers. She was on her bed, in her party dress, weeping. He could tell she was weeping silently, a pillow against her breast and face. Taking shallow staccato breaths, the lines of her belly panting in gulps of pain. A witness to this personal tragedy he abandoned whatever thoughts he had of them together, this night. Even through the sliver of drapes, her pain was poignant.

In retreat, he brushed a sleeve across his eyes. A snowflake on his cheek. He should go back to the house of his father. Back to witness the sober regret and the mixing of the plaster. The working of the trowel to smooth the damage. It was a task done silently and alone. Working first this way, then that, scraping the excess. The sanding and the painting, but never quite making the match. A permanent scar if you knew where to look.

But instead, he drove to the city and slept in his car outside the Students for a Democratic Society office. It wasn't until the afternoon that Shaw showed up to let him in. His full name was Jack Shaw, but people just called him Shaw. He had been a delegate to the national conventions in Kewadin and Clear Lake. He went to the University of Wisconsin to protest the presence of na-palm-maker Dow Chemical at a college job fair. He had his head split when the Madison cops took to night sticks and tear gas, his bloodied face was photographed and pictured in newspapers across the country, a mark that elevated his credibility. He wore a Pancho Villa mustache, like many of the SDS'ers. Shaw made the call to Reggie.

She wasn't able to come until much later and Tommy was teetering on the precipice of returning home. Home to a mother who must be worrying and home to a father whose regrets had him on the precipice, too; supposing a way down. Down to the Bar Bill and down to the company of men and a bottle. But he stayed for Reggie.

She arrived looking haggard. Eyes still red from a night of alcohol and tears. She wouldn't look at him and was methodical and detached as she assessed his situation.

"So what would you like to do now?" she asked, as she might say to a fella off the street; a complete stranger.

"I don't know what to do, Reg," Tommy said, seeking answers.

"Well, you can't stay around here, that's for sure. If you just would have waited," she scolded. " I think Canada's your only option. They'll find you if you stick around."

Of course, he thought, that was the plan all along. Why was she acting like this? It had been discussed ad infinitum. Just go to Canada. Discussed often on those nights when he longed to be close and he dreamed of crossing the bridge with her at his side.

"I can always just report. Go home," Tommy said dejectedly. It was a card he was loath to play in her present state, but she left him no choice.

"Just like that? You'll just go home? And what? Show up for induction?" She was teetering, too.

"It's not too late for me," he pressed.

"So you'll just go home then?" She seemed on the verge of crying. He had nearly put her back in the room after the Jeep had fishtailed.

"Maybe," he said. "I mean, if I go to Canada I'll just be alone up there. I don't know anybody in Canada."

"Yes you do. You know Bruce Freed." Bruce Freed was one of the guys from that day at the Unitarian Church.

"He's in Montreal. I'm not going to Montreal."

Reggie took him by the hand and led him back to the lounge, away from the office and Shaw. The lounge was a dim place with old chairs and floor lamps. It was the place they sat around and chewed on politics and listened to records. There was a refrigerator with left-overs and beers. She gave Tommy a beer, but couldn't stomach one herself.

Tommy opened his beer and looked at her directly, "I saw you last night."

"Saw me? I was with Robbie, you know that."

"I was at your house. When he left you," Tommy swigged and confronted her. "I came to your bedroom window. I wanted to tell you. You were crying."

"You were spying on me?" she asked with a hint of indignation.

"I wasn't spying. I came to you, because you said you'd help. You'd be with me," Tommy felt crappy about calling her out. They both felt crappy.

"I am with you. I'm helping you, right?"

"Why were you crying? Did he dump you?"

"I suppose you'd know?" she accused.

"How would I know?"

"Ask your sister," she snapped.

So it was true, Debbie and Robbie were a thing, more than just friends. He felt it, but didn't believe it and had not seen them since the night at the movie house.

"You think they're together?" he asked, playing dumb.

"How could you miss it?"

"Well, I didn't know anything about it, Reg. If they're together it's news to me... and my folks. They wouldn't let Debbie date anyone, not even Robbie Clark," he stated, keeping his suspicions to himself.

"Well they are. He told me," she said, doubting his sincerity.

Tommy sucked on the beer and asked her, "So you're through then?"

She was stuck at the question. Even then she couldn't bear it. Her eyes were wet and she turned away, not wanting to show.

"Well, I'm not going to Canada if you're not with me," he said, letting her off the hook.

She said back, softly, still not facing him, "Tommy, I was never moving with you. You knew that, right? I'll be with you, but I'll be here. I'll come and visit when I can. I'm going to school. My life is here."

"And mine isn't?"

"Well, of course, but..." and she realized how ridiculous she sounded.

"I'm not asking you to come with me, but I'm not moving if I can't see you again. I'm not moving away and never seeing you again. I'd just as soon go get killed," Tommy said.

That was the confession of love she had sought all along. A confession of devotion and respect and the understanding that comes to soulmates, when one connects completely with the other. A bending that brings them closer when fowl winds blow. Unfortunately, the confession had come from the wrong boy.

She came across the room and snuggled in with him. He wanted to finish what he started that night by the river, but she took his hand from her breast and deflected his lips to her neck. His devotion was too much to bear. She was too broken for the burden of his love. He knew this, too. She needed to set his love aside and rest. Her soul needed rest and distance before contemplating something else. It was the toughest part of her journey. The grade was steep and her body was already forging beyond understanding.

She placed her arms around his neck and pulled him close as a sister might, "I'm not leaving you, Boy. I promise I'll come and see you. I'll come and stay with you in Toronto when the time is right."

"You'll come?"

"Yes. I'll come and be with you... when I can. I'm not saying it won't be hard for you. Sure, at first it will be hard and you'll be lonely, but I'm not leaving you. I won't abandon you."

"Good," he said, there upon her. "I won't make it, Reg. Not without you. I know you're in love with him, but I won't make it without you."

"Then you'll make it," she said.

Tommy spent two more nights at the SDS house and there were many powwows about his exodus. Reggie made an effort to stick around for each of them, advocating on his behalf. Shaw had already taken a couple guys across and it was agreed he would be the one. As much as Tommy wanted Reggie, Shaw insisted more people makes for more problems at the border. They had to go before his induction date; before he was a deserter. Canada had a clear policy on conscientious objectors, but the policy on deserters was less friendly. He would likely be turned away if they knew it was past his induction date.

They got Tommy a cheap suit from the Salvation Army and cut his hair short. They gave him a thousand bucks which he would show at the border as a means of support. Money to be returned after crossing. Someone from the Toronto Anti-Draft Programme drove down to Buffalo with a job offer from a company that sold paintings door-to-door. With just a high school education and no real work experience, Tommy would be a borderline candidate for landed immigrant status. Canada used a point system and a person needed at least fifty out of a hundred to be considered for legal status.

The person who came down with the job offer knew the work schedule of a sympathetic border agent. They would make a run for it then. A sympathetic border guard could curve the numbers to make the difference between going and staying.

A room was arranged on Baldwin Street off Spadina. That's where all the boys who refused to fight landed if they went to Toronto. Once a neighborhood of working-class Jews, it had become a ghetto of American draft dodgers. Cheaply-rented, narrow clapboard houses in various states of repair, not too far from the University of Toronto and the bustle of Bay Street.

It was a Saturday morning when he packed his things into the Nova. They would drive up in his car and Shaw would return it to Reggie. She would make things right with her dad, regarding the job and the car. They drove to the bridge in two cars. It was a frigid

January day and the winds off the lake funneled down the cut of the river making it feel like ten below. Shaw drove ahead and Tommy was back in the second car with Reggie. At the foot of the Porter Avenue entrance they parked and said their goodbyes. She gave him a lover's kiss and held him tight, reassuring him. Letting him know it wasn't all a big tease. Letting him know there was a possibility of them.

"I will come to see you," she said. "When you're settled I'll come up for a visit."

"You'll be my girl?"

"We'll see," she told him truthfully.

"We'll share a bed?"

"We'll see. We'll just have to wait and see," she told him.

"When will I see?"

"Just get settled. I have a break in March. I'll come then."

"Can't you come before?" he prodded.

"In March I won't be so stressed about school. We can spend time together then," she said.

"I'm not happy about that."

"I know you're not," she said closely, feeling warm as his lips tickled her neck under her hair. "Call me when you get a phone. We can talk on the phone. If you have to, just call me collect. Use a pay phone. You have my number."

"At school?"

"Yes, call me there."

She got out and walked with him to the Nova. On their final kiss, he opened her winter coat and put his hands on her waist. There were tears in his eyes and she smiled to calm him.

"I love you, Reg," he said for the first time, meaning it.

"Take care of yourself, okay?" she said, as best she could.

He and Shaw crossed up and over the Peace Bridge. To the left Lake Erie, frozen as far as the eye could see. Below and beyond, the Niagara flowed dark and swift. Over the hump of the bridge they passed the flags that delineated the two places. Their colors blowing straight and in sync. Between them a line through the nothing that means something different. The stars and stripes waving indifferently as they passed.

# 32
## ଔ Toronto

How easy to discard your life and start over. Just follow the recipe. Take one second hand suit, fill completely with a neatly-trimmed coward, add two cups of cash and fold in the promise of work. Bake for one hour with a sympathetic immigration official and sprinkle with bullshit to taste. Let cool until born again; this time an orphan in a foreign land. And so Tommy was.

When they were younger, each summer his father would take them to the amusement park at Crystal Beach and that was his only experience with Canada. Even though Toronto was just two hours up the Queen Elizabeth Way, he had never been. Soon it would be home.

Their first stop was at 11½ Spadina Avenue, the offices of the Toronto Anti-Draft Programme. Cozy and cluttered, you entered through a bright yellow door, a peace symbol hand-painted in reflex blue. A Canadian maple leaf hung along the back wall. Cork boards were pinned with leads on apartments and jobs. A huge poster of Benjamin Spock followed you from across the room. Fliers with protest announcements, political rants and motivational thoughts taped thick and haphazard throughout the office. Above the file cabinets another peace symbol, this one a construct of discarded draft cards. There were pamphlets stacked on windowsills and desks. It was part work space, part social club, not unlike the SDS office in Buffalo, only busier. You could see there was real business conducted here.

Heather was expecting them and asked, "No troubles at the border?"

"Piece of cake," Shaw said.

She was involved in a mound of paperwork and explained, "When I first started here we might get three calls a week. Now, I get ten times that every day. It's crazy. Nixon's got us on our toes."

She placed a call for someone to come get Tommy and he handed the thousand bucks back to Shaw.

Heather told him, "We got you sharing a house and I'm sorry, but it's really cramped. Don't worry, it's just a half-way house until you get on your feet. Like I said, we're so busy we just don't have the space for all the new guys showing up. Tommy, you can settle-in today, then pop round the office tomorrow and we'll start working on a job... get you acquainted with the city."

"What about rent?" Tommy asked.

"The rent is covered until you get some work, but you'll need to take care of your own food and necessities. Do you have any money?"

"Yeah, I've got some saved."

"Good. It usually takes a month or two before you find something. But don't worry," she said, reassuring him.

A fellow came into the office with no gloves and no hat and he hadn't bothered to button up his peacoat. He was blowing warmth into his hands and he looked like so many of the anti-war types. Long hair, a fortnight beard and blurry eyes.

Heather introduced him as Pete Sommers. He said, "Holy hell, it's bloody cold out there. You the new guy?"

Shaw drove them back to the house at 106 Baldwin Street, just around the corner. A dilapidated three-story Victorian row house. They carried his stuff in; his worldly possessions in a single trip.

Tommy was assigned a cot on the first floor. There were two more cots in the small room. It had once been a dining room, back when a family lived there. A blanket tacked above the archway served as a door. The blanket provided no peace from the little black and white television and commotion in the parlor. There were a couple guys watching *Reach for the Top* and blurting out answers. The place was cold and dark, a mustiness painted with the stench of cigarette smoke.

Tommy said so long to Shaw and so long to his car before Sommers gave him the low down.

"This is my place. I'm the de facto chief of this house. I'm your daddy. What I say goes. Capiche?"

Tommy listened and nodded as Sommers continued, "I'm in charge of keeping the expenses in line. The thermostat is set at sixty-four degrees. Anyone caught messing with the thermostat gets a demerit. Capiche?... Lights are only to be used at night and only if you absolutely have to. When you leave a room you shut the light. Anybody that leaves a room and doesn't shut the light gets a demerit. Capiche?... There's one phone and it's in the kitchen. It's only set up to take incoming calls and make collect calls. If you ab-solutely need to make a phone call and can't do it collect, there's a pay phone on the corner of Spadina and Baldwin... No fighting. Like the television, for instance. The group decides what to watch. Anyone caught fighting over the television gets a demerit. Capiche?"

"What's a demerit?" Tommy asked.

"A demerit, man. It's a kick in the ass. It's a demerit, you know? You get kicked in the ass often enough and pretty soon your ass is out on the street. Capiche?"

"Capiche," Tommy said.

"Cleaning. Everyone's responsible for cleaning. You make a mess, you clean it up. I got a bathroom schedule on the wall. Every day one guy is responsible for cleaning the bathrooms. And I'm not talking about some little candy-ass wipe, 'cause that ain't gonna cut it. There's cleanser and a scrub brush in both bath-rooms. You get in there and scrub that mother like you mean it. You scrub that mother until the porcelain is about to peel. Every time I take a shit I inspect the bathroom. If it's your turn and you ain't scrubbed it to my standards, whatta ya gonna get?"

"A demerit."

"That's right. You're gonna get a kick in the ass," Sommers finished.

Sommers introduced the roommates in the television room, but Tommy soon found himself miserably alone on his cot under a blanket. He would always remember the first night at 106 Baldwin as the loneliest night of his life.

The despair was palpable. He thought of his mother and the pain he was visiting upon her. His father had been buoyed with pride over his son, the Marine. But this, this desertion, that would only fuel more anger and disappointment. It would lead to a run of drinks which would ultimately come to rest on the back of his mother. Debbie, too, she would feel the wrath of the old man's fits. Tommy imagined his father's pain, when he would have to tell his buddies how his son was a deserter. How his only son had turned tail and run. Better dead than red, his father had often said. Undoubtedly, to the old man, he was dead now.

Then he thought of Reggie and how his *I love you* had not been echoed. How he wanted one back as they hugged goodbye at the border. She still loved the other and there was nothing he could do about it. Yet here he was. It was incomprehensible how abruptly his life had pivoted. One moment on his way to southeast Asia and three days later, destiny plucked him away to the cold of this lonely city.

Hours to days to weeks and a month was gone. He found work as a runner at The Brunswick House. The bar was a fixture on the corner of Brunswick and Bloor. University of Toronto students had started to infiltrate the older crowd of working stiffs and scoundrels, immigrants and tramps. Kids drawn by the cheap beer and the campy atmosphere of talent shows and pickle-eating competitions. The tables were lined in long rows and there was a small performance stage. A pianist was ready to accompany anyone drunk enough to sing. Karaoke, old style. At the Brunswick, enthusiasm always trumped ability.

Strong-armed waitresses slung trays on their shoulders jammed with thirty glasses of draft beer. Almost everyone bought off the trays; no special orders, no mixed drinks. The only question for the willing patron was how many? For twenty-five bucks you could purchase the whole tray. Fights were common. The bathrooms and pickle alley were always getting slopped with the barf of kids and women who couldn't hold their beer. There was never a night when Tommy wasn't mopping up the remnants of poor decisions.

Ruth started at the Brunswick a couple weeks before Tommy and she mentored him on bar backing and puke mopping. She was the mop queen of the ladies room. Like Tommy, Ruth was fresh out of high school and new to the big city. She was a small town girl from Cape Breton and took the bus from Sydney to Toronto. She lived with her brother and his girlfriend in a two-room apartment off the Danforth. She was a simple, plain little thing who immediately took a shine to Tommy. To his knowledge, she's the first girl to ever have a crush on him.

Ruth had an overbite and mousy straight hair with a mild complexion problem, but Tommy liked watching her tight little body. He would find himself disguising peeks at her ill-fitting jeans as they rode snugly up her thighs to highlight the lines between her legs. Like Tommy, she was living on a little and trying to make it in the big city. She was a girl with no outward ambition, beyond taking it a day at a time.

Ruth would ask him to come over or go to the show, but he would always make an excuse. Reggie was still on his mind and he wasn't about to cheat on her... even if she wasn't his. But March was rapidly approaching and then she would come. Reggie would come and all would be right. It was the thing that kept him sane.

Reggie called the Baldwin house on Sunday evenings. Sundays were dry days in the city of Toronto, so the Brunswick was closed. The conversations were short and general. She would inquire about his well-being and he avoided conversations that got around to Robbie. He always reminded her of the commitment to visit in March. That all changed in February. She called late on a Wednesday after the house had gone quiet. It was unexpected.

Her voice cracked as she told him, "Robbie's missing."

Tommy was waking up  and trying to comprehend, "What's that?"

"He's gone missing. His platoon was in some kind of a fight. They think he was shot or captured, I dunno. He's missing."

She was quiet on the other end, unable to continue. Tommy struggled for the right words and failed, "So, what can I do about it?"

He could hear her struggling without speaking. The audible gulp of someone trying to hold it together. "His sister just called me. Tommy I..." It was all she could choke out.

Collecting himself, he said, "I'm sorry, Reg. They don't know for sure, so maybe he's okay."

"The Army sent someone to the house. Some guys showed up at their house. That doesn't sound good to me."

"I'm sorry, Reg." He could hear roommates crying in the background and wondered if Karen was one of them. If it had been him, who would've cried?

She was still struggling. Struggling to speak, struggling to cry, struggling to accept what her body was telling her.

"When are you coming?" Tommy said stupidly. Just trying to fill the void.

Now he could hear her crying. The short little breaths that come audibly and uncontrollably. He thought of the night at her window. If it was true that Robbie was shot, dead even, he didn't feel the same.

"I'm sorry, Reg. I don't know what to say."

"I know," she said, sniffling. "I'm sorry to lay this on you."

"No, I'm glad you called. I wish I was there. I know you love him."

And to speak of that broken love, irreparable love, it set her into an open bawl. Sobbing forth the words, "He can't be dead, Boy. Not Robbie. Not him. I'm sure he's just captured or lost, right? He couldn't just disappear if he was dead, right Boy?"

"I don't know, Reg."

This despair of hers was cutting him, too. And not because of what happened in Vietnam. But Tommy was wounded, too. His wounds were tangible and painful. Cuts that bled in lonely tears of separation and regret. Reggie his only remedy and here she was placing him second again. Her salve of concern spent on the boy who didn't love her, leaving Tommy to fester and decay in exile.

"He's not dead, right?" Reggie pressed.

"I hope not," he said without conviction, resenting the other boy and almost hoping for the worst.

But Tommy did not know the other thing she knew. How could he? A compounding of the tragedy by a second trauma. This, too, a trauma of Robbie's concern. A thicket born of a single seed. Left to grow, it would overrun the garden she once imagined. It was something she alone knew. She would wish it away each night before bed and each morning it would return in fits of nausea.

"Are you coming in March?" he asked.

"How can you ask me that? How can you expect me to think of that now?"

"He left you. Remember?"

And she hung up. She hung up on him and didn't call the next Sunday or the Sundays after that.

# 33
# ⌘ The Sisters in Vietnam

Helen Clark refused to accept her son was gone for good. Advance a theory, no matter how absurd, and she would cling to it. *Perhaps a bullet to the head left him with amnesia. Perhaps he had been converted to the doctrine of Ho Chi Minh. Perhaps he had found a woman and was living off the grid. Perhaps they were still holding him captive, this son of an influential businessman; a future bargaining chip. Perhaps it was a bad dream.* Delusions of a fragile woman unable to cope.

Their father spent hundreds of thousands of dollars going through foreign intermediaries and back-door channels before Vietnam was opened to the west again. He hired mercenaries to infiltrate the country, sent gifts to officials of the new Socialist Republic of Vietnam and he was scammed by refugees who said they knew of Robbie and how to find him.

Helen sought the advice of the spiritualists at Lily Dale. A woman there described Robbie with enough vague familiarity, she just had to be authentic. The fact she conjured things that were public knowledge, or things you could guess at with a high degree of certainty, didn't matter. She was a thread of hope. She told Helen that Robbie was alive and trying to contact them. She saw him in a bamboo cage and he was telling her to look along the Laotian border. The psychic was put on personal retainer and was even given a room at the big house. Just another scammer.

The day they found out about Robbie's disappearance, the farm boss drove up to the big house with the captain and chaplain in their Army service uniforms. Helen collapsed in the doorway before they could speak. They carried her to the bedroom and a doctor was called to sedate her. Her husband was summoned home from the plant and the casualty notification officers stood in the foyer, waiting.

The soldier stood erect, at attention, and said it sympathetically, but without overt emotion. His delivery perfected through the misery of other families and soldiers lost. He recited without notes, "Mr. Clark, we've come on behalf of the Secretary of the Army. I'm sorry to inform you that your son, Robert Clark, has been determined to be missing in action. Robert was involved in a reconnaissance mission on February sixteenth near the village of Thoun Loc in Quang Nam Province, Vietnam. Robert's platoon came under heavy enemy fire. A member of Robert's company, Private Calvin Jones, witnessed Robert take fire while advancing on enemy positions. Private Jones says he saw your son fall wounded, but could not determine the extent of his injuries. The platoon was forced to temporarily withdraw their position until additional troops and equipment were called to engage the enemy. Upon withdrawal of enemy combatants, an immediate ground and air search was conducted to locate Private Clark. To date, the search has not yielded any results and the Army is not certain of your son's location or condition at this time. However, rest assured, we continue to vigorously pursue this search and we are determined to find your son."

The father still standing, now slumped against the doorway, asked, "Do they ever find these boys?"

"Yes, sir. I believe they find them more often than not. It's also possible he's been taken alive into enemy hands."

"Do you think he's alive?"

"We can't say with any certainty, Mr. Clark. I believe it's in God's hands now," the chaplain said.

There was a long pause, the elder Clark not wanting to ask questions there were no answers for. He thought about how he acquiesced. About how he failed his son that day at the plant when they met man to man. About how his wife would blame him.

The Captain handed him an envelope and said, "I'm going to leave you a copy of the investigation, including letters from Robert's Platoon Sergeant William Dickerson and Private Jones, both were friends of your son. My contact information is there. You will be immediately notified if we have further information regarding your son. The Secretary extends his deepest sympathy to you and your family during this trying period."

After their mother's suicide and when Vietnam opened to American tourists, Linda, Judy and their father made the trip to try and find some piece of Robbie. They hired a guide and visited those places they knew their brother had been. They took his service records and searched the countryside where he was supposedly shot. They spoke to villagers and no one had recollections of that particular battle or of an American GI, wounded or killed. They talked to local authorities who seemed eager to help, but had nothing to offer but conversation and sightseeing advice; or why they should patronize a particular establishment owned by a relative.

They wanted to hike up to FSB Rhonda, but the locals dissuaded them. There could be mines and everything was pilfered and overgrown anyways. They left feeling like rubes, seeming further away from solving Robbie's disappearance.

This time, though, Linda and Judy made the trip with nervous excitement. They were going to the place he spent the past forty-five years and they would see his daughter, their niece. There was a good chance someone could tell a part of his story.

They spent two days in Hanoi in an executive suite with a garden at the Apricot Hotel. Using that time to acclimate to the culture and the time zone and do a little shopping. But they could hardly wait to depart for Que Trung.

Upon learning about Mai's existence, the girl's were eager to meet this piece of Robbie. Eager to make amends for past failings. There had been much discussion between them about what was to be done with Mai, her husband and two boys, their great nephews. What would be theirs.

The Clark estate had long been settled. The sisters were sole inheritors and sold their joint interest in the company upon their father's death. The fortune was entrusted to professional money managers. Large piles of cash parked around the world in diversified funds. Neither Linda nor Judy had any interest in running a business, or even kept particular track of the fortune. There was more than enough to do anything they wanted.

Mai was a Clark, too. It was a delicate business and they fussed over how much would be enough, not wanting to turn them into those lottery winners who would squander their windfall in short order, only to find themselves penniless and worse off for having known money. Plus, does more money make a person happier? By all accounts the family was content in their circumstance as subsistence farmers.

Consulting with their financial advisors it was decided Mai's children would have enough money to pursue any education they wanted. There would be a trust that could be converted to cash over time, given the meeting of certain life goals; marriage, children, levels of education and employment. Additionally, a trust fund would be established for Mai and her husband. Enough money so that they would be considered wealthy in Vietnam. A lump sum would be distributed at the time of each sister's death. A sum that would be life-changing money. It was hoped by then, Mai and her husband would be familiar with the responsibility of money.

There were similar discussions with regard to Madeline and Roberta, and Roberta's children.

Que Trung was a collection of farming villages near the Thu Bon River. Mai and her husband lived in Trung Phouc, a cluster of farms off the main highway, connected by dirt paths traversable only by foot or motorbike. From the rice fields, they hiked up a path snuggling through banana trees and bamboo houses with palm thatched roofs, their interpreter and guide asking directions along the way.

Mai and her family were expecting them, standing by the stairway of their stilted bamboo home. Under the house a cow was tethered and there were baby chicks in a pen. A dog was sniffing patterns through the geese in the yard. A concrete pen held some pigs, their squeals punctuated by the crowing of unseen roosters. Clothes hung drying from a beam under the house. Colorful birds flitted back and forth in bamboo cages hooked below the roof edge.

Mai and her husband, Huy, greeting them with a small bow and gentle handshakes. Their two boys stood behind Huy and clung to the edge of his loose-fitting trousers, peering out curiously at the two older American women. The taller boy had light, blondish hair that stood out from other children they had seen in Vietnam. He had thick pouty lips and a distinct brow line; both sisters pointed at him with an identical reaction.

"Oh, my God," Linda said with a smile.

"I thought the same thing. He looks just like him, doesn't he?" Judy responded.

Linda and Judy could not resist looking curiously at Mai for those parts of Robbie in her. Her features were lighter than the typical villager and she had the strength in stance that Robbie had. Strong, muscular arms and the square, tilted chin of their brother. Her eyes hinted of places west. She, of course, understood the stares and did not resent them for this.

With the shutters open, the house seemed like a park pavilion, barely more than a roof. But for it's airiness and rustic construction, the interior was comfortably decorated. There were family pictures on the walls, large bureaus with ornate mother of pearl inlays; family treasures. The bamboo floor creaked and bent under foot. Open wires strung along the ceiling were connected to exposed light bulbs. There was a television and a picture of Ho Chi Minh.

The cooking space was traditionally in the center of the house; a charcoal stove and pots hanging over a fire. They motioned for Linda and Judy to sit in the front room, but the women asked if they could watch and assist with meal preparations. Mai was outwardly nervous about the meal, correcting Huy as he fussed with the fire.

She explained to them about the supper, the pork and bean paste rolled in bamboo leaves. A pot of pho hung over the fire on a metal rod. Mai showed them the spices she used; mint, coriander, basil and chilis. She dipped a spoon in the pot and let them taste it; nervously awaiting their approval. There was another pot of sticky rice. Fresh fruit had been placed on a tray.

Linda and Judy remembered from their first visit, eat heartily as a guest in Vietnam, but when finished, leave a little bit on the plate; a signal that the guest has been completely sated and couldn't eat another bite, no matter how delicious.

After the meal they sat in the large, open room drinking tea and opening gifts they had brought from America. Clothing and toys and household essentials the interpreter had portered up from the car.

It was only then they began telling Mai stories of her father. They told her of his exceptional athletic ability. About how he was a rower and wrestler in high school. About how he was one of the best polo players in the country for his age. And then they explained what polo was. During the telling Mai dropped her guard for the first time. She looked at them openly, wanting to absorb every inkling of her father.

They told her funny family stories about how Robbie would play tricks on them, fixing faucets to spray at them, loosening salt lids and other childish pranks. They told her about how he wanted to come to Vietnam and did so against his parents' wishes. They told about how much he was loved by everyone who knew him. Then they thought they said too much, when they told her about their mother's suicide because she couldn't live without him. At this, Mai teared up, causing the same reaction in Judy and Linda.

Of course the whole point of the stories, of the trip, was to learn about Robbie. It was Judy who said, "So, Mai, what can you tell us about your dad? Do you have any stories you can share with us."

Mai gestured for them to follow her. In a corner of the room was a small altar. There were fresh cut flowers, two candles and fresh fruit on the little table. Mai lit the incense sticks in the brass bowl and poured two cups of tea into painted porcelain cups for the spirits. Then, they all got down on their knees and bowed. On the altar was a picture of a woman and the US Army patch from Robbie's uniform was pasted sideways on her photo.

"Is that Mai's mother? What was her name?" Linda asked of the woman in the photo.

The interpreter told her, "In Vietnam, it is bad luck to speak the name of the dead. They will only call her Mother."

"I hope she wasn't offended by our stories."

"When I translated I substituted the word Brother for you," the guide said.

Mai explained the woman in the picture was her mother. And she pointed to a stone on the altar with her name inscribed. *Tien.* She died in 2011 from something they think was cancer, but she was sickly for many years. A second stone was inscribed *Clark Robert E.*, the text taken from his dog tags. There were other scraps of Robbie's uniform and his boots were beside the altar, as well. And there was a photo strip of a young girl, trying to smile.

Mai asked if the young girl was either of them.

Judy said, "That must be Debbie Donohue."

Mai said the pack with the letters also used to be there. She replaced it with the cross from his grave.

Then they all sat around a low table before the shrine and Mai began to tell her story.

When she was a girl no one ever spoke of her father. Her existence was a great family shame. Both she and her mother were ostracized by villagers. Merchants in Que Trung would charge extra or refuse to sell to them if business was good. But, as the years passed, people got tired of going out of their way to treat them poorly and they were largely forgotten and ignored. Still, Mai grew up ashamed of her light skin and western features. Children would tease her at school and play. She laughed when she said how desperate poor Huy was, agreeing to take on such a homely girl.

Not long before her death, Mai came upon her mother walking alone in the fields beyond the bamboo forest. It was a place she often disappeared to. It was late in the day and the last of the sun sat like a crown on a distant hilltop. Her mother was moving slowly with more pain than usual. Mai thought the tears were from the cancer. But when their eyes met, her mother collapsed in a ball. Mai yelled for Huy, thinking they would need to rush to the clinic in the town, but her mother shooed him away, pulling Mai close. Clutching her. It was there in the fields, as the sun disappeared and the million stars of a cloudless night emerged, that Mai learned the true story of her father.

# 34

##  Tien's Levy

Mai sat in the darkened field, her mother's hand tight around her wrist.

"I want to tell you about him," she said. "I need to tell you, before I go. How what was said was untrue. How I'm the one."

Her mother sat beside her, catching breaths shortened by sickness and emotion. Mai remembers how the sky was clear and thick, with stars stuck like starch spilled upon a bed of tar. Her mother's chest moving with effort, trying to catch the air; the breath required for the words. The words to tell their story.

"Your father was a good man," she began.

◇   ◇   ◇

Que Trung was situated on a route the Northern Army used to move between the Ho Chi Minh trail and positions east, along the coast. While many villagers were sympathetic to the North, Tien's parents were in no way political. Survival and happiness their only doctrine. Nonetheless, it was common for the soldiers to coerce villagers into supplying food and aid.

Tien was a young woman of twenty-two that night Ho's army came through. They were in quick retreat, under pursuit by American troops. She remembers a man from the village coming late to their house.

"Wake up. We need to talk with you about some business," the man said.

"Business? At this hour?" her father said, pulling a shirt over his pajamas.

Her father left with the man and returned a short time later in the company of two Northern soldiers. She watched through a crack in the shutters as the soldiers dragged a lifeless body up the hillside. She thought the person must be dead from the careless way in which they conducted him. But then the body let out a moan and it struggled in the grip of its captor.

The soldier kicked and cursed him, "Shut up you motherless dog."

She remembered the Cong soldier instructing her father, "You can keep him chained, just for a few days. We'll come back then."

"Where will I keep my cow?" her father asked. Back then, as now, they kept the cow in a concrete and bamboo pen under the house. It had a strong iron ring, cast in cement, to which they tethered the animal and that's why their house was chosen.

"Keep your cow in the pen, too. It's okay," the soldier said.

Tien's father said, "He looks like he could die. What if he dies?"

"If he dies before we get back, you can feed him to your pigs. Just leave us the head so we know he didn't escape," the soldier said, making her father's responsibilities clear.

Of course, Tien's father wanted no part of this, but no one cared about the concerns of a poor farmer. So, the prisoner was chained and kicked once more for sport. The soldiers reminding her father again, "If you feed him to the pigs, be sure to keep the head, that's all."

Tien didn't sleep that night knowing what lie chained and battered under their house. Her parents didn't sleep either. Tien could hear the muffle of frightened whispers coming from their bed. What if the Americans come and find the soldier? They would surely kill them. It was a great strain on everyone. They secretly hoped the soldier would be dead in the morning, so they could feed him to the pigs and hide the head.

The next day, after their morning meal, Tien prepared a plate for the prisoner and she accompanied her father to the cow pen. Her father carried the blade they used for butchering the pigs and chickens. It would be useful for protection, or for securing the head.

They crept quietly upon the pen, her father peeking around the edges, not wanting to be ambushed by the American. He took an offensive posture with his blade, and despite the tension of that moment, Tien remembers how funny that gentle man looked pretending to be a warrior.

To their surprise the prisoner was awake and sitting up against the wall, near the cow. He was locked in leg irons and secured with a chain used for pulling heavy equipment. His hands were tied uncomfortably behind his back. The man from the village kept the key to the lock for himself.

The prisoner saw them and did not seem particularly frightened. He smiled at Tien and she looked away. She remembers being so shy at that moment, her father calling several times to bring the food. She was ashamed for blushing. Her father took the plate and set it beside the American, freeing his arms from the rope and using hand gestures, inviting him to eat.

Her father saw the blood-soaked pant leg and knelt beside the prisoner, lifting the rip in the fabric. Tien's stomach nearly sent back her breakfast when she saw the torn flesh, open clear to the bone.

"We need to clean and bandage this," her father told her. "Go ask your mother for some cloth to make bandages. Make some hot water and bring some alcohol."

The prisoner was looking at the wound, too, so Tien felt safe in looking at his face for the first time. She thought how he was just a boy. She had never been so close to a *mi chang*. His skin and hair unlike anything she had seen before. Although filthy with blood and dirt, she thought his face the most beautiful she had ever seen.

Her father told her a second time, "Tien, go get those things I asked for."

And the prisoner, smiling through his pain looked up at her, their eyes meeting for the first time. She should have looked away, but he held her gaze, for just a beat. Tien told Mai her heart stopped the moment their eyes met. The beat that never was.

Tien's steps were quick and her body flush with a maiden's upset as she returned with hot water, linens and some liquor. Her father removed the prisoner's trousers, cutting them off, for it was the only way. Filthy and blood-stained, the pants were an invitation to infection. As well, his underwear was soiled, so those were cut and discarded, too. His shirt barely covering him. Tien's father took a piece of the cloth meant for bandages and covered him further.

Her father held the bottle to the boy's mouth and he knew to drink deep and quick. Then he poured some of the alcohol on another strip of cloth and began washing around the gash in the leg. Just touching near the hole caused the boy to writhe in pain and scream out. Her father handed her the cloth and alcohol, before grabbing his blade. For a moment she thought he was going to kill him mercifully, as one might slaughter a pig, gripping the blade with both hands and positioning it by his neck. Then he slid the blade into the soldier's mouth and his teeth bore down on it.

"Now clean inside the wound, Tien," her father said sharply.

"But Papa, I can't."

"Do it," her father said firmly.

She looked into the boy's eyes and he was frightened, but there was a nod of approval. She poured more alcohol onto the cloth and dipped it into the wound, touching all the way down to the bone. The boy struggled to keep his composure, but his torso went rigid and his muscles tensed as grunts of pain escaped through his teeth, so forceful it seemed the blade hummed in chorus. When she touched a certain spot, his body contorted off the ground and the cloth that covered his groin flew off.

She was going to cover him, but her father said, "Forget that. Finish the wound. Finish it quickly, Daughter."

Tien was holding her breath and dabbing as the boy struggled. When she finished, she saw the tears in his eyes. Her father dropped the blade and told Tien to hold the leg as he wrapped it tightly. By then the American was nearly unconscious from the pain and alcohol.

Her father directed, "Use the hot water and clean the rest of him."

Tien gently bathed the boy, washing his face and arms and neck and hands. She went to unbutton his shirt and he recoiled, crossing himself defensively with his arms. Thinking the soldier was hiding a weapon, Tien's father scooped up his blade once more and held it to the prisoner's throat. The boy understanding, slowly unbuttoned his shirt revealing a flattened field pack, the straps wrapped tightly around his chest. Her father took the pack and looked inside, the prisoner watching and hoping for understanding. Hoping, if only, to keep those letters and the picture of the dark-haired girl. His expression communicating the depths of his soul. Tien's father placed the pack close beside the prisoner, reassuring him these would not be confiscated.

Tien began to scrub his chest and below, trying not to look in his eyes, nor below, but she saw both fully. Despite the gravity of the situation, blood was pushing hormone-steeped adrenaline through the fabric of her being.

He instructed Tien, "Go ask your mother for things to make a bed and tell her to fix something we can cover him with."

She and her father crudely altered an *ao dai* as a robe for the prisoner and they prepared a makeshift bed of straw and blankets. The man from the village, who visited this misery upon them, came up to check on the prisoner. Tien casually took the prisoner's pack and slid it under her shirt.

"Why are you wasting good cloth on this dog?" the man asked suspiciously. "And why are his hands loose?"

Tien's father knew this man to be Viet Cong and he could make their lives miserable. He said, "He was making loud noises from the pain. I didn't want loud noises in case someone should be looking for him."

"Well, then, take a piece of that cloth and stuff it in his mouth," the man said, pulling a pistol from his belt. He put the pistol to the prisoner's head, saying, "If he continues to make noises I will plug his throat with a bullet."

"It's okay now," her father said.

"Well, his hands have to be tied or he might escape; maybe even attack you... *or your daughter.*"

Tien's father looked in the eyes of the boy, the gun against his temple, and tied the hands once more behind his back.

Each day, Tien would volunteer to take the prisoner his meals, accompanied by her father and his blade, lest they be set upon. They would untie his hands so he could eat. Tien would nurse the wound which showed little signs of closing. Each day she worried the soldiers would return and take him away. Each day her father worried they wouldn't.

The prisoner would speak to them, but neither understood, so they would communicate with hand and facial gestures. They would untie him for meals and keep watch for the man from the village, ready to bind him quickly if necessary. Surprise visits were common.

When the man would come, her father would ask him, "I thought they would come back for him by now."

"Don't worry. They'll come. You don't need to feed him. Let him die if you want."

"It's easy for you to say," her father would say, pretending not to care about the prisoner. "It's me who will have to answer for him."

Tien's father worried most about his daughter. She was not good at hiding her budding affection. The tenderness she bestowed upon the prisoner and the special touches she would add to the meal, sometimes taking extra spices and testing things for taste, as one would an honored guest. She even was caught sharing her meat and fish, things which were dear to them. He tried to remove her from these duties, but she would still follow him down and he didn't have the heart to stop her.

The first day she went to visit the prisoner without her father, she secretly saved some fish soup and *banh mi*, fresh from the baker in the village. It was raining and her parents napped after dinner. He sat up when she came and she avoided eye contact, untying his hands. She set the food beside him and sat away, not looking. The boy ate greedily, all the while watching her. Then from under her shirt she produced his pack and the letters. She watched as he removed the letters and read them; a tear gracing his cheek as he looked at the photo-strip of the dark- haired girl.

That night many years later, under the stars, Tien told Mai, "After finishing the letters, he motioned for me to come and tie his hands. He held his wrists behind his back and as I reached over him, he placed his head against my stomach. He was crying. Of course, I should have tied his hands and been done with it, but I couldn't. I couldn't just leave him and be done. It was then I dropped the rope and I put my arms around the boy and ran my hand through his hair. It was soft and yellow. The boy, your father, wrapped his arms around my legs and spoke to me in whimpers I could not understand... As I petted him I said, *I won't let them take you.*"

From that day forward she would secretly spend time with the American boy whenever possible, and it was often convenient at night, when the house was quiet. Each time she would take a candle and his letters. Each time after reading them, their arms would linger longer, and their lips even longer. She could feel him wanting all of her and each day she feared she would lose him; either to the soldiers who said they would come back or to the leg, which was not showing much improvement.

Tien delicately explained to her daughter she was not without experience. She had been betrothed to a boy from the village who was co-opted into the Northern army. It was years before and she assumed him dead, for other boys in that circumstance always managed a message to family and sweethearts. And yet, she accepted his suspected death with the stoic certainty that comes from living with war. In war, life comes and goes with a matter-of-factness incomprehensible to those in peace.

Tien had obliged her fiancé on a few occasions, in the fields or at the home of his parents, and so developed the taste for passion that comes from experience. A taste gone unsated since.

Tien said, "The American, we would talk in whispers to each other. Whispers in strange and foreign sounds, yet whispers that passed through the shadows of our hearts and made us understand."

When she spoke of the sex to her daughter, under the stars, it was veiled in the parlance of poetry. It was intimated, discussed like the glimpse of a woman's thigh, revealed in the lift of a skirt by a passing gust. It's meaning elevated beyond the physical, beyond the carnal, beyond the instinctual. They were soldiers of consequence, marking time by moments. Understanding time was finite and their love would be in the moment and of the moment. That's all. He, trapped in confines of her cow pen, and she, trapped in the confines of his beauty.

Her thoughts were constantly mired in the desire to cut his chains and run off with her *mi chang*. Once his leg was good again, then she would take an ax and they would run to the Americans and she would become his wife. That was her fantasy.

She said to her daughter, "Mostly, our times came at night. At night we could rest freely together. Together as one, in spirit and body. It was unusual for opportunity to come by day. Until that afternoon. I believe that afternoon was chosen by fate. That day my parents were traveling to a sick relative in another village. My father instructed me to leave the prisoner alone until he returned and did I know how to use his blade?"

But she couldn't leave him alone. With the irons on his ankles, it was customary for her to take the top, but in the light of day he wanted to take charge. She remembers how playfully they started and how they struggled to position themselves with the weight of the chains and the weakness in his leg. She started with her head in the blankets, but as he became enraptured in his mount, her head shifted into the dirt of the pen floor and she put a hand under her face to keep the dirt from her eyes. On this day he was the bull. The quiet they kept when she was in charge was impossible under his tutelage.

It was from this position their love-making turned. He was always gentle under her guidance, but like a violent schizophrenic, he suddenly broke his rhythm. From love-making it turned to pain and sadism. How could she have been duped by the prisoner? It seemed at once he was going to kill her and manage his escape this day.

He did not tell her what he saw as he violently ripped the hand from under her face and wrenched it securely behind her back. And because of what he saw, when she tried to question him, he drove her head into the dirt, holding her tightly around the neck, preventing her from breathing. Did she really mean nothing to him? He continued his thrusting as he punched her ribs, all the while snarling obscenities in a language she didn't understand. Finally, he viciously bit her back, letting go of her neck long enough for an awful scream to escape.

Tien told Mai, "I remember thinking I was going to die. Your father was going to kill me. This violence it started as we made love like animals and he had become the animal. While it seemed a long time, it all took place in seconds. My scream had barely sounded before the thunder of a pistol at close range echoed through the cow pen. I could hear the thump of the bullet passing through his head. After the shot, he collapsed on my back, going limp. I was covered in blood and parts of his head. That was our last moment together."

Tien took Mai's chin and turned her face so their eyes met, "The man from the village, the Viet Cong, he kicked the prisoner off my back and told me, *I told you this could happen if you didn't keep him tied. You are lucky I was here to save you.* Of course, now everyone would know I had been attacked. The man would tell everyone about how it was he, who saved me. A moment sooner and he might have even stopped the seed from penetrating the soil... Do you understand, Daughter? Your father was a good man."

# 35
# ☙ That's One Dead Buffalo

Ann Donahue was called to school and met privately with a counselor and the principal. The counselor described it as symptomatic of an anxiety attack. Ann said there was a lot going on at home.

It happened during a math test, something that came easy to her. She was always prepared. She always did her homework and read the book, reviewed her notes and did the end-of-chapter practice tests. No one could say she was not a good and reliable student.

> Line $m$ and line $n$ are perpendicular.
> Line $m$ has a slope of 3.
> Line $n$ contains the points (5,8) and (2,$y$).
> *What is the value of y?*

Who gives a shit, she thought? Who gives a shit about *why*?

The teacher noticed her head down, looking at the paper, trance-like. When she started visibly shaking, the girl at the next desk raised a hand and said, "Mrs. Reed, I think there's something wrong with Debbie Donahue."

The teacher came to the desk and said, "Are you okay, Debbie? You haven't even started and there's only 15 minutes left. Just guess if you're not sure."

At that moment, Debbie shoved all the papers off her desk and screamed out his name. Every face in the room now on her, she ran out slamming the door, loud enough to bring a cluster of teachers into the hall. They found her vomiting outside in the mud and melting snow, apoplectic and inconsolable.

For a while now, Ann knew her daughter was in a dark place, but they all were. She tried to understand, assuming it was this business with her brother and the precarious state of her own marriage. When she arrived at the nurse's office, Debbie was sitting on a chair and she broke into tears running to her mother's open arms. It was decided the family physician should make sure there was nothing physically wrong, and they discreetly gave Ann the calling card of a child psychologist.

After a cursory exam, the family doctor asked Debbie's mother to wait outside. He had been treating the girl since she was a baby. She was always thin and proportioned. When checking for abnormalities he detected a slight bulge in her belly. The doctor was in family practice for over thirty years and it was something seen often enough to diagnose at first blush. She sat on the examination table and he sat in the chair where her mother was. She knew what he knew.

Alone he asked her, "Do you have a boyfriend, Debbie?"

"No," she whispered.

"I asked your mother to leave, because I noticed a small bump in your belly."

"What do you mean?" she said softly, knowing.

"Have you skipped your period?"

Debbie's face flushed with embarrassment.

"It's important we rule out a tumor or something more serious. If you've missed your period and you've been sexually active, the first thing I'd like to do is test for the possibility that you're pregnant."

"I don't want to," Debbie said sullenly.

"I know," the doctor said sympathetically. "But you can't hide a pregnancy forever. At the end there's always a baby. If you are pregnant, we need to take steps to make sure you and the baby are healthy. Does the boy know?"

"He's dead," she said, angry at having to say it.

"What do mean, he's dead?"

"You're a doctor aren't you? You know what dead means, right?"

He sent Debbie out of the office, calling Ann Donohue back to discuss his suspicions.

On the ride home, Debbie sat morose and aloof, her mother groping for the questions that would provide the answers. How could this happen? She was involved in her daughter's life. There were no boys coming or going, calling or otherwise. Debbie had always been a good and reliable daughter.

When she refused to answer her modest inquiries, Ann said flatly, "Who's the boy?"

"It doesn't matter."

And sharpening her tone, her mother pressed, "Of course it matters. This boy needs to take responsibility, too. It's not just your mistake."

"I told you, it doesn't matter!" Debbie barked as her mother parked the car. "There's nothing you can do about it now."

The girl ran upstairs to her room and locked the door. Ann was left to face yet another crisis which would echo in the foulness of her husband's temper. She wanted to smack her daughter, but mostly she wanted to protect her from the coming storm. She did not speak of the baby again for two days, hoping her daughter would come around. Instead she made plans.

Then she cornered Debbie in her room. "Since you won't tell me how this happened, or who the boy is, I've found a doctor whose going to take care of this."

"What do you mean?" Debbie leered at her mother.

"I mean, this baby is the last thing this family needs. Your father is already out of his mind over Tommy. You're not going to complicate things further."

Debbie closed the distance and rushed to her mother, falling upon her knees. Grabbing the end of Ann's skirt, she begged, "No, Mom. You can't."

"We can't bring this into our lives now. Who knows what your father will do? You can't have this baby, I'm sorry."

"No, Mom. You can't take this from me," she pleaded.

"I'm sorry, Debbie. I've already made the appointment."

"Unmake it. I won't! I just won't! I'll run away, I swear."

Her mother used this leverage and demanded, "Then tell me who the father is."

Debbie let go of her mother's hem and crouched in a ball on the floor, her voice muffled as she spoke into herself, into the place where his baby grew, "It's Robbie. It's Robbie Clark. We only did it one time and now he's probably dead. I love him, Mom."

"Robbie Clark? You're lying Debbie. You know he's dead and you're lying to protect someone."

Debbie sat up straight and looked her mother in the eyes. Looking so straightly that it couldn't be a lie, "It's true. It was just once. Robbie Clark and I spent the night together. On New Year's. You can ask Michelle. She knows."

Even with this knowledge her mother did not unmake the appointment, nor did she tell her husband.

Then over supper the night before the appointment Peanut said to her father, knowing the consequences, "Daddy, I'm sorry, but you need to know something. I'm sorry, Daddy. I'm pregnant and I'm sorry I didn't tell you... Mom is making me get rid of it. She's taking me to a doctor for an abortion. She's making me get rid of the baby tomorrow. I'm so sorry, Daddy. Please! Please, don't let her do it."

Jimmy Donohue looked around the table. His daughter watching him with mournful eyes and his wife looking fearfully into her supper plate, bracing for the backlash. The backlash that starts with a slamming door and a walk. A walk of three blocks down to the Bar Bill. And there the rage would ferment, bubbling quietly as the pressure increased, waiting to be opened for his wife's consumption.

After the door slammed, she told her daughter, "If you think this changes anything, you're wrong."

It was into the next morning when the house shook with the banging of walls and the tossing of things from counters and tables. Things that bounced and broke and dented in expressions of anger and disappointment and the irreconcilable differences of lives gone stale. Jimmy Donohue letting his wife know, in no uncertain terms, that she wasn't taking that baby. And who the hell is the father?

Like Debbie, she wasn't about to say. She was not about to let him cause a scene at the home of the missing boy. It was only when he finally did it, when he finally hit her with conviction, for the first time in their life together. It was only as she lay cowering on the floor and he cocked his fist for the second time and she knew it was coming, then she said, "Don't! Please stop... It was that Clark boy. That boy who's missing in Vietnam. Please don't hit me!"

Truth be told, Jimmy Donohue didn't want this baby anymore than she did. Truth be told he couldn't stand the fact she had gone behind his back and made this decision specifically to keep it from him. That's what burned him. His son may have pulled a fast one, but his goddam wife and daughter weren't getting away with this.

When Jimmy came home from work the day after hitting his wife, he was alone. He noticed she had taken some things with her. Her closet was empty and, so too, her drawers in the dresser they shared. He looked in his daughter's room and things were gone there, too. He came home expecting to make amends, to apologize for hitting her. To let her know she was forgiven. Instead he went down to the market and there was some hard cider on sale.

It was after midnight when his daughter returned, having jumped from her mother's car. Her shoes and pants muddied from running through the wintered cornfield. She was cold and hopeful her father would be remorseful and thankful for her allegiance. And perhaps he might have been, but the cider was on sale. With his wife gone for good, now there was no one else to hit.

He called in to work the next day and forced his daughter to come with him up to the Clark house. They didn't stop to ask for permission or directions, instead just driving straight up to the big house, Debbie pointing the way. She had become a shell and she would do it for the baby. She would suffer the indignity, the wrath and the humiliation of being his daughter, if only the baby would survive. And why wouldn't they want this baby, this piece of their son?

Jimmy Donohue, unshaven and uncouth and stinking of cheap alcohol, pounding repeatedly on the big house door. It was Helen Clark who answered, frail and in mourning.

"Are you the mother of the missing soldier?" Jimmy asked, Debbie hiding behind him.

"Who are you?" she asked, not fully opening the door. She told the housekeeper to fetch the farm boss.

Jimmy grabbed his daughter and placed her in front of Helen Clark, like she was some garbage left in his yard, "You know this girl?"

"I don't know her," she lied. She lied because she knew her son.

"She's pregnant. Your boy is the father," Jimmy said menacingly, looking for a fight.

"I'm sorry. I don't know this girl. My son is in Vietnam. He's missing in action," she said, trying to shut the door, but he pushed it open.

"Your son was with her on New Year's. Tell her," he said to his daughter.

"I was in your pool," Debbie said quietly, Aunt Enid's necklace conspicuous over her turtleneck. "Robbie and I were in the stables on New Year's. Above the horses."

"That's impossible. He was with our family and his girlfriend on New Year's. Your daughter is not being truthful," Mrs. Clark said.

"The hell she isn't," Jimmy Donohue said.

"Daddy don't," Debbie said when her father kicked the door open, just as the farm boss pulled up.

"What's going on here?" he demanded of Jimmy Donohue.

"Her son knocked my daughter up. And now she's trying to cover it up."

"Hold on there, mister."

"I'm telling you my daughter isn't lying about this. She was with her boy on New Year's."

The farm boss was older than Jimmy Donohue, but he had the cut of a man who worked the land all his life. A life of long days with dirt and barns and livestock. He was a man not easily intimidated by a harsh word or a close step.

"This man is mistaken. Robbie was with us and his girlfriend. He knows my son isn't here to account for himself," Mrs. Clark told the farm boss.

"Yeah, and conveniently he's not here to deny it either," Jimmy said back.

"How dare you," Helen Clark said, near to tears. "How dare you, when you know full well my son is missing in action! How dare your daughter pull something like this knowing he's not here to defend himself!"

All the while Debbie was struggling to disappear. At one point her eyes met those of Robbie's mother, the elder's eyes darting away, almost in fear or perhaps, shame; she knew her son.

"Look it. You're gonna have to leave. You can't just come in here and make these claims," the farm boss said, getting between Jimmy and Helen.

"She's pregnant and he's the father, goddammit! I wanna know what they're gonna do about it?"

At that point another truck with three farm hands arrived, all young and strong and loyal employees of the Clark family. When the farm boss grabbed Jimmy Donohue, he shook him off and knew he couldn't win this one. He put Debbie back in the car.

A few days later an attorney for the Clark family came to their house, in the evening, when Jimmy was home. The lawyer was accompanied by a big man who had nothing to say, but stood over the lawyer's shoulder as he showed Jimmy Donohue the papers. Sworn affidavits that put Robbie with his family that night. There was a second signed statement from Regina Albach swearing that she had spent the night with Robbie in an old caretaker's house. It would be impossible for Debbie to have been with Robbie.

The lawyer also had an offer of $1000 for Jimmy Donohue. It was a gift to help his daughter with the expenses of birthing the child. It was charity and nothing more, since the child could not be Robbie Clark's. The money was his if he agreed to drop this ridiculous claim. Jimmy called Debbie into the room and showed her the statement by Regina Albach.

"That's a lie! That's a stinkin' lie," Debbie shouted at the attorney. "He broke up with her. She hit him in the face and he spent the night with me. This baby is his."

Jimmy stood by his daughter and ordered the lawyer and his companion to get the fuck out of his house. On the porch the attorney told him, "Unless they find the boy, there's no way you can prove your claim. You won't get this offer again. You'll get nothing."

"You stay the fuck off my property," Jimmy Donohue yelled as they drove away.

Jimmy called in again the next day. He stayed home and drank. The cider was on sale and he drank all night. Staggering through the house and cursing the Clark family in bursts of rage. Debbie slid out for school while his head was down on the kitchen table. That morning he gathered himself together and took another glass for courage. He got the Weatherby 22 magnum bolt action he kept in the footlocker by his bed. He bought it for deer hunting.

He knew the way to the big house and this time when he banged on the door, he was brandishing the rifle, spare cartridges in his pocket.

He yelled, "I know you're in there! You can't buy my daughter for a thousand bucks! You people think you can just buy us off for a thousand bucks?"

There was the sound of trucks coming up to the big house and he let off a warning shot; over their heads. He kept the barrel pointed as he reloaded, the spent cartridge bouncing in the driveway.

The trucks stopped and the farm boss yelled, "There's nobody home! You have to leave!"

"Yeah, I'll leave when I get what I've come for!"

"We called the police. You can hear 'em."

Jimmy fired another round into the air and started walking towards the men in their trucks, reloading as he went. The sirens were winding up from the village as the men slowly reversed down the driveway. When he pointed the rifle, they ducked behind the dashboard and veered off into the grass. The small herd of buffalo was grazing nearby. Jimmy steadied his barrel on the top of the fence post. He pulled the trigger and the animals spooked at the sound, running as one in the opposite direction, except for the dead one.

# 36
# ᑲ The End of Ruth

In March Tommy secured a furnished apartment on the third floor at 77 Baldwin Street. It was a one-room dormer with a shared bath on the second floor. There was a cabinet with a few plates and utensils, a hot plate and an electric kettle. He was lucky to get it, being in the anti-draft office when the listing was posted.

The couple who owned the house were expats from Philadelphia. Sick of America, they just up and left. He was an adjunct professor at the University of Toronto in the political science department and she was a photographer. There was a small gallery on the first floor at the front of the house. She did street photography, specializing in vignettes of the homeless and common man. She took a shot of Tommy with a long lens through the dormer window. She staged him with his head down, forlorn and a half-face bathed in the soft light that came over the top of the house. She framed it and hung it in the gallery. The sticker on the back said 10 dollars.

With Reggie gone and a room of his own, Tommy was less eager to keep Ruth at arm's length. He began answering her calls. Seizing opportunities to extend their chat. Letting her sit close in the break room, looking over his shoulder as he thumbed through the sports pages of the *Star*, feeling her hair as it touched his face. He would playfully hold her nose in the mop room as they emptied the slop of the puke buckets.

One night in the dim of pickle alley after the house lights were shut, they sat on the floor warming their backs against an old cast iron radiator, sharing four glasses of stale beer left behind on tables. She leaned into him and he grabbed her leg up high enough to remove any doubt. She took the lead, sliding over his lap and straddling him tightly. As they kissed he lifted her shirt and felt the taut flesh of her waist. They could hear the rattle of dishes loading in the kitchen.

"Do you wanna come home with me?" he asked.

"Sure, that would be nice," she said, working herself against him with enough technique that he nearly finished right there.

Ruth was the kind of girl who could mold lovers from boys. The women who came later, the proper women who get taken home to mother, restrained by the mores of their parentage, they would benefit from Ruth's study. Men blessed with a Ruth in their youth are free to explore the mysteries of all things female. Free from judgement, free from expectations and free from shame. Ruth's love came carte blanche.

There was nothing off limits and she loved to chronicle their exploits, checking off boxes as they went. From the top and rotating the points on a compass. From behind, standing up, like a pair of scissors, in the tub, in front of the mirror and sitting in the dormer window in the dim of night; this she liked most. On the wicker chair in his lap facing out and her legs open, feet perched on the wide windowsill acting as their rudder. Looking out over the darkened sidewalk and daring to be caught.

Ruth liked to count orgasms, particularly his. She would set goals and hold him to it. How many times could she please him in a night, in a weekend? And then there were the oral treats. She loved to take all of him when he was spent and swish him around between her tongue and teeth, tempting him back to form. She showed Tommy how to take her that way, complete with instructions on how to make a proper job of it. Heaping praise when it was well done.

Within a month of his apprenticeship he had mastered the ability to come second, and this he did selfishly. His excitement multiplied when he could hear her first. When movements went rogue and she broke into a spontaneous litany of feminine lamentations, her fingernails denting the skin on his back. And she would stay that way until he joined her, ending in gasps that relaxed to sighs and eventually he would melt away in the comfort of her arms.

Ruth loved him, but still, he couldn't commit. She wanted to move in and he kept putting her off, though it could be said they were already roommates. A collection of her clothes were in permanent residence. It was unusual for them to sleep alone.

Though Ruth wasn't around the day he heard the soft creaking of stockinged feet, in tandem conversation, coming up the third flight of stairs. Tommy's door was open, sucking up the heat from the lower apartment. His landlord said brightly, "Knock, knock. Are you decent? Company."

Tommy was trudging through *Slouching Towards Bethlehem* which Heather recommended. She lent him her copy from a stack of books in the office. He looked up to find his landlord in the company of a redhead who hung him out to dry several months before. His landlord sensed the moment and excused herself, skipping the small talk she was accustomed to.

Reggie worked on her smile while parking the car. She said to Tommy, "I bet ya didn't expect to see me."

"How the hell did you find me?" he asked, scanning the apartment for evidence of Ruth. Her nightshirt was under a set of panties on the chair by the bed. Too late now.

"I stopped in the draft-thingy office and they told me where you were. How have you been?" she asked, looking at Ruth's pile. Her hands were in her coat pockets, open at the front, and she was in a loose fitting sweater disguising her figure.

Tommy answered, "I'm fine. I miss home, but I'm okay. How about you?"

"Hmm, where should I start?... It was wrong of me to just leave you hanging like that, Tommy," she said. And then she had to know, picking up Ruth's undies, "You've got a roommate?"

"Just a friend," he said.

"Interesting, Boy," she teased, like back when Karen had tutored him.

"You stopped calling, so I found a friend."

"It's okay, Boy. Really," she said. "Is your friend coming home soon?"

"Not until later. We both have to work tonight. We work at the bar together."

"I guess I won't be bunking here, then," she said nonplused.

"You were planning on that?" he wondered.

"I know, presumptuous, right? Especially after I treated you so poorly... For the hundredth time."

Just like that. He was her toy again.

Just the sight of her face and the husky bass that harmonized under the girl in her voice. He didn't love Ruth and hated himself for using her. Reggie was here and now he would dump Ruth. This simple little thing from Cape Breton, who gave so freely of herself and he took it without conscience. The things she taught him, now to be spent on Reggie. It was Reggie's body he would wait for tonight, holding on for the sounds she would make; melting in her arms tonight. All he imagined since that night in the cabana, it would happen tonight.

"Stay here. I want you to," he said.

"Just the three of us?"

"I'll call in sick. I'll tell her she can't."

Reggie came over and looked at the book he put down, commenting, "Joan Didion? You've come a long way from Louie L'Amour, Boy."

"I like to read about the end of the world as we know it. Didion doesn't much care for the peace and love movement, you know?"

He came up behind her and grabbed her hips, pulling her back into him, owning her confidently. He pulled the coat from her shoulders and kissed her neck, poking his tongue between his lips as he dragged along the space between her cheek and shoulders. Nursing tenderly on the pappy skin below her cheekbone, caressed by the scent of freshly-bathed hair. She instantly knew this was not a Boy to be trifled with, and certainly not the Boy she used to know. She was no longer calling the shots and it left her off-kilter. She was supposed to drive the bus and he couldn't get off until she opened the door.

Attempting to right the ship, she ducked her shoulder away from his lips and asked, "You know, I've never really spent any time in Toronto. Can we walk around the city? I'd love to go to the Riverboat. Do you know it?"

So he spent the afternoon showing her. They walked over Dundas through Chinatown and Reggie said they should get takeout on the way home. They passed the new modernist-style city hall on the way to Yonge Street. They browsed the stacks at Sam the Record Man and A & A. They stopped in the boutiques on the way up to Yorkville.

It was a time when Toronto was shaking off the pallor of its stodgy colonial sensibilities. The city was becoming younger, more open and it was a brighter, more optimistic mirror of America. Reggie found herself completely in love with the place from the start. Everything was cool and fantastic and how lucky he was to be in the middle of it. The whole day they never really spoke of them and their lives before.

She wanted to go to the Riverboat; her friends had been and she wanted to say she had been, too. The walls had performance photos of Joni Mitchell, Neil Young, James Taylor and Gordon Lightfoot, all who cut their chops in the narrow confines of the basement coffeehouse. They had tea and strudel and listened to readings from a beatnik poet.

And then they stood on the subway at rush hour, looking into each other's eyes, arriving back at 77 Baldwin with Chinese as the sun settled orange and pink behind the rooftops. Tommy thought about Ruth starting her shift at The Brunswick.

They set a table on the floor with candles in the middle. Ruth filled jelly jars with colored beads and set tealights on top. She liked the way the beads glowed under the radiance of the candles. Tommy lit them and brought out a bottle of wine to go with dinner. Reggie curiously asked for a glass of milk and settled for water. They sat cross-legged opposite each other, a carpet their table cloth and jelly jars for light.

Reggie said, "So have you heard from home?"

"Only what you told me about Robbie."

"How about your folks?"

"I called, but my mom said I should live my life. Not to call except in an emergency. She was afraid of my dad. My sister answered another time and hung up on me. I don't get it. I never did anything to her."

Reggie reached over and grabbed his arm, "God, I'm sorry, Tommy. I'm sorry you've had nobody. I should have been here for you. I said I'd be here for you."

"So what's the story with Robbie?" he asked again.

"Nothing. No news," she said sullenly. She was making a mess of the food, insisting on using the chopsticks from the bag. "But... I have some news."

Tommy waited for it and she slid around next to him and took his hand and put it under her sweater, on her belly. She pressed it and he could feel there was more to her than before. Under the bulky sweater her figure had been hidden, but now she was telling him, directing his hand to know without saying.

"So, no wine," she said.

"Is it his?" he asked.

"Yes," she said. "I would hide it from you, but I can't. I've tried to wish it away, but it just keeps growing."

"You don't have to keep it."

"I can't do that... Maybe, if I knew he was alive. But in my heart, I know I'll never see him again. I know it's awful, but I feel certain he's dead and he's never coming home. Is that a horrible thing to say?"

"He dumped you."

"Yes."

"He loves my sister."

"I dunno."

"So, why?" he wondered.

"Because I loved him. Because I know he loved me once. Because this is all that's left of him. Do you understand?" she asked, still gently kneading his fingertips, back and forth, up and over the little life that was growing inside.

"If I love you, I suppose I have to... If I love you, I'll love this, too."

And she wrapped her arms around him and wet his cheek with her tears. Tears for him, for the first time.

"I love you, Boy" she said.

"For now or for good?"

"How about we start with tonight? Tonight's a good start."

And it was a good start. The unlikely intersection of fantasy and reality. The convergence of desire and chance; a melding of fate and want. The exception of a hundred lives. Here she was with him and the food was left for fancy on the carpet.

She felt small in his arms as he carried her to the single bed. He removed her sweater and unbuttoned her jeans, opening the fly to reveal her nylon knickers. He left her bra on, delaying desire to heighten arousal. He stood by the bed and she fumbled to help him. He kept nothing from her, she delighting him with a pet and a lick before he dropped to his knees beside the bed. He leaned across her belly and kissed the little bump, running his face over it, rubbing his lips and his nose and the ridge of his brow against it. A layer of muscle and fat between he and the little one. Reggie ran her fingers through his hair. He stuck his tongue into her belly button and she shivered and pulled his hair, telling him no.

His words coming as warm gusts of breath upon her tummy, speaking to them, "I know I'm not him, but I love you. Love isn't straight. Love makes no sense. Love kills me... and yet I still love you. I've always loved you and I'll love you always. I love you beyond a thousand deaths. Do you believe me?"

"Yes," Reggie said, her own breaths coming deep and her belly filling to meet his face. Longing to touch it again; deep-held breaths that dawdled upon the stubble of a day-long beard.

"I wish you were mine and I've always wished that," he said.

The lines were blurred between her and the womb. Which words for who? Was he declaring to both?

And after he climbed into the bed, her breasts undone and feeding his contentment. Bringing nourishment to the empty barrel; the void of want no more. They gushed warmth upon the vacance of his spirit and brought light to the darkness in his soul. Lifting the curtain she had shadowed him behind.

And for her, now there would be a new tenant. The old one left a mess, to be sure. She left this new one free to tour the property. He went down to the basement and she told him of the ghost who lived there. He checked the foundation for cracks and checked the doors and windows for alignment. It wasn't all cosmetic, but perhaps they could fix these things on the cheap. They would fix them together with sweat equity and perseverance.

As he came back up to her face and the fragrance of her flesh, sheer muslin over the workings of a fine craftsman. Her muscle and bone chiseled into a beauty so deep it hurt, just to be close. As he took the first step towards their life of intimacy, he was hesitant, barely inside and she understood his reticence, saying, "Don't worry, you can't hurt the baby."

And at first push she sounded. As he imagined, her tones unrestrained, culminating in the raw baritone of her most personal salacity. Deep sighs and her neck swiveling from lips to pillow and back again, legs clenched and aching to restrain his essence within her tenderness. The sound of her in sweet surrender, succumbing to his will, that is what set him off. Never had he become so unhinged, so willing to be openly unburdened in his own lamentations. Together as one. The first of but a thousand and one for-evers. It would never be the same again. It would never feel the same, sound the same, nor glue their souls in timeless bliss again. They would live a lifetime together and it would often be good, but it would never be like that again. This moment of bliss.

And then there was everything before. Then there would be those things to come. There was nothing in between.

# 37

# ೮ Coda

Robbie's return was testing everyone and they were all passing with flying colors.

When Linda called with details about the memorial, Regina offered their spare room for her visit. It was an offer extended cursorily, politeness to be followed by a gracious refusal. Regina was shocked when Linda replied, "If it's okay with you and Tommy, I would love it. Will Madeline be home? I'd like to meet my niece."

She came in two days before the service, Regina and Madeline met her at the airport. They drove by the old estate and through the village. It had been ten years since her last visit and she couldn't get over how much things had changed, what with the trendy shops on Main Street and the gentrification of the old village.

Since the letters, Debbie returned to the church and sought forgiveness. Not the forgiveness of her sins, but the strength to pardon those sins against her. The acceptance of Jesus into her life for a second time had healed her. Her reasons selfish, to seek the holiness that embodies forgiveness, so she could enter God's kingdom and see him again.

Mai and her family stayed in Rochester, guests of Judith, but they drove in the night before to attend a dinner the Clark girls put together at The Roycroft. They paid to reserve the loft. Even Debbie, Bertie and her two youngest came. Framing it as a dinner in Robbie's memory put everyone on their best behavior. Old grudges kept at bay in a veneer of civility and curiosity; particularly with Mai. The sisters and the translator were seated together at one end of the table, while Huy and the children served as a buffer between Debbie and Reggie. The antics of the little ones helped to keep the conversation light.

Back home after the dinner, Linda and Madeline talked into the early hours of the morning, long after Reggie and Tommy said their goodnights. Sitting alone in the front room where Madeline's mother once tugged on a heel and tempted Robbie a lifetime ago. Only feet from where the Polaroid was taken in front of the Christmas tree. Regina took the faded snapshot from its box and left on the coffee table for them. Displayed to remind them they were young once, too. How on that day, she and Robbie became bound by Madeline.

At the funeral, Robbie's daughters gave the readings. They sat on the right, alone together and side-by-side in the front pew.

Bertie had chose a reading from the holy gospel according to John:
*Jesus answered them:*
*The hour has come for the Son of Man to be glorified.*
*Truly, truly, I say to you,*
*unless a grain of wheat falls into the earth and dies, it*
    *remains alone;*
*but if it dies, it bears much fruit.*
*Whoever loves his life loses it,*
*and whoever hates his life in this world will keep it*
    *for eternal life...*

Madeline read from E.E. Cummings, adding her own preamble:
*Dear Regina, Tien and Peanut, the keepers of my soul;*
*Through your heart, your sacrifice and your love*
    *I live forever:*
*Carry your heart with me - I carry it in my heart,*
*I am never without it (anywhere I go you go, my dear;*
*and whatever is done by only me is your doing,*
    *my darling).*
*I fear no fate (for you are my fate, my sweet)...*
*I carry your heart - I carry it in my heart.*

Mai created her own reading, and she practiced with the translator, pausing line by line.

*Confucius asked "If we don't know life, how can we know*
    *death?"*
*My father knew life and from him I know death.*
*I never knew my father, yet from him I exist.*
*Without him, I am nothing.*
*Without him, this circle doesn't close.*
*Without him, my sisters would be seeds of*
    *another pod.*
*Without the father, this day does not exist.*
*While he has died, we experience life.*
*While he has left us, our journey continues.*
*Because of him, I have sisters.*
*Because of them, I don't mourn alone.*
*Because I have sisters, I know there is life.*
*Because of my parents, I know there is death.*

The honor guard folded the flag and presented it simultaneously to the girls, *On behalf of the President of the United States, the United States Army, and a grateful Nation, please accept this flag as a symbol of our appreciation for your loved one's honorable and faithful service.* Mai would place it on the altar in her home, where he died.

After the service, the small procession left the Basilica escorted by the Lackawanna police. They traced a route along the lake, past the shuttered mill of Clark Steel, into the city and winding through the tree covered lanes of Forest Lawn. Into the place where he would call home for eternity. The Clark's had an agreeable plot looking across the road and over the lake in Delaware Park. If it weren't for the trees you could see the house where Enid first laid eyes upon the carpenter, Albert.

It was a small contingent of mourners who gathered at the family stone. All those others who once cared about Robbie, mostly dead. For May, the day was dreary and cold. *Taps* played as the casket was lowered. A solitary bagpipe droned out *Amazing Grace* and flowers were tossed in the hole. A persistent rain left everything wet. The leaves of another season sucked upon the bounty, taking as they could and dripping off the rest.

After, the mourners gathered in little groups in the rain, taking time before leaving. Regina and Tommy stood uncomfortably with Debbie.

Reggie said, "Look."

Off to the side were the girls, these levies of devotion, sharing an umbrella and smiling about who knows what. Comfortable in their new-found company. Grateful for life and that time they would have as sisters.